# OF SWORDS AND STARLIGHT

WREN JONES

# OF SWORDS AND STARLIGHT



Cover Illustration by Kateryna Vitkovska
https://www.vitkovskaya.art

Typography by Amphi Studio
https://www.amphi.studio.com/

Chapter Illustrations by Willoy Tea Art
Instagram: @willowyteaart

ISBN 979-8-9942402-0-5 *(print edition)*

ISBN  979-8-9942402-1-2 *(ebook)*


1 2 3 4 5 6 7 8 9 10

**www.wrenjones.net**

To the magical girls.

May you always remember your light
in times of great darkness.

# CHAPTER 1

# THE PRINCESS AND THE SPACE CAT

Under any other circumstances, a night like this would have been beautiful. The glow of the city lights bounced back off the thick clouds in a brilliant amethyst haze. The stillness of the buildings, empty offices and high-rise apartments filled with sleeping people, would have been comforting.

A whole bustling city, finally quiet and at peace...

But Harlow couldn't see the stars.

And that was a problem.

She was pinned against a brick wall, her hands held up over her head by a massive claw. Painfully, and much to Harlow's frustration, slowly, the grip on her wrists tightened, hoisting her higher.

She grit her teeth with equal parts physical exertion and fierce determination.

This was bad.

But it wouldn't be the end.

Harlow arched her back, pressing her shoulders into the wall as she kicked a booted foot at the giant monster. Her kick landed and hit its broad chest. Her eyes widened as she watched the monster's face. All her effort, and it hadn't even flinched.

She pulled it back, grimacing at the sensation of freezing needles pricking up her leg.

Pain shot through her arms and down her back as the monster raised her higher until she was off the ground. Harlow stared into its galaxy-filled eyes, blood running down on cheek, a snarl on her lips.

It would have been beautiful, she thought for a moment, to gaze into the large, deep black eyes. They were two portals. Endless voids of nothing flecked with starlight and streaks of dark purples and blues.

She could get lost there. It would be easy to drift away...

The monster smiled at her. It was going easy on her.

It would be its final mistake.

*Hopefully.*

Harlow glanced up, fighting through the ache in her joints and the throbbing in her head.

The stars were still gone. But the moon was a carved crescent.

And Carina didn't need to see it to use it.

This time, it was her turn to smile. Her half-grin twitched up despite the pain, and she kicked again.

"That won't work, Princess," the beast growled, ignoring the hit to its body.

It truly was a beast. No matter what captivating depths its eyes held. No matter that it could use language. Its hands were monstrous, clawed and terrifying. Its smile was at the end of a snout. At eight feet tall, skin and body made of ever-moving cold silver moonlight and swirling darkness, it couldn't be considered human, though she knew it once was.

It couldn't be considered like *her*.

Harlow spat blood and defiance. Her own smile widened, and through her teeth she managed to grunt out, "Look up."

The slightest tilt upward of its wolf-like head –

A blur of midnight blue and pink burst down from the sky.

Harlow hit the ground. Air knocked out of her lungs.

A stinging pierced her chest as she forced herself to breathe in and pushed up from the hard concrete.

A howling, ripping sound ahead compelled her up despite everything in her wanting to catch her breath and heal her body. She rose, her feet planting in a wide stance as she held a hand up to the sky just as a patch of cloud parted.

A rush of warmth flooded through her fingertips and down her arm as she spun the single point of starlight into a pale, glowing dagger.

Ahead, Carina and the monster battled in a brutal blur.

Her guard was smaller than the monster, but swifter. She moved about the alleyway as though she were swimming through the air, dodging the monster's heavy swipes and gnashing mouth. She ducked, bitting at the skin that bled moonlight. It poured from the creature like water.

Carina retreated again.

Harlow held her dagger firm. Her heartbeat slowed, taking the scene in with sharp focus. Her grip tightened, and she saw her opening.

Carina darted down and Harlow threw the starlight with sharp precision.

A wail filled the night as it hit the monster in the shoulder.

In a flash of pale white light, the monster was gone.

She smiled, though she stumbled on suddenly unsteady legs. Harlow slumped to the ground.

And laughed.

Carina, in this strange giant cat form, was nearly at her eye level. She towered over Harlow now as Harlow sank down a little more. "You better wipe that smile off your face," the guard scolded.

Harlow ran her hands through her hair and tried to stifle her laughter. It hardly worked. The rush of excitement, the euphoria of being incredibly lucky, and the lingering hint of fear were too much. She did her best to seal her mouth, though her grin was still glaringly evident.

Carina glared. She had always been the more grounded of the two, despite this form being derived from moonlight.

She was a simple-looking calico house cat by day. But at night, when she needed to, moonlight poured into her and she became – this. A five foot tall cat-like creature. Black as the darkest night, but glowing with brilliant pink and silver starlight that moved around her skin and radiated out of her like a delicate, swirling nebula.

She was beautiful and powerful.

And absolutely done with Harlow's nonsense.

Carina nudged Harlow's shoulder with her head, her long pointed ears melding into Harlow's cheeks for the faintest moment. "Get up," she said. "There might be more."

Harlow grunted as she used the wall to steady herself. She stretched her shoulders back and a dull ache in her arm socket intensified. She hissed a breath in, then doubled over. Her lungs were still shallow from the fall.

"Harlow!" Carina cried. The space cat crouched down to her, ears pressed back against her neck.

With a clenched jaw and her hands on her knees, Harlow pushed herself up as she let out a heavy groan. "I'm fine," she said. "But let's get out of here just in case."

Carina sighed, as much as a giant space cat could, and in a bright flash, she turned back into a little calico.

Harlow looked down at her as they began their walk out of the darkened alleyway. Her little guard, with patches of orange and black dotting her body, trotted along with silent steps.

"You're being too reckless. You can't go looking for a fight when it's starless out," Carina said as they turned a corner out to the street where closed boutique shops lined the road. The streetlights illuminated the windows and reflected off the few puddles in the otherwise dark street.

"I wasn't *looking* for a fight. The fight found me," Harlow lied with a shrug. She looked around them as her stomach growled.

No chance anything would be open now... It'd have to be cup noodles or vending machine chips for dinner. Again.

Ignoring her grumbling stomach and disinterested gaze, the cat went on, "It was going easy on you. You're lucky."

Lucky. That was a word that got thrown out a lot whenever Harlow's name was mentioned. But she never considered herself lucky at all.

She didn't think it was lucky that as a young girl she had woken up to strange powers she couldn't explain, fractured memories of an alien past life, and a talking cat who transformed with moonlight into a giant beast.

It wasn't lucky that her aunt had been waiting for that moment to throw her nights into practicing harnessing starlight, studying battle strategy, and learning all the creative ways the monsters who had been trying to take Earth could kill her.

It wasn't lucky that her home planet had been destroyed in a great battle between the starlight wielders and those who had been turned monstrous by moonlight. Or that she had been reborn on this strange planet, never feeling quite like she belonged among humans despite her outward appearance.

Harlow's eyes followed the road, then drifted to the large windows lining the street. Her reflection looked back at her, but she peeled her eyes away. Her chin-length hair, blue at the top and pink at the ends, was horribly disheveled. She had a cut under one eye and a bruised nose.

She'd heal quickly, but she certainly didn't *look* like the monster was taking it easy.

Still, with a half-smile and one raised brow, she put her hands in her pockets as casually as she could and said, "I'm not lucky. I'm prepared."

"Fine. You're not lucky or reckless. You're arrogant," Carina teased her and trotted up ahead.

"It's not arrogant if it's true." Harlow hurried after the cat.

She was running late.

# CHAPTER 2

# THE OBSERVATORY CURSE

Not much bothered Harlow, much to the confusion of nearly everyone in her life. She had a lot to *be* worried about. Finishing graduate school, for one. She wasn't exactly excelling in any of her classes. And her night job that kept her running on energy drinks and vending machine dinners, for another.

From the outside looking in, her plate was stuffed to the brink of overflowing.

From the inside, to the few who truly knew her, her plate was full, on fire, and spinning rapidly on the brink of collapse.

But this? The run-in with the monster who dangled her like a doll and mocked her? *This* had been bothering her. The look the moonlight monster gave her like it was taunting her flashed through her mind as she walked the tree-lined sidewalk toward the massive observatory on the edge of the university grounds.

She looked up at the starless night sky and breathed in deeply. If she didn't look to her sides, only up at the gently swaying tree branches, she'd think she was somewhere far away. Somewhere where monsters made of moonlight weren't constantly leaping out of alleyways to try to kill her. Or where, more often, she wasn't going rogue and hunting them down.

Usually, they sprung up at random, it seemed. Sometimes they appeared somewhat organized, but she had never been able to really get an idea of their patterns. They'd show up, try their best to kill her or her friends, and then either flee or fall to her sword.

Quickly, generally.

This was the first one that had toyed with her.

The feeling of being lifted off the ground and thrown aside like she was small and weightless was unnerving. Carina was right. She *had* been lucky. The thing could've killed her fairly easily without her starlight weapons if it had wanted to.

So… why didn't it?

Harlow huffed and pulled her jacket tighter around her body. She peeled her eyes from the sky. She wasn't somewhere far away with no problems and no stress. She was running late for work, overtired, and stuck to the university grounds like it was a cage.

Some people were just mean. There was no reason for it or deeper meaning behind it.

She supposed it was the same for the monsters.

To her, they were all the same. But she supposed they did, in fact, have personalities.

Harlow entered the observatory with her keycard and did her best to banish any lingering thoughts of monsters or other world-ending problems.

The lobby was dark. Dim overhead lights that never turned off, no matter how many switches she had curiously pressed, lit the mostly bare circular room with a buzzing yellow glow. Four vending machines in various states of disrepair lined one curve of the wall; the other was filled with framed and faded posters of strange planets from the last interstellar telescope transmission long ago.

She stopped at the first vending machine and waited, her foot tapping the tile floor impatiently, as her bright pink energy drink descended before she moved on to pay for three bags of chips.

Harlow held the drink in one hand, popped the tab with her thumb and balanced her chip bags in the other as she made her way to the deep interior of the building. She swiped the second set of doors behind a front desk, climbed the stairs up to the top as she sipped the first bubbles from her can.

She swore to herself that *this time* she would focus on the actual data instead of spending most of the night talking to her coworkers and playing phone games. She needed something to focus on so she wouldn't waste the whole night strategizing for something she had no real knowledge of.

The motivations behind the attack, and any other lingering problems she had with that part of her life were for Morning Harlow. She would be better equipped to deal with what was going on after a nap and protein. Night Harlow was fueled by pink caffeine and stubbornness, a bad combination for battle planning.

Harlow pushed the last set of doors open with her elbow, finally banishing any last thoughts about moon monsters or close calls.

Here, she was safe. Or, at least, safe from anything lingering outside in the shadows.

The telescope room was a round space with a big domed ceiling made of old stone, metal, and glass. The massive telescope system took up most of the back wall; its huge optical tube was as wide as she was tall, narrowing down to a comically little eyepiece. Beside it, there was the world's most uncomfortable chair, a small desk with stacks of paper and a single pen that the professors were all very attached to.

Along the curve of the wall, a row of four desks, with their old computers and squeaky rolling chairs, waited for her. She had a favorite spot, the one closest to the telescope, though that one was also farthest from the vent and was warm on summer nights. And she had a least favorite. The one closer to the AC had the slowest computer and the squeakiest chair.

But every desk was a second home to her. Or, she thought, a third. Earth was her second home, she reminded herself.

Earth, however, was still strange to her in many ways. For instance, the concept of the university in general made her somewhat uneasy. She wanted to learn it all, and the idea of spending money on it felt like a crime.

Begrudgingly, Harlow had learned she *shouldn't* triple major and had long ago changed her two majors from astronomy to journalism, having decided that she dealt with enough space in her night hours to be both-ered going into debt learning about it. Though, if she was being honest, the heavy math had more to do with it than anything else.

So, she stuck to her library books, and kept in touch with the students and professors, though always at arm's length until she gained a reputation for her tenacity and practical skills. Over time, she had learned enough to obtain, and keep, her job here.

Analyzing and charting data points was pretty easy, anyway. At least it was fairly black and white and followed rules. Unlike almost everything else in Harlow's life.

But as she sat down at the desk, illuminated by the very old green-topped lamp, she realized that while she was safe here from monsters and the shades of gray that dominated her life, she was *not* safe from Rainey.

"You promised me you were going to try to get actual food this time," Rainey said as she sat down beside Harlow with a narrowed glare at the pile of chips and open energy drink.

Harlow raised a brow. "I did try. I battled epically, actually, but... the chips won," she said, her tone seri-ous. "And besides, chips are food. It's potato."

"You're going to die of Red 40 poisoning," Rainey countered. She tied her hair into a low ponytail, but her eyes stayed fixed on the bags as though they really were a deadly poison.

Harlow leaned back in her chair, lifting a bag of chips. She pointed at the green leaf in the top corner of the packaging. "No artificial coloring," she read. "See? It's basically a health snack. And three snacks makes one meal."

Rainey rolled her eyes and let out an exasperated sigh. "Fine. It won't kill you right away. Years off your life, though, you know. Eating the crap, and worse—" She pointed dramatically to the can that Harlow was now downing in several large gulps. "Do you even know what's in those? If you need the caffeine, just drink coffee, I beg!"

Rainey, a fellow student, had taken it upon herself to become a pseudo-mother to Harlow, though she had never indicated that she needed one.

It must have been evident.

Harlow had never talked much about her past, how she didn't really have parents, or even a steady adult presence for most of her life, how her aunt had been more of a boss than a trusted adult.

She caught herself dropping little hints here and there over their long nights working together, though, and she cringed every time some sad comment made its way out of her mouth.

Secretly, Rainey's worry over her eating habits and attempts to make her try to take better care of herself warmed Harlow's heart.

It had become a ritual.

Get a can of garbage, listen to Rainey berate her, insist that coffee just didn't hit the same no matter what Rainey said, then wait for Gigi, who would inevitably be running even later than Harlow, before they got to work.

Tonight was no different, and Harlow was glad for the routine. Though as she turned to Rainey with a bright smile, her sharp features catching the light of the desk lamp, Harlow knew she was *really* about to be in for it.

"Harlow! What happened to your face?" Rainey asked with a gasp.

*Damn it.*

Harlow turned away quickly; she touched the cut on her cheek. She wasn't sure what would be harder to explain: how it would be completely healed by tomorrow's shift or how she got it. Great. Now she'd have to wear a fake band-aid for a week. She scrambled to come up with an excuse, her eyes lifted to the dark ceiling. "Oh, you know, Carina and I got into it... again," she said, hopeful it came out casually. It was a basic excuse, but it always worked. Cat scratches happened all the time, right?

Rainey just shook her head slowly. "That cat, I swear... Are you going to get her on meds or something? My mom's dog had to go on an anti-anxiety. Completely cured his food aggression."

Harlow raised another brow at her.

"Okay, not completely, but still. I'll bet it'd help."

Harlow shook her head and opened her bag of chips. She leaned back further in her chair and put one leg up on the corner of the desk, her booted foot hanging limply over the end. "It's fine," she said with a wave of her hand. "She's just... unique. I'm used to it." She popped a chip into her mouth and chewed loudly. before offering the open bag to Rainey, who merely shook her head sadly.

The door opened with a loud thud against the wall as a hurricane of a woman blew in, though neither Harlow nor Rainey even bothered to look up from their desks.

Gigi huffed as she threw her oversized bag on the floor and nearly crumbled into the chair beside Rainey. She tossed her head back over the chair and let out a disgruntled groan.

Rainey reached out to hold Gigi's shoulder with a

practiced motion. She gave it a few light squeezes. "Everything okay?"

Harlow shrugged and continued eating her chips.

"No," Gigi said as her arms hung loosely at her sides. "I'm going to get fired if I keep showing up late but no matter *what* I do, I'm always five minutes late!"

Harlow's eyes shifted to the large digital clock on the wall.

1:13 am.

Not egregious. But not five minutes either.

Luckily, if anyone was checking their badge swipes, they had never found her tardiness to be enough to write her up. Harlow doubted any of the professors had the time, or the energy, or even the give-a-shit to care to check. As long as the work was done, everyone seemed to find the arrangement agreeable.

Harlow leaned forward to try to catch Gigi's eye. "Maybe, and this is just a gentle suggestion," she said from the side of her mouth, "you can *not* do a full face of makeup before the overnight at an empty observatory?"

Rainey shot Harlow a wicked look that she was certain read 'shut up and eat your poison.' Aloud, she told Gigi, "You look beaut–"

"It's not the makeup. It's the *curse*, Harlow," Gigi cut Rainey off with a practice dramatization. "Besides, it's like my makeup ritual. It calms me."

*Yes, so calm*, Harlow thought as she opened her next bag. She leaned over Rainey, shaking the bag at Gigi.

Gigi took two chips with well-manicured fingers. "Thank you," she said. Then, as if remembering that she was just in the middle of a tantrum, she sighed heavily again, pointing a chip at Harlow. "Besides, what if there's a fire?"

Rainey sat up straighter. "A fire?"

Gigi nodded, her expression serious. "Yes, a fire. And then..."

Rainey shrugged. "We...?"

Gigi gestured for her to keep going, the chip still between her fingers.

"Die looking pretty?" Rainey suggested.

Gigi deflated. "So pessimistic." She bounced back quickly enough, her posture changing to look like a damsel in distress with one hand on her brow. "No, we save ourselves. But then we get to chat up hot fire-fighters while looking our best. *Obviously*." Gigi ate her chips with a loud crunch as though it was the period to her point. She pushed her light, pixie hair behind one ear. She smiled teasingly at Harlow. "And, who is going to get their phone numbers? Me. Because I look amaz-ing." She waved her hand around her face.

"I think I'm good without the phone number,"

Harlow grumbled as she handed the last bag of chips over to Gigi for her to continue snacking.

"Stop it, you two," Rainey scolded. She bristled as she listened to the two of them crunching on chips. "If I wasn't broke, I'd be bringing you horrible people actual meals." Her chair made a sad, broken plastic sound as she pushed herself up from her seat.

Those wheels never quite rotated the way they should.

Harlow kept promising to come in on off-hours and replace the busted wheels. After all, how hard could it be? But that seemed to be one promise she just couldn't keep.

*One of many*, she thought harshly.

"Girl," Gigi grabbed Harlow's arm just as Harlow swung her legs off the desk. She stared at the cut on Harlow's cheek, eyes bouncing from it, to Harlow's confused expression. "You and that cat have *got to* form a truce."

Harlow laughed. It sounded fake. "Yeah, a truce... Maybe." She pulled Gigi up with her as she rose from her seat at last.

Gigi examined Harlow's face more closely, though she had to tilt her head up to see. "I'll sew you a cat-bite arm. Like the ones they make for police dogs."

Harlow shrugged with a noncommittal grumble.

Gigi leaned closer. "No, for real, I can make one. Lightweight. Study. You can use it as a buffer, at least."

"What about full body armor?" Harlow said. "It's *that* I need."

"Honestly, it's not being late that's going to get us fired, it's the fact that it takes us a solid half hour to get started..." Rainey said under her breath. She was busy reading the handwritten log attached to a worn clipboard. Louder, she said, "Gigi, there's some new stuff in your files to go over. Harlow, want to log some points for me?"

Harlow and Gigi exchanged quick glances, then moved to their respective locations, Gigi at the desk by the door again, and Harlow at one closest to the telescope lens.

Rainey positioned herself at the stool and fiddled with the telescope for a bit before she settled in and gazed into the dark night sky. Occasionally, she read off a series of numbers, and Harlow would record them diligently.

That is, until Rainey gasped. "Another meteor," she said as she sat up straighter, blinking a few times to clear her eyes.

Harlow's brows furrowed. "Another?" she said.

"They've been getting more frequent, right? I'm not going crazy?"

Gigi leaned back in her chair to get a better look at them. "No," she said, "they've been getting more frequent *exponentially*." She clicked around on her computer, pulling up a line graph. She turned the big computer to face them. "I've been charting them on the side. This is with the data over the past three years." She scrolled along the chart that had a few small hills and valleys before she got to the end, where the line went up. And up. And up. "Here's the last two months."

"Weird," Rainey said.

"What?" Gigi crossed her arms. "The chart is pastel, so what?"

Rainey's eyes grew wider, realizing she had offended her. "Not your chart, the frequency," she clarified quickly.

Harlow's heart grew heavy in her chest. She had no idea what it meant. All she knew was that it couldn't be a *good thing*. She liked her celestial bodies and debris right where they were. Floating about in space. Far away from her.

But it seemed no matter how hard she wanted them to stay there, strange things were coming to Earth. And they were coming fast.

# CHAPTER 3

# BATTLE BY NUMBERS

The best part of working the night shift was the vending machine snacks. The second best was the good company of humans that Harlow could *maybe* someday down the line consider friends. But the third was leaving the building and seeing the sun rising over the university buildings.

It cast everything in a cozy golden glow, illuminating the world as if the night before had simply been a wild dream. As Harlow left the observatory, she gave

Rainey and Gigi a little wave and they smiled back brightly. The warmth of the rays on her quickly healing cheek reminded her that it was time to start over. It was a new day, full of possibilities.

A sense that everything was going to be alright washed over her with the morning sun.

The sun rose every day.

And so did she.

Her bruises, for instance, no longer ached dully, and the cut on her cheek was patching up quickly. Soon, there would be no evidence of the battle from which she almost didn't make it out of.

She could go about the day, secure in knowing that any monsters she'd run into would be people. And while she wasn't exactly good at 'peopleing', dealing with them was still easier than summoning swords from starlight and fending off beings made of moonlight. At least with people, the rules of engagement were fairly stable.

But the rules of battle were changing on her.

She and Carina had been fighting these creatures since she was a teenager. It got easier, like most things did, with enough practice. They learned something new with every encounter, got better with every bruise and gash, grew faster with every swing of her sword.

Saving people from bloodthirsty monsters hell-bent

on overtaking the world had never been a *consistent* hobby. There were the occasional anomalies, nights gone wrong for reasons she wasn't able to foresee. But it wasn't until recently that things got noticeably... *different.*

It was subtle enough that Harlow hadn't tuned into it all the way until last night. Little things here and there snuck up on her, like the gentle warming of the water, only to realize she was being boiled. There was no denying it now. She was in hot water.

They seemed more organized, more methodical, as though everything they were doing was leading to... something. And no matter how hard Harlow tried to stuff down the increasing dread, the same sinking sensation kept creeping back up.

But not now.

Now, the sun was shining.

Harlow made her way to the coffee shop at the edge of the open grassy mall. The bell above the door chimed as she stepped through to the familiar scent of rich roasted coffee grounds and sweet caramel syrup. The steady sound of the machines all working to fill huge carafes of coffee and the low hiss of the milk steamer welcomed her like a familiar greeting.

The night shift had its downsides, but another positive was that she got to be one of the first inside *Espresso*

*Yourself*, the (relatively) new shop on campus. And that meant that the coveted corner booth on the second floor loft, nestled between large bookshelves, was hers for the taking.

It was quiet up there. The conversations from below carried up to the loft space in muffled frequency was like a soothing balm for her loneliness. The lo-fi coming from the speakers blocked most of her spiraling thoughts out so she could get her work done in a calm, steady, caffeine-fueled rhythm.

She ordered her usual: a hot coffee with an obscene amount of vanilla and caramel pumps, then climbed the metal stairs with the mug balanced precariously on the saucer to find her little nook space...

Taken.

Harlow's eyes narrowed at the man sitting in her seat.

Sure, it wasn't *technically* her seat, but that didn't stop the feeling of entitlement that shot through her upon seeing him there, or the deep frown that immediately formed.

There *were* other places to sit in the upstairs loft. There was a long wooden bench built into the wall with an equally long table. Those seats were still completely empty. But the wooden bench was hard, and the table situation could get... weird, depending on the next person's boundaries.

Too often, she had found herself sitting next to someone who had clearly never heard of having a personal bubble, casting dagger glances at the strangers until they finally got the hint.

Plus, getting out of it was a nightmare if it got full. It was a team effort; everyone sliding out to make way for the person in the middle.

Once, she had simply gotten up onto the bench, stepped onto the table, and walked across it with the nonchalance of a cat to get out of an awkward conversation with someone who scooted too close to her.

She was certain that if she pulled a stunt like that again, she'd be banned.

The doors had *just* opened a few minutes ago. How early was he up to make it here already?

Her eyes darted to the table where his laptop and notes were splayed across the dark wood. He didn't have a drink.

Harlow shifted her bag on her shoulder and held her mug aloft to get his attention subtly, but he seemed too focused to notice. A pen hung from his mouth absently, and his hands were busy organizing the papers with slow, methodical movements.

"Fox!" the barista's voice rang out above the music from below.

The man looked up, eyes widening when he saw Harlow standing near the stairs. But an easy smile quickly replaced his initial shock. As he pulled the pen from between his teeth, his face only lit up brighter as if she was an old friend.

He was handsome, with dark curly hair falling into his round brown eyes. Not an undergrad, most likely. He was too well dressed, his expression a little too tired. His outfit, black slacks and a button-down shirt, open at the collar, looked both effortless and also strangely formal for being so early in the morning.

Still, Harlow couldn't help but smile back, though her feelings of quiet resentment lingered, as did the little crease between her brows.

"That's me," he said as he tossed the pen on top of the scattered notes and rose from the couch. He gestured to move past her with an open palm.

Harlow, realizing she was in his way and staring, let out a little sigh. "I'm just going to take this to go," she grumbled and turned back toward the stairs.

Fox put his hands in his pockets as he approached. He was a head taller than her, well over six feet, and as he grew closer, she noticed he was slouching slightly to make himself smaller. There was something about the way he moved, like he didn't want to frighten her, that both eased her and compelled her to firm her stance.

He cast his head toward the corner couch, indifferent or unaware of her inner conflict. "Not a fan of the bench?" he asked.

Harlow shook her head. "It's no problem." She turned to walk back down the stairs. Slowly. But not slow enough. As soon as her foot hit the second step, a little of her steaming coffee spilled out over the side of the mug and onto the saucer. "Damn it–"

"I can share the couch," he said, not following her down. "I'm just going to be here for another twenty minutes or so."

"That's okay," Harlow said, eyes fixed on the cup in her hand.

"Suit yourself."

She took another cautious step, and a little more of the coffee splashed over the rim. She would never complain that they filled it to the brim... but this was ridiculously full. Harlow looked back up at him. "Actually..."

Fox moved aside with one hand outstretched to usher her along.

"Thanks," she said as she passed him, coffee splashing to the side with every step. For the amount of gracefulness it took to fight monsters all night, she certainly seemed to find it hard to keep it together during the day.

Harlow watched him disappear down the steps with far more poise than she managed to muster.

At least the couch was big enough to sit on the far end of the L-shaped sectional and not be too much in each other's way. She wouldn't have to worry about gesturing at something and spilling her drink all over his stuff.

Harlow set her mug down among his papers, eyeing them with a suspicious gaze as she got out her own laptop slowly. Her expression soured at the numbers and equations on the pages. Of course it was math. Math people were up at ungodly hours. At least, her freshman roommate had been under the impression that she simply could not do math unless the sun was on the horizon, much to Harlow's annoyance.

She set to her own work just as Fox came back up the stairs, two cups in his hands, and, once again, significantly more graceful than she had been. He was long, lean, and agile. He moved with purpose. *A math nerd who also danced?* She looked down at his two ceramic cups. At least he was also just as addicted to caffeine as she was.

Fox set the mugs down and slid one across the way to her. "Since yours ended up half full by the time you made it to the table," he said with a light laugh. "I asked the barista for your order. Six pumps of vanilla *and* caramel drizzle? You like to live dangerously."

Harlow's eyes flicked to the mug of dark, steaming coffee. The rule on taking drinks from strangers was clear. Don't.

Not that she had ever had anyone offer to buy her a drink. Or even been out at a place where that would conceivably happen.

But this wasn't a bar. It was a coffee shop.

At 6 am.

And it wasn't like he could do much to poison it from the counter to the loft.

Fox, noticing her hesitation, simply smiled, took a large drink of his own hot coffee, and then poured half of the coffee he had offered her into his own mug and took another small sip. He gave her a single nod, then began looking over his equations, pen back in his mouth and brows slightly furrowed.

"Thanks," she said at last, but if he heard, he didn't acknowledge her. Harlow sipped her own coffee and booted up her laptop. She worked on cleaning out her inbox, occasionally casting a sideways glance at him, his notes, and the extra cup.

As though he had an internal alarm, Fox rolled his neck gently, then finished his coffee after almost exactly twenty minutes. He looked up at Harlow at last, who held his gaze over the top of her laptop. "It was nice meeting you," he said quietly under the din that had formed around them as students began to populate the long bench.

"Yeah," she said. "Thanks for the extra coffee."

"Fox," he said as he held out a hand over his own computer.

"Harlow." She shook it twice.

"Maybe I'll see you around," he said, gathering up his papers, careful to keep them in a particular order.

"First one to the couch wins," she said as he rose, slinging a leather bag across his chest.

"I don't mind sharing." He flashed another grin, then made his way down the steps and out of sight without another word.

Harlow grabbed the other cup as soon as he was gone.

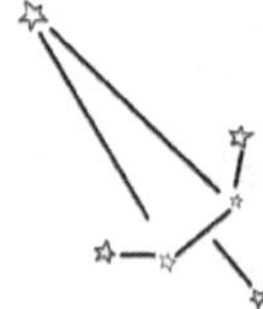

THE COFFEESHOP WAS PACKED by the time Harlow left. The sun was brighter, and the mall began to bustle with students gathering and hurrying to their morning classes.

She adjusted her bag and set out into the crisp fresh air. She was in no hurry but she knew her friends would be. Harlow was content to make her way places at her own speed.

Especially on a day like this.

The sound of people laughing, birds singing, and the rustle of leaves in the wind was like a calming symphony. It harmonized together so perfectly that all she wanted to do was find a sunny spot on the little hill, close her eyes, and soak it all in.

That is, until the buzzing of her phone broke her peace like an ominous crack of thunder.

Harlow fished her phone from the depths of her bag with a sudden urgency. Her phone vibrated angrily, loudly blaring a shrill tone at the bottom of her satchel until she finally grabbed it, silencing it quickly as she answered with a curt, "Hello."

"You got one last night?" Her aunt's voice was sharp. She cut through any pleasantries, as usual.

Harlow shifted the phone to her other ear. She held it between her shoulder and cheek as she secured her bag across her chest. "Yes," she said. "I texted you. One."

"Good," her aunt said. "Any problems?"

Harlow's heart sank. She wasn't sure how her aunt

knew, but, somehow, she must have intuited it. She never asked if there were problems. Harlow stifled her sigh. "It was anomalous," she said quietly, her eyes shifted to the people around her as she continued her walk through the grass. "I'll fill you in later, yeah?"

"I don't understand your methods sometimes."

Her aunt, the Queen of her former kingdom on a planet and time far away, had never really trusted Harlow's judgment no matter how Harlow continued to prove herself. She also didn't trust technology, far preferring an old-fashioned phone call or face-to-face meeting than a text. It made Harlow's life... inconvenient.

She would rather be left alone to deal with things her way, send a text occasionally, then wait hours to respond to any follow up on her own terms. She got the job done, after all. Harlow figured that should be all that mattered, but her aunt saw things differently.

Harlow held the phone firm in her hand now. "I'm your general." She narrowly dodged the shoulders of a group of people who walked directly in her path. She glared at the group as annoyance flared through her.

There was a long pause on the other end of the line, followed by, "Debrief later."

"Of course." Harlow didn't wait to end the call. She stuffed the phone into the back pocket of her leggings just as another group crossed her path. But this time, she slammed straight into one of them.

A smaller girl grimaced, casting a dirty look up at Harlow before the man beside her growled, "Watch it."

"You cut me off," Harlow bit back. She wasn't even sure it was true. But pent up anger boiled in her chest. "*You* watch where you're going."

The man squared his shoulders.

The corner of Harlow's lips twitched up, her fingers clenched.

Harlow, tall and with her pink and blue hair, was never one to blend in a crowd, but no one could stop and make heads turn quite like Len.

Her friend materialized as though by magic at her side and the group paused, one of them mid insult. The man's mouth fell open as he looked Len up and down.

Len was taller than all of them, towering above them all like a goddess. She looked down at them with half-closed eyes, as though she was bored by the near fight. Her elbow length silver hair, cascading down her back, and her flowing purple dress, so unlike anything anyone on campus wore only added to her enchantment. She smiled, faintly, at the group then she put a long, strong arm around Harlow.

Len guided Harlow so that her friend had no choice but to follow under the weight of her shoulder as she continued to walk by the group. "You have eyes, too," Len said to the man as she passed, her voice firm and deep. As she continued to whisk Harlow away, in a hushed tone, she added, "Can't have you making any bad decisions either."

"Hey–" Harlow started, she tried to shimmy away from Len but her friend's hold was steady.

"You know I'm right," Len said, looking down at one of Harlow's clenched fists. "Phone call that bad?"

"The usual." Harlow shook her head and loosened her fingers. She let herself be led by the taller woman, leaving the bad phone call and the annoyed group, who she felt really owed *her* an apology if anything, behind.

"She has her reasons for worrying about you." Len gave Harlow a gentle squeeze. "Come on, with that cut on your face? I know what you were doing all night."

"Not *all* night. I made it to work."

Len let her arm fall and her posture straightened. She seemed ready to scold Harlow when another young woman, petite and chipper, bounded up to them.

"Picking fights alone again?" Dessa asked as she looked up at Harlow's cut. The charms on her bracelet jingled as she moved her body closer to inspect Harlow's face. She tucked a lock of dark, chin-length hair behind one ear, exposing several gold earrings, each with a little brightly colored gem that shimmered in the sunlight.

"Look," Harlow said, exasperated, "not *picking* fights. Fights find me. I'm innocent in all this."

Dessa's amber brown eyes flicked to Harlow's chest. Her cheeks reddened slightly. "You haven't been wearing the protection charm." It was an accusation, though Harlow was sure Dessa tried to make it sound like a question.

Harlow's heart sped up as she moved her head to avoid Dessa getting a closer look at her pained expression. "It makes it harder to find them–"

"So you *were* looking for them?" Dessa said, a single finger raised at Harlow. "Why you absolutely *refuse* to include us, I will never know. You must hate me, it's the only explanation. And it's so rude. Inconsiderate, really, when all I've ever done is love–"

Len cut in, her pace quickening. "We can't be late. Rodriguez will lose it."

"Maybe if we tell him you were using your free speech rights to keep Harlow out of trouble... that she causes herself," Dessa grumbled, as if ending her rant was a quiet admission of defeat. Her eyes fixed on Len. "Yes, I saw."

"Protecting people is what I do," Len said with a shrug.

Harlow's shoulder slumped. She wasn't sure if Len meant protecting her from the group or the other way around. It was true that at night she did go looking for fights. But by day, conflicts truly did seem to find her. That, or she was just unable to turn off her soldier mode...

"But it won't get us out of being chewed out in front of the class," Len went on.

She took a few longer strides to avoid finishing the conversation and Dessa hurried to catch up.

"Wait!" Dessa called.

Harlow stuffed her hands into the pockets of her athletic jacket and trailed behind. She watched as Dessa talked excitedly to Len, who simply nodded as they entered the shadow of the tall journalism hall.

She had no idea what had gotten Dessa all riled up, but whatever it was, Len was taking it in stride, absorbing details and all of the emotion well.

Len always did.

She was, after all, the shield.

# CHAPTER 4

# SAVE THE BEES

For as long as she could remember, it had been the three of them.

Harlow, Helena, Odessa.

The sword, the shield, the bow.

They had once been a group of ragtag, wayward children who found themselves bonding with each other through shared miserable life experiences. Though, it seemed, that fate had planned their meeting and detachments from humans long before they knew their destinies, because no matter how Harlow had tried to avoid the two of them, Dessa and Len managed to find their way to her again and again.

Harlow hardly had any memories before she knew who she really was, the great responsibility of her past life, and her present dire circumstances. Her aunt had taken her in very young after the sudden death of her parents. The Queen had raised her with honesty and ferocity.

She couldn't remember the first conversation where her aunt told her that although she had been born on Earth, she was not *from* Earth – that she wasn't even human. Not really, at least. Harlow assumed that they must have talked about it once, or perhaps, her parents had. She couldn't really remember them and her aunt never spoke about them.

For all her missing memories, Harlow counted herself as somewhat lucky.

Her friends' powers had manifested much later. Their past life memories were beyond fragmented, mere kaleidoscopes and fractals of images and emotions. Their disbelief had served as a massive hurdle in their development when they were younger.

It took Harlow several months to convince them that their dreams and abilities were real at all, no matter how strong the pull to their different abilities was.

It wasn't easy living with the Queen of a dead alien species fighting a losing war, but at least she didn't have a panic attack the first time she saw a monster and pulled a sword from the stars.

Dessa and Len had been a different story.

Though, as she had explained to them all those years ago, the signs were all there. Strange dreams that felt so real that waking up hurt, the feeling of never quite belonging, the inhumanly fast healing... they only finally believed her when their guardians showed up.

After all, it was hard to deny a talking cat.

Cats, even the reincarnated space kind, had that tenacity about them that made them impossible to ignore.

But now that the ragtag, wayward children had grown into polished, tenacious adults. And they grew increasingly unhappy about Harlow going off on her own. Which was abundantly evident now as Dessa stared at her from across the elevator with a deep frown and narrowed eyes.

"For someone so smart, you sure are stupid," she said, crossing her arms.

"Dessa!" Len gasped, alarmed by her friend's deadpan delivery amid complete silence.

Harlow scratched the back of her head and

shrugged. "Yeah, she's right." A half-smile lit up her face. "I *am* smart."

There really was no winning against Odessa. The best Harlow could ever do was try to get her to laugh. At least that kept her out of trouble.

Usually.

Temporarily.

Dessa's gaze only narrowed further.

No getting out of it this time. Perhaps she could roll over and play dead. At least dropping to the ground would be so shocking Dessa would at least snicker at the commitment to the bit.

The elevator dinged.

The three stepped out and down the narrow hallway, filled with bright sunlight.

Rodriguez was already lecturing about the importance of being early to interviews as they all huddled inside the small classroom, heads down.

Len raised a hand up in acknowledgment, offering a silent, "Sorry."

Times were tough for a starlight wielding fighter, especially as the monsters' tactics changed and her friends grew increasingly tired of her renegade outings.

But if there was one thing Harlow could count on, it was at least that Rodriguez was consistently in a bad mood.

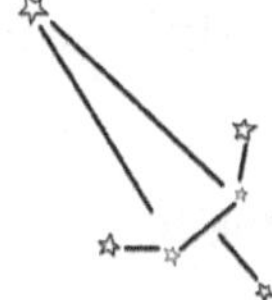

THE CLASS OVER, and her face entirely healed, the group made their way across the street to the sandwich shop, grumbling the whole way about what a waste of time it was to attend live classes.

At least, Harlow had been protesting.

Len seemed neutral.

"But it is nice to have discussions, bounce ideas off each other," Dessa said as Harlow opened the door for them.

The inside was small and narrow, a long line zig zagged from the door to the small counter. The air was buzzing with noise from all the little conversations and the loud pop music playing from overhead speakers.

"Meh." Harlow mumbled, hopeful that no one else in the crowded entryway heard her. "That could all be an email."

Dessa rolled her eyes. "You think everything should be an email."

"Yeah, then everything's in writing," Harlow said as she tapped her temple. "See? Smart."

"Oh my god! You're right. You're *so* innovative." Dessa said, sarcasm heavy in her tone. She was smiling wide, but it didn't reach her eyes. She held Harlow's gaze for a beat, then threw her hands up. "See? Then you can't get tone or body language, *smart ass.*"

At least it was loud here. The din of the small shop drowned out the bite in Dessa's words.

Harlow shrugged one shoulder. "Fair enough."

"Neither here nor there," Len said quietly. "You're not going to change the system by ranting about it in a Shelley's Sammies."

"Yeah, yeah," Harlow said. "White flag. I surrender and see the error of my ways."

"Mhm," Dessa hummed, casting Harlow a dismissive side glance.

"I'm just hangry," Harlow said as they finally made it to the counter. She leaned over the butcher block, inspecting the menu board as Len ordered for the three of them.

Len knew Harlow was getting her usual. She was a creature of habit no matter how she feigned looking interested in the other items, or tried to pretend that she was spontaneous.

Harlow pushed off the counter, accepting her second defeat of the day. "I'll find us a table," she said and moved through the crowd of waiting students to the outside patio.

Outside, the shaded courtyard was even busier. All the little blue bistro tables were full.

She sighed, scanning the space for any signs of people about to leave so she could swoop in. Everyone seemed to have just gotten their sandwiches, or were only half way done, their paper plates and napkins littering the tabletops to keep anyone else from approaching.

"Looking for a table?" A familiar voice asked.

Harlow turned to a table tucked away between the restaurant wall and the large water station.

Fox rose to meet her.

Harlow's posture shifted. She looked down at his table, his empty basket, and then back to him. "Oh, hey," she said. She looked him up and down for a moment, though the sudden loud buzz of a bee beside her made her flinch, breaking her gaze. She waved her hand at it, grateful for something to do besides stand there awkwardly, even if she was sure she looked a little wild while flailing at a bee.

Fox tossed his trash beneath the water station, his head cocked just a little as he watched her fight off the little bug. "You know they're disappearing," he said. "I think we should want to keep as many of them alive as we can."

Harlow grimaced, still waving at it as it moved

closer to the pink of her hair. "I'm not trying to kill it," she said. "Just... get it away." She whacked at it again.

Fox stepped closer gracefully, his large frame blocking the sunlight so she was drenched in a cool, sudden shadow.

Harlow stopped flailing as he held out a long-fingered hand, palm up, in a slow, methodical movement between them.

The bee shifted its chaotic course, then landed gently in his hand. His eyes softened at it as it moved across the lines on his hand. He looked back at Harlow with an easy smile.

Harlow took in a quick breath, watching as the bee charted his palm, its antenna twitching as it moved. "They don't like being swatted at," Fox whispered, his smile growing as he looked back at the bee.

Harlow's brows rose as she followed the little black and yellow fuzz. The bee paused along the curve of his palm, then it flew off.

Fox's eyes flicked up. "Try staying still next time."

She smiled back at last. "Yeah, staying still... I'll try that."

Fox cocked his head. A short exhale, almost like a laugh, escaped through his parted lips. His gaze burrowed into her with a swift intensity, as though he had only now *actually* noticed her. "Your cut is healed," he said quietly as his eyes dropped to her cheek.

A flush flared across her nose. She lifted a hand to her face and felt the smooth skin. "I'm a fast healer," she said with what she hoped was a casual shrug.

"Same," he said, though if her tone had come across as nonchalant, his was anything but. His gaze swept across her face as if trying to find a secret hidden in the details of her expression before finally settling on her eyes with the increasingly familiar stare. "Harlow, do you believe in fate?"

She recoiled at the sudden question but he was calm, his eyes kind. He let out a soft laugh as though he couldn't believe he had said it, then his eyes moved up over her head.

Harlow followed his gaze to her friends walking out of the restaurant, plastic baskets of food in hand. She stood on her toes to wave them over but a sudden shock ran through her wrist as Fox grabbed her.

Delicately, as though she only felt his cold shadow, Fox's fingertips ran from her forearm to her hand where he slipped a folded up paper. Instinctually, her hand clenched around it.

"Let's talk about it soon, Hatysa," Fox's voice was a low rumble behind her.

Chills surged through her at the sound of her name.

Her past name.

*How did he–?* She turned back, but Fox was already turning the corner and out of sight.

"No tables?" Len asked, her head on a swivel as she scanned the patio.

Dessa's mouth drew into a tight line. "Who was that?" she asked, an objection thinly veiled by a question.

Harlow's stomach turned. From hunger. From the sudden feeling of unease she was not accustomed to. From Dessa's judgmental stare.

She hadn't heard that name in a long time. Her own Queen hardly used it. But whoever he was, he recognized her. Somehow. He had *seen* her.

*It could be a trap*, the part of her mind not overwhelmed cut through her other, racing thoughts.

She shook Dessa off as casually as she could. "No idea," she said as she stuffed the folded paper into her pocket.

Len swooped in on Fox's previous table, hidden away by the giant glass container of water and plastic cups stacked precariously close to the edge of the wire tabletop. She motioned for the others to follow.

They did, though Harlow dodged Dessa's glare along the way.

She didn't want to give anything away before she

was ready. Not before she knew what this was and if it was safe.

They sat down and she stuffed a big bite into her mouth to avoid talking.

Dessa held her pickle spear between her ringed fingers with trepidation. She gestured to Harlow who simply nodded in return. Dessa tossed the pickle onto Harlow's plate, taking the tomato from Harlow's sandwich as payment.

"So your aunt called?" Len asked.

Harlow nodded, making a show of her full mouth.

Len rolled her eyes. "Any updates?"

Harlow swallowed. "No," she lied.

# CHAPTER 5

# BEFORE THE
# STARS SHINE

Harlow stared at the slip of paper on the table like it was about to spontaneously combust. It had been a full day since Fox had given it to her and she had run through every scenario that she could think of since.

She could burn it. Let the ashes settle into the vanilla candle wax, never to be recovered. But something told her that if her curiosity wasn't satisfied, that she'd find him again. Somehow.

She could text him. But then he'd have her number, and he'd be able to find all kinds of other information about her. That was how it worked... *Right?*

She had no idea. But it felt risky.

And if he didn't manage to find anything about her, but they did meet? He could attack her. He could attack her with starlight.

Or moonlight.

And she'd be leaving her friends vulnerable. Maybe it was all a ploy to get her away from them. They weren't as strong as she was.

Her eyes narrowed at the series of numbers. She lifted the paper gently and studied it again, as though it were encrypted with some kind of message.

On one hand, reaching out to him seemed to have only negative ramifications, whereas not meeting was simply risking unsatisfied curiosity. The choice was clear. There *was* a right path.

Still, she couldn't shake the curiosity. She never could. As her eyes drifted from the paper to Carina, perched high on the kitchen counter, Harlow suddenly understood a cat's urge to take their little paw and gently tap, tap, tap the breakable thing until it came crashing down brilliant shards. She understood the need to know what would happen – the hope that maybe *this time* gravity would be different.

"What?" Carina asked when she noticed Harlow's stare.

"Nothing." Harlow shook her head and crumbled the paper in her fist. Dessa and Len would be home soon, their own guards would be close behind. They never let them too far out of their sight when twilight approached. Though they lived in different units, they'd see her coming out of her apartment, no doubt.

And then the questions would come flooding in.

Before she could talk herself out of it, Harlow rose, her head nearly hitting the hanging light above the table as she did. She dodged it quickly. "I'll be back."

Carina's eyes narrowed. "Where are you going?"

Dessa and Len had lost their fights with their guards long ago. Harlow, however, was far too stubborn. Carina relinquished most of her control back when Harlow was still a kid.

"I'll be back soon," Harlow said, trying her best to sound comforting. She zipped up her cropped jacket to her throat and tapped the front of her boots to be sure they were secure.

Carina grumbled in response but went back to looking up at the corner of the ceiling with her intense stare. "There's a leak in the roof," she said quietly.

Harlow smiled and slipped through the front door

of the apartment, the phone number clutched tightly in her hand.

She was down the block before she dared take it out again. Her heart began to thud beneath her ribs as she typed the numbers into her phone.

> Hey. It's Harlow

It beat faster as the response, immediate and confident, came through.

> Glad to hear from you, Hatysa.

> Harlow

> Harlow

> Grab a drink with me?

> who are you

Grab a drink with him? Bold. Or insane. Neither was good. Yet, her heart thudded beneath her ribs at his confidence.

Bubbles appeared on her screen. He was typing. Her throat tightened.

What was she doing? No good could come out of this. But like a stupid moth searching the dark for some trace of light, she'd light her wings on fire.

Let's talk in person

Harlow let out a shrill groan. All that build up. For that?

Please?

I'll explain everything I know.

Fine. But before the stars are out

Bubbles again...

Her request was reasonable. And if he knew her from before, when she had been a mighty warrior, a princess, heir to the throne... then he'd understand.

That's fair. It's getting dark now.

Tomorrow? Noon?

where?

You tell me, princess.

A flush of heat exploded across her cheeks. She looked up from her phone and down the street, as though her face had burned so brightly it became a beacon. She laughed, releasing the tension from her body at last. Her shoulders relaxed into the giggle that radiated up from her throat.

It was a stupid nickname. She'd command him to make sure he didn't use it again if she had to.

> there's a park on campus, the one with the little red bridge

I'm familiar.

> see you on the bridge

Goodnight. Stay safe until then.

Harlow thrust her phone in her pocket. Her heart was still racing, a shiver tight in her stomach ran out into her fingers until they shook. She stuffed her hands under her arms to quiet them.

*Stay safe.*

It felt ominous. And caring. And... the addition of 'until then' felt strangely intimate.

Harlow huffed, threw open the door to their building, and climbed the stairs with heavy feet all the way back to her apartment.

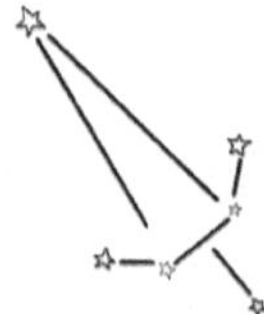

IT WAS twilight when she heard the front door open, the familiar sound of the key fumbling in the lock, sticking just a little as it was shoved forward, and then the old hinges creaking faintly as it swung and the space ignited with chatter.

Dessa threw a set of keys on the counter with a loud *clank*, her bangles jingling as she moved about the small living room, inspecting quickly as if she expected there to be something hidden among the furniture. "What's that smell?" Her nose crinkled a little.

Len kicked the front door shut, her dark eyes peering over the large paper grocery bag to be sure she didn't step on any of the cats who had bounded in. "It's two-day-old trash," Len said as she set the bag down beside Dessa's keys. "I thought you said you'd take it out, Harlow."

"I'll do it now." Harlow rose from her seat on the couch but Len stopped her with an outstretched hand.

"It's fine," she said. "I'll light a candle."

"A strong one," Dessa added.

Their weekly movie nights had been a source of joy for Harlow since their sophomore year of college. After being sick from loneliness, and nutrient deficient cafeteria food, Len had decided that enough was enough. She wasn't going to let the three of them go hungry or grow lonely.

"After all," Len had said, "we can't fight monsters if we're sick all the time."

But Harlow and Dessa had known, even then, that it was merely an excuse to care for them. A kindness they happily accepted then and several years later.

Harlow liked living alone, or with Carina, *mostly* alone. But on the weeks that they had to skip their tradition, the loss was felt deeply in her heart. Even though they saw each other all the time either in classes or out in the alleys under the moonlight, it wasn't the same being under one roof when the stars were burning brightly outside.

Dessa dug through the bottom of Harlow's little entertainment center. She was crouched down, skirt tucked nearly under her knees and a playful smile on her lips. She cast a glance at Harlow from over her shoulder. "I'm thinking maybe two candles," she said. "Where do you keep them these days?"

Harlow flushed with embarrassment. The place really was a chaotic disaster no matter how she tried to keep things tidy. No matter how she knew, logically, that her friends really didn't care, she still wanted to impress Dessa. Even if it was just something simple as an organized drawer. But she couldn't even manage that. She shook her head and tried her best to shrug nonchalantly. "I dunno."

Dessa rolled her eyes, then slammed the entertainment cabinet shut. "Carina, how do you live like this?"

The cat, busy finding a space on top of the couch to call her own now that the other two cats had invaded the small living room, simply flicked her tail in response.

Vela, a thick coated cat, and Dessa's companion, swiped at Carina's tail, amused. She was always trying to play. Though they were an ancient, alien monk, Vela certainly never let that define her and took any opportunity to act like an entitled, lovable, silly cat.

Harlow often wondered if in their past lives, Vela had chosen Dessa because she saw something similar within her – a playfulness underneath the sarcasm and smugness.

Meanwhile, Ara, Len's sleek cat pranced by the two of them as if she hadn't seen a thing. At least they were similar. Ara and Len never let much of anything get them down for long, even the squabbles of their closest friends.

Before Harlow knew it, the sounds of chopping vegetables, the water bubbling, a movie blaring, and Dessa and Len's voices all blurred into the familiar white noise.

It usually brought her a sense of peace. Of calm and happiness.

But as she glanced out the window and into the sky growing dark, all she felt was a sense of dread.

# THE SUNLIGHT THROUGH THE TREES

The park was mostly empty as it usually was just before noon. It could hardly really be considered a park. It was a patch of grass at the edges of the university grounds. A few large trees clustered together to block the sunlight, creating a feeling that the patch grass was farther away than it was. In the middle, a small pond full of students' abandoned goldfish with a small bridge and a gold plaque that had long eroded to the point that no one knew who had donated it in the first place was a popular spot for people to walk across, holding their breath to make a wish.

She wasn't sure how that tradition started. All she knew is that freshmen often came before finals to walk across it and hope that their late night cram session could make up for weeks of slacking off. She knew that the bridge had no such powers. Or, at least, it hadn't worked for her and she had to retake her abnormal psychology class to recover her GPA.

Harlow pulled her attention from the bridge. She squinted at her watch.

She had arrived early, hopeful she'd spot him and be able to discern something new about him, some kind of clue about what sort of person he was.

She waited behind a large oak tree where she could see the little red moon bridge easily, but was obscured enough by the rough trunk to not be noticed if someone was waiting there.

No one was.

It was nearly noon.

And Fox had failed to show.

Unease settled into her spine, tingling from the base of her skull down to her booted feet. With his nice, tailored outfit in the early morning, he didn't strike her as the type to be late.

But then again, she didn't know him at all. Even if he seemed to know her.

"Harlow."

She spun behind her quickly, hands already clenched in fists.

The leaves above rustled in the breeze. Spotted sunlight danced across the dark crown of his head. A beam caught his eye, but he didn't blink. He only smiled a little as she looked him over with a suspicious gaze.

"I'm glad you came." His voice was warm. He put one hand in the pocket of his black pants as if he was a little nervous, despite his easy tone.

Harlow glared back.

Fox gestured with his other hand to the bridge. "Walk with me?"

"I said the bridge," Harlow bit back. As soon as the words left her tongue, she flinched at her own abrasiveness. She hadn't meant to sound rude, but she wasn't sure what to make of any of this. Of the way he looked in the speckled sunlight, the way he seemed at ease with her, or the way a part of him seemed a little afraid of her, too.

"I wasn't sneaking up on you," he said at last. "I was

coming from this way when I saw you. You're... easy to spot."

Harlow's shoulders relaxed slightly as she let out a small sigh. He was right. She was. "Let's go," she said, and turned on her heel, walking quickly.

Fox caught up with a few long strides. He matched her speed, though he kept his gaze straight ahead.

She snuck a glance up at him but he didn't look her way. He seemed focused on their destination, as if she had given him a command and he had to follow it, see it through to its completion. Even if it was something as simple as 'Let's go'.

She peeled her eyes away from him as they neared the bridge, focusing instead on the sounds of the gentle splashes ahead as the large fish glided through the pond.

Harlow led the way to the middle of the bridge. She leaned her forearms on the railing and fixed her eyes on the surface of the water. It mirrored back a distortion of their reflections, murky and turbulent as the light breeze blew over the water. Gold, white, and red fish breached the surface. Their reflections rippled out and away, replaced by scales gleaming as they caught the stray beams of sunlight through the canopy above.

"How do you know my name?" Harlow asked at last.

From the corner of her eyes, she watched him as he

focused his gaze on the water. He leaned down beside her, his fingers interlacing loosely as they hung over the railing. The edge of his mouth quirked up. "It was scary," he said gently. "You know? Getting those memories back. It started slowly. In dreams. A few, at first. Then, more frequent. But almost all of them... with you." His fingers tightened. "Then, flashes here and there in my waking hours when something triggered them. That started small too. But when I sought them out – When they finally all came back... It was hard to believe for a long time, still. Was it like that for you?" His head tilted toward her as though he expected her to whisper her response.

Harlow felt her words stick in her throat, choking her before they could come out. She wanted to whisper. And scream. To grip the wooden bridge until it splintered under her pressure. She *didn't* have all her memories yet. She had been satisfied in knowing that she may never remember them all, at least, told herself that she was.

The only people she knew with at least some of their memories intact were herself, her two friends, and her aunt. She knew there were others out there. Thousands, maybe, who all had been reborn here. But how many of them knew what they were? She had assumed none...

Other than the ones who were tempted by the moonlight.

Her sideways stare broke away. He hadn't answered her question. At least, not really. She didn't need to answer his. "You knew me?"

Fox took a deep breath. His hands untangled and he let them fall over the edge of the bridge again. He lowered his head, tuffs of hair falling into his eyes so she couldn't quite make out his expression. "Yeah, I knew you. You would have been my Queen."

A burst of heat rose in Harlow's chest. She didn't know why – couldn't pinpoint the reasoning behind her sudden unsteady feet. 'Princess', she was familiar with. 'Queen' screamed sacrilege. The Queen held her title closely, dearly, fiercely. "What was your name?" she asked at last, the only question she could manage.

Fox let out a little laugh. "You know, that's the one thing I *don't know* yet."

Harlow held the railing tight and leaned back a little on her heels. "Do you have a companion? A guard?"

He shook his head, eyes still forward. "No, that's reserved for royalty."

"You weren't..." Harlow's words faltered as they came out, carried away by the gentle ripples of the water below them. "How did you know me?"

At last, Fox rose to his full height. He stood beside her, shoulders back, as confident and tall as he had been the first time she saw him. "You really don't remember me?"

Harlow's eyes searched his. She analyzed each fleck of honey in the dark brown depths, each burst of amber that shot through them as the sunlight hit his face. She moved up to his forehead, the line of his curly hair spilling over, to his sharp cheek bones, and angled jaw. She lingered on his full lips, parted slightly as she stared. None of it looked familiar in isolation. Hardly any of him looked like someone she knew, even in full. But as her gaze landed back on his large brown eyes, she found herself captive. Trapped in their depths. She wasn't sure what she found there yet, but there was *something* there that pulled her in.

The corners of his eyes crinkled as his lips drew up into another kind smile. "Don't get a headache."

Harlow's brow furrowed. She took a step back. "Alright, then."

"Hey," Fox said as his smile grew. "I'm teasing. I'm not used to people studying me like that."

Harlow narrowed her eyes.

"Look, I'll be honest. Since I remembered you, I've been trying to find you. The most important thing is that you're safe. I'll save our old rapport for when it's earned." He looked at his feet, hands finding their way back in his pockets. "What *do* you remember?"

Harlow took another step back. From the corner of her eye, she caught a group of people walking toward the pond. She stood taller, a sense of urgency flooded through her. "Why are you so concerned with my safety?" her voice came out harshly. She couldn't help it, and wasn't sure she wanted to.

"Isn't it obvious?"

"I'm *the* princess. The general."

"And I served you in both."

"You were in my army?" Her arms crossed over her chest.

Fox's eyes met hers again. This time, his stare was hard. "Yes."

"I had many soldiers under my command."

"I was different."

"How?"

"I loved you."

Blood turned to ice in Harlow's wrists, her fingers clenched into tight fists as they fell to her sides. It wasn't just his words but how he had said them. As though he had said it to her a thousand times before. As though he expected her to say it back. As though it broke his heart. But Harlow couldn't understand. The crushing weight of his words and tone pressed onto her shoulders. "You what?"

Fox let out a breath, his shoulders squared. "Where is the Queen?" he asked, his sudden change in subject hit Harlow like a slap.

"I'm not telling you that."

Fox shook his head sadly. He closed his eyes. "Be cautious of her," he said.

"My own aunt?" Where ice had been, fire flared. She stepped toward him, her right hand already reaching out for starlight that wasn't there.

The sound of laughter and happy voices broke them apart as the group approached the bridge. They seemed blissfully unaware of what they had just walked in on.

Fox backed away with unhurried steps. "Just be careful. Stay safe," he whispered. "We'll talk more soon."

Harlow wanted to shout after him. Something quippy like 'doubt it' or 'in your dreams'. But instead, he turned and made space for the group of young women to step onto the curved wooden bridge and continued his way out of the park without looking back.

She wanted to race after him. Or throw something at his head. Craft her sword and demand at blade point who he really was and what his intentions were.

But instead, she went the other way, leaving behind the happy sounds of the women laughing, her head swirling like stardust.

# OBJECTIVELY OBJECTIVELESS

Harlow spent the rest of the day walking through the city in a haze. Rushing thoughts quieted to a deep set numbness until twilight at last descended upon her. She was blind to the people around her, deaf to the sounds of the busy streets, and unafraid of the empty alleyways. Nothing seemed important compared to the revelation that there were others like her. Others who knew who they were and had been on her side. At least, so he said.

She stopped at tall buildings. Stared up at their glass exteriors, and wondered how many people were there. How many of them might be like them, just... not awake. How many were really a strange, aimless little alien reborn as human, always wondering why they just couldn't quite fit in. Was anyone staring out the window, looking for something familiar just the way she was?

She wondered what it might be like to be blissfully unaware of the dangers that roamed their streets under the pale moonlight. Perhaps she'd always feel a little different, a little strange, like she wasn't in the right clothes or skin – but at least she'd be able to sleep better at night not knowing that monsters were real.

She longed for a good night's sleep...

Harlow found herself at empty dead end alleyways where she could overhear conversations of the people on the floors above her. She stopped at corner stores, busy with the bustle of people getting last-minute dinners.

She was surrounded by people.

But they weren't really *her* people.

She was home in the concrete and steel maze. She had learned its twists and corners so well she could navigate it blindfolded. A place where modern architecture ruled but weeds still sprouted from cracks in the sidewalk. A place with an old university at the center. A one mile square of brick and stone buildings, the little park with the little bridge, and an observatory that stubbornly kept looking up into the stars even with all the light pollution casting a heavy purple glow at night.

She knew it all well.

Her home.

But... not really.

She had heard of people saying they felt like they were born in the wrong time. It seemed to be a human feeling, something that connected them all together, even her.

Nostalgia. Anachronistic. Loss.

But no matter how the root of the feeling was the same, it hurt that she couldn't explain that she had always felt out of place *here*. Not only from a different time, but a different space. A different culture. A different world. One with magic and gods and talking cats...

Harlow shoved her hands into her pockets and kept walking as twilight darkened over the city, drenching the skyscrapers in a golden, pink glow.

Fox had said to be careful. To stay safe.

He promised they would talk again soon.

The words itched at the back of her mind like an uncomfortable tag on her collar that she couldn't yet cut out. But she wanted to – she wanted to rip it free and finally scratch at it until it was raw.

No matter how she turned his words over, the mystery behind them was still there. Still irritating like a form of slow and tedious torture.

There was no solving this on her own.

She pulled her phone from her pocket and texted the group with Dessa and Len.

can we talk soon? URGENT

Len: Don't you have work tonight?

goddamnit

Dessa: We'll meet you on the way

Dessa: What's so urgent?

see you in a bit

Dessa: Fun!

Dessa: See? That was sarcastic.

Dessa: This is why not everything can be an email.

Len: You're so clever

Harlow couldn't help but laugh as she put her phone away.

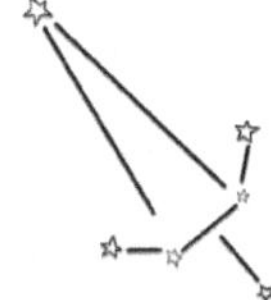

IT WAS dark by the time she made it back to the campus but there was plenty of time before her shift began. Still, she would have preferred to not talk about it in the open, beneath the stars. Though the campus was often quiet and empty at night, it still felt... vulnerable.

As she sat on a high wall, legs dangling over the side to a steep potential fall, she was able to at least see most of the mall, the library, and the food court. Every now and then, a small speck of a person zooming on a bike would pass by, then disappear from sight.

From up so high, at least she felt detached, like a sentry waiting for something to happen but with no stake in the outcome.

The light clipping sound of heels on the stone walkway jolted her from her thoughts.

Dessa, looking put together and gorgeous as always, with her cat Vela darting quickly between her calves, smiled at Harlow with a gentleness that only the night brought. She put one hand on her hip as she stood beside Harlow. In the light of the half moon, her jewelry glistened against her skin. She looked out at the campus below with the same detached, but kind expression.

Harlow fidgeted beside her. She picked at a thread that had come loose from the hem of her jacket absently as she watched Dessa from her peripherals, trying hard to look like she was too busy to notice her despite her heart beating faster.

"What's this about?" Dessa asked. Her voice was steady, calm. She had that way about her – a duality that always caught Harlow off guard. Most of the time, she was bright and sarcastic. Funny, usually at Harlow's expense. But when they were alone... a softness settled in her tone, a kind of patience that Harlow had never known from anyone else.

A kind of patience she was sure she didn't deserve.

Harlow looked down at her hands in her lap. Her feet swung a little so her heels tapped along the gray stone wall. "Do you think there's a way to... activate our memories?"

Dessa's poise remained unchanged, her back straight, head forward. Only her eyes moved to look at Harlow. "You shouldn't be sitting like that," she said, her voice suddenly shifting to the familiar hard edge. "You could fall."

Harlow shrugged. "I'm a fast healer."

Dessa's shoulders loosened as a small snort escaped her. She leaned her forearms along the wall. Her gaze moved back to the space below them as Vela leaped up to meet them with silent grace. Dessa held a hand out to the cat, who pressed her face into her knuckles gently. At last, she spoke, "I don't know. I'm not sure I want to. The ones I have are..." She turned to Harlow, then looked back quickly, as if she had spoken aloud something outside of her control. With a confident voice, she went on, "No. I think the more we know, the better. Is this what's so important? Do you have a way to unlock them?"

"Unlock what?" Len's voice broke them apart as she approached from the other side, her own guardian trailing alongside. Her long dress swept across the stone, looking more like a fairytale princess than a student, as she approached with light steps. "Where is Carina?"

Harlow looked at the two cats, then to the others. Carina. Carina wouldn't approve of any of this. Her friends' guards were with them because of how unsafe every night was. This was no different. If anything, things were getting exponentially more dangerous with each passing moon phase. "This was a mistake," Harlow blurted before she could stop herself. If she wasn't smart enough to figure this out on her own, she'd have to learn. She swung both legs over the side of the wall and landed swiftly on her feet. "I'm sorry."

She only made it two steps away when a spark shot

from her arm and down her spine. Dessa held Harlow's hand in hers, pulling her back. "I don't think so," she said as she turned Harlow back to face them. "What's going on?"

Harlow looked to Len for help, but all she got in return was Len's impassive, intense stare under the glow of the moon. Her eyes shined as she scanned Harlow's face.

Harlow sighed as Dessa let go. There was only one way forward. Brute honesty. "Okay, so you know that guy you asked about at the sandwich shop?"

Dessa's jaw tightened.

Harlow went on before she could convince herself otherwise, "He said he knew me. From before. He called me Hatysa."

Len and Dessa exchanged quick looks. Their cats, each hunting little bugs before, suddenly fell still. Ears twitched as they both turned to Harlow.

"He's one of us?" Len's voice was a whisper.

Dessa shot her a look. "We don't know he's one of us. He could be a Mechoida. A smart one. Where's his guard?"

"Good point," Len said.

Harlow's shoulders slumped a little. "I know. Listen, his name is Fox–"

"Sounds like a code name," Dessa grumbled.

Harlow went on, ignoring her for now. "He said he knew me and remembers everything. He said he was under my command back then. Look, we didn't all have guardians then, and not now. He's not... *one of us.*" The last words came out wrong, but she wasn't even sure how. He *wasn't* a royal, that much she knew. She wasn't even sure if he could craft starlight yet. But if he did...

If he was another on their side, another with all their memories intact... it could be exactly what they needed to start changing the tide of this losing war.

A loud crack erupted from the other side of the wall followed by a low growl that rumbled from the ground.

Dessa and Len darted to the ledge, each leaned over the side of the wall to get a better look.

"Mechoida," Dessa spat under her breath. She took a few steps back from the wall as Vela began to glow. "Don't," she told the cat with a hand raised. "We got this."

Vela nodded and raced off with Ara. "I'll tell Carina," the cat called back, no longer caring about speaking in the open as the sound of claws tearing up the brick echoed behind them.

Len's eyes were wide as she reached for the stars.

"I got this," Dessa told her, crafting her own long bow from the starlight. It rained down around her like electric sparks, glittering in bright white and yellow as it began to take shape in her hand.

But Harlow was faster. Sword in hand, she leapt over the side of the wall and landed the two stories below in a quick roll. Heart pounding in her ears and Dessa's cry from far away echoed as Harlow sprang up onto her feet. She squared her body at the monster, twice her size, glowing in the dark with pale purple light.

Harlow pulled a sword down from the sky with a quick motion. It shimmered in her grasp and she pointed it at the creature with a narrowed gaze.

The monster snarled at her. A clawed hand swiped.

Harlow dodged the claw, but if she was quick enough or if the monster had retracted from the starlight arrow that whizzed between them, she couldn't be sure. She glanced up a moment to see Dessa nocking her next arrow. "Leave this to me!" Harlow shouted, swinging her sword hard at the monster's chest.

"We're out in the open," Dessa replied in a sing-song voice, as though placating a child in the midst of a tantrum.

The monster looked up at Dessa. It smiled. An arm went up, brightly burning a deep blue. A burst of moon-light launched from its fingertips and up to her friends.

Harlow's mouth fell open, her muscles in her arms and legs tightened.

Len's shield came down just before the impact.

Moonlight and starlight exploded in a brilliant glittering mist.

Harlow's sword found its target, though just the tip sliced through the monster's chest.

It cried out, an animalistic sound cutting through the air as moonlight poured from the wound. Before Harlow could get another hit, it turned to all fours and ran off into the shadows.

Harlow slumped over. Her forearms found her knees, her sword still held tightly in her grasp. She was breathing heavily, a bead of sweat dripped onto the stone sidewalk.

"What the actual fuck was that?" Len cried from the top of the wall.

Harlow glanced up, chest still heaving with heavy breaths. The corner of her mouth turned up despite herself. She almost never heard Len swear. But when she did, it always came out like this.

Len peered over the wall to get a better look. "Is it gone?"

Harlow nodded, though she wasn't sure that Len could tell in the dark. She straightened her posture, then looked into the darkness surrounding her. Trees rustled with the cool wind, at the end of the sidewalk far ahead, a dull orange streetlight flickered.

"Get your stubborn butt back up here," Dessa called. She was leaning over the wall now, too, half her body sticking out dangerously.

Harlow nodded again. She released her sword back to the sky and hustled around the wall to the stairs that lead back to her friends.

At the last step, she was met with Dessa's hard open palm. It stopped her with a heavy hit to the chest. Though she was little, when Dessa planted herself, she stayed put.

"Next time use the stairs or maybe let me deal with it when it's far away," she scolded Harlow. "What're we going to do if you break an ankle?"

Harlow looked down at her chest, where Dessa's hand stayed firm. "I'm fine," she said with a shrug. A part of her, a small part she wished wasn't, was glad that Dessa was worried.

Len hurried to their sides. A little crease formed between her brows. Her frown grew. "Did you see that? The beast *threw* moonlight!" her voice was an urgent and low whisper, as though she was afraid to wake the campus with her words. She turned back around to be sure no one was coming.

And honestly, Harlow was surprised no one had. At

the very least, the burst of the moonlight had to have drawn *some* attention.

But it seemed, for now, that the monster had picked its time well. No one was around.

"And it attacked in the open like that..." Dessa finally lowered her hand. She looked at her own open palm like it was one fire. "I had that shot," she added painfully. "You need to trust me when I say I got it."

Harlow's heart sank. A chill rushed through her. "I do."

"Then let me handle it when I say I can handle it," the other woman shot back. She turned on her heel. "And wear your damn charms. It might have found us because we are all out here in the open together."

Len's hand went to her throat, then traced down the open neckline of her dress. She wasn't wearing hers either, it seemed.

Dessa sighed. Her shoulders fell inward, but only for a moment. "They're getting bolder," she said at last. She led the way back to their position along the wall. "There could be more."

Harlow shook her head as she followed behind. "They travel alone."

"Usually," Dessa said. "But they usually don't *throw moonlight* or attack us in the open either."

"It's unnerving," Harlow agreed.

"You could use less nerve," Len said. She straightened her posture, long neck craning up to survey below again.

"What if that was Fox?" Dessa said as she crossed her arms. "Sure is awfully convenient for us to be debating whether or not we can trust a stranger who says he knows us and then a monster shows up."

Len's eyes shifted to Dessa, catching the moonlight as they did. "I'm thinking not. If he's up to something nefarious, I doubt he'd be stupid enough to do something like this. But..." Len paused for a long while, letting the silence creep between them. "It does feel connected. He's here suddenly, and the Mechoida are changing just as quickly."

Dessa's brow furrowed as she seemed to be considering the options. She always saw things from way high up, considered every angle, observed the entirety of the picture before she acted, and then, when she did, it was swift, decisive, and brutal.

If she decided that she couldn't proceed the way Harlow wanted to, that would be that. A final line in the sand that no one would be able to cross.

Harlow had learned that long ago. In another life, and in this one, too. Dessa and her guard looked sweet, and they usually were. Until they needed to be otherwise. She *had* to get in front of Dessa's distrust if she was ever going to get her to give Fox a chance.

Harlow took a step to stand between them quickly. "If they're changing rapidly, then I think we need all the information we can get. Maybe it is all connected, but it's also *fate*. He might be all the missing pieces we need."

Dessa's lips drew into a line. She crossed her arms, fingertips dug into her skin.

"I just think it's worth considering hearing him out. We have always talked about wanting to find more of us. More people who have woken up. And now we have. We finally found someone like us." Harlow's words tumbled from as though she was worried they wouldn't come at all. She wanted to add that *she* was the leader. *She* was *the* princess. And that she was going to explore this. She was going to do this with them. Or without them, if she needed to.

Dessa's stare hardened.

Len leaned forward, her silver hair spilling over one shoulder. "But we didn't find him. He found us."

"He found *you*," Dessa corrected as she put one hand on her hip again.

Harlow looked down at her feet. This was going exactly the way she should have foreseen. There was no sense in including them. It could only hurt. Hurt their relationship, or even potentially get them in serious trouble. Fox had alluded to his concern for her safety around the Queen. She couldn't get her friends caught between her aunt and the Mechoida.

But she couldn't do this alone either. Especially not as the rules of engagement kept changing on her.

"Let's all meet with him," Dessa said at last, as if reading Harlow's thoughts. "Anything he can say to you, he can say to us."

"We're a team." Len nodded.

"And then we'll all have all the information. No hiding, no misinterpretations. Nothing lost in translation," Dessa went on. "In cases like this, I think tone and diction matter. I want to get a read on this guy."

"I don't like this…" Len's voice trailed off. "I think we need a plan."

"We'll meet in daylight," Dessa said. "All together. Confront him and ask him the hard-hitting questions. We're in journalism school, for starlight's sake!"

Harlow's breath was shallow in her chest though relief coursed through her on every inhale.

"Our objective is to find out who he is and what he wants," Dessa said.

"That's pretty loose." Len shrugged. "But alright."

Harlow checked the time. It was getting late. "Time

for work," she said, grateful for the excuse to cut the conversation short.

"Call out," Dessa said, nearly an order.

Harlow shook her head. "And what? Go home and be miserable about a new kind of monster?"

Dessa scoffed. "I'll work on battle strategy."

"I'll work on a bread recipe," Len added.

Dessa raised a brow at her.

Len shrugged again. "Carbo-loading."

As her friends went one way, and she another, a pain in Harlow's heart blossomed in waves of dull ache. She was supposed to be the leader. But she just felt like a fraud.

# CHAPTER 8

# THE METEOR

It was rare that a Mechoida escaped her. Rarer still that one escaped all three of them. But, Harlow supposed that it was also rare for them to attack in the middle of a potentially crowded area, and hurl moonlight like cannon fire.

The whole situation reeked of danger, as though smoke from a wildfire surrounded her. She wasn't sure she'd be able to control it in time before it spread further, damaging everything.

She stuffed her hands into her pockets, careful to

keep her fingers loose in case she needed to grab at starlight again.

The whole walk to her work, she had been on edge. She whipped her head behind her at any sound of a branch snap, a rustle in the leaves, or even the buzz of a moth flocking to the glow of the orange pathway lights. She kept her head turning, moving in a zig zag along the sidewalk.

She glared daggers at the one person who passed her on the sidewalk, eyeing him suspiciously as though he was going to transform at any moment. She felt a little bad about it when he ducked his head and sped up. The poor old man was dressed well and looked exhausted. He was probably just a professor trying to get home after accidentally falling asleep at his desk.

At least, that was the story she had made up for him after she walked through the observatory doors and she no longer felt a threat of attack lingering in the depths of her stomach.

Now, Harlow's head was resting on the desk in the darkened observatory. She hadn't been home all day and had been so preoccupied with everything that she forgot her wallet. And so, there she sat with the greatest threat of all and a new kind of pain: hunger. She held one hand to her loudly grumbling stomach. Chipless.

This was the real travesty.

The sound of a large canvas bag hitting the table beside her shook her back to the present. She rolled her head to the side and looked up at Rainey with a pathetic expression she hoped would inspire pity.

"I brought extra," Rainey said with a calm smile. She pulled her blue floral bento boxes from her tote and handed one to Harlow.

Harlow sat up straighter, her enthusiasm back as swiftly as it had been depleted. "How did you know?"

Rainey shrugged. "I just like to surprise you guys from time to time." She looked around the room, then to the clock on the wall and let out a little laugh. "Gigi?"

"It's the curse," Harlow said as she opened the bento box with wide eyes. A burst of rich, earthy aromas filled her nose and her stomach gurgled louder. It all smelled amazing and was still warm at the bottom as she held it close.

"Well–"

The door burst open and Gigi hurried through. "I made it!" she declared when she got to the desk.

Rainey checked the clock again. "Two minutes–"

Gigi cut her off with a raised hand. "I don't want to hear it. If it's under five, it's on time."

"Isn't it if 'you're early you're on time, if you're on time, you're late'?" Harlow asked from the side of her mouth, cheek stuffed with rice and pork.

Gigi rolled her eyes dramatically. "What is this? Military school? I get paid to look at stars." She shifted her stance, her gaze landing on the unopened bento box in front of her desk. She clapped twice, bouncing on light feet. "For me?"

Rainey slid it closer to her. "I had extra."

"No," Gigi said as she sat down. The squeaky rolling chair protested slightly. "You love me."

Rainey laughed. "Sure, sure."

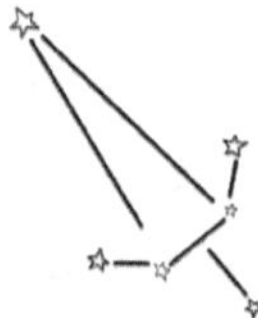

BELLIES FULL, and enough chatter out of the way about how the day had gone, (with Harlow carefully dodging every question) the three got to work.

Rainey, busy at the telescope read out measurements from time to time as Harlow charted and Gigi busied herself at the computer. Every so often, Gigi would ask a strange question to pass the time like: "If you could be any breed of dog, what would you be?"

"Basset hound," Rainey answered confidently, her head still glued to the eyepiece.

Gigi turned to her, a look of fake horror on her face. "Not your *favorite*. The one you'd *be*."

"Yeah. Basset hound," Rainey said.

Gigi huffed. "No, you're a golden retriever. Harlow is an Akita. And I am a Maltese."

Harlow's brows furrowed, trying to imagine each of them as dogs. It wasn't readily apparent in her mind. "You could have just told us."

"I wanted *you* to tell *me*," Gigi said. "It's more fun."

"Not if you already have the answers," Rainey said with a snort.

Harlow pointed at Rainey. "She's right."

"Fine." Gigi turned back to her computer. "What is your *favorite* breed?"

"Basset hound," Rainey said, too quickly. She shot Harlow a wink.

Gigi threw up her hands. "Oh my god!"

"What about favorite color?" Harlow offered.

"That's basic."

"Hang on..." Rainy's voice was low, urgent. She peered into the telescope lens as her whole body sank around it.

Gigi's brows furrowed.

Harlow joined Rainy's side quickly, though the other woman didn't move from her spot. It was clear that Rainey wasn't giving up her position at the telescope.

"I thought I just saw like a flash or something," Rainey whispered.

Gigi's fingers flew across the keyboard, her acrylic nails clicking at the keys like a rainstorm. "Let me pull it up." A few more quick taps, and the image appeared on her screen.

It was, in fact, a quick flash. Of dark purple, and navy, and flecks of blinding silver moonlight.

Harlow's fists clenched. "What the hell?"

Gigi looked up at her. "What was that?"

Rainey flinched, sucking in a quick breath of air through her teeth. "Another one!"

"A meteor shower?" Gigi wondered aloud.

Harlow's muscles tightened. *They wouldn't.*

The Mechoida had never attacked her when she was around humans. Even earlier that evening, it waited until the campus was empty. Sure, it was a risky move on its part, but it didn't feel like one that put too much of a spotlight on itself. They didn't seem to want to harm humans, either. Their goal seemed solely to take her and the shield and bow out. Hell, they never even went after the Queen.

Harlow had moved about the night with confidence when humans were around. Until tonight.

There was no way...

A deafening boom shattered through the roof. Harlow grabbed Rainey and covered her with her body as debris from the stonework above rained down between the telescope and the computers, creating a low barrier between Rainey and Harlow from Gigi.

Dust and cold night air filled their lungs.

Rainey coughed violently as Harlow held her down, arms tightening around her back. She turned her head over Rainey's shoulder to check that Gigi was alright.

Gigi sat in her chair, eyes wide and mouth agape in terror as she stared up at the massive hole in the ceiling. She was frozen, petrified with terror, but unharmed.

Harlow breathed out a long exhale and let Rainey go. She rose to her feet, shoulders back, hands out at her sides. She looked up past the damaged roof and to the starlight shining bright above.

Fine.

They wanted a fight.

They'd get one.

A flash of purple light burst through the dark observatory.

The Mechoida crashed to the floor, cracking the tile beneath its legs. It rose up to its full height, towering over them with broad shoulders, an empty darkness in its limbs even more opposing as more sparks of electricity fell from the hanging wires above them. It turned to Harlow, eyes filled with shimmering moonlight, glowing bright as the sparks around them finally faded, drenching the room in black and gray shadow. A clawed hand lifted as if to summon Harlow. A snarl cut through its face.

Behind her, she heard Rainey scream.

Harlow stepped forward, squaring her body between her friend and the monster. A half-smile on her lips mirrored the creature's. She had already warmed up earlier that night. She was ready.

Harlow's hand reached for the sky. She closed her eyes and spun together the starlight, enveloping her in a golden glow as the sword materialized in her grasp. She set her stare on the Mechoida and thrust the sword forward with ease. "Come on," she challenged it, voice bold in the dark.

The Mechoida growled.

One step closer to her.

"Come on!"

Another slow step.

*Squeak.*

The sound of the faulty wheel on the tile cut through the room.

The Mechoida stopped. Slowly, curiously, it turned.

Gigi's hands flew to cover her mouth, knuckles white as she gripped her face hard to stifle her scream. But she was too late.

Harlow's legs ignited in burning exertion as she propelled herself forward. She leaped onto the debris, one foot pressing swiftly into the rubble as she tried to get up over it as fast as she could.

The Mechoida's claws came down hard.

Gigi's cry pierced the space between them, but then, she was silent.

Harlow swung her sword up. The tip of it caught the Mechoida's back, slicing up from the base of its spine to the tall shoulders.

It howled, back arching as moonlight poured from it and, like mist, evaporated into the night. It spun on its heel to face her again, mouth open in a wide black hole.

Harlow's gaze was fierce as she readied her sword again, positioning her stance so she wasn't so easily knocked off her feet. "It's me you're after," she said through gritted teeth. "Or is your brain too rotted to know the difference between your princess and a human?"

It only snarled in response, reaching out for her with one long arm.

Harlow jumped forward. Her sword drove through its chest before she, or the Mechoida, had time to think. It stuck there, right in the middle, and with a hiss and a blinding darkness, the Mechoida vanished.

Harlow's breath came out in bursts. She thrust her hand skyward, returning the sword back to the stars. A shimmer of light surrounded her, lifting her hair from her sweaty brow before the sword disappeared completely.

Rainey scrambled over the fallen stone, clumsy, but brave. "Gigi!" she cried as soon as she made it up over the obstacles.

Harlow hurried to Gigi's side. Fear, for the first time that evening, flooded through her as she rushed forward.

Gigi curled up on the floor, her hand pressing down hard on her cheek as bright red blood flowed between her fingers and down her arm.

Harlow pulled Gigi's shaking hand away with a gentle, firm grip.

Gigi let out a small whine in protest.

"I'm just seeing how bad it is," Harlow whispered kindly. Though, as soon as the words came out, she wished she had thought for a second about what to say. She winced, at both her own stupidity, and at the two long gashes running from Gigi's forehead down her cheek and all the way to her chin.

Gigi's wide eyes searched Harlow's in a panic. "How bad? Is it bad? Did it get an artery? Am I dying?" Her questions came out of her in rapid succession. Her body began to tremble, hard.

From behind her, Harlow heard Rainey's voice cut through the panic. She was repeating an address, explaining that her friend was hurt. She told them to hurry.

Gigi pulled her hand free from Harlow's grip then pressed it back to her face. "What was that?" she whispered.

Harlow's gaze bounced from Gigi to Rainey. She had no idea what to say. All she knew was that things were escalating. Exponentially. And that despite her fear and confusion, she was glad that the creature hadn't hit Gigi harder. It could have been worse. It could have so easily been fatal.

Her own body started to tremble under the weight of it all. The feeling of loss. Of coming so close to something catastrophic.

Gigi would be alright, she told herself through the haze of adrenaline pumping into every vein.

At least, mostly.

Guilt tore through Harlow's insides as Rainey crouched beside them. "Paramedics are on the way," Rainey said as she gently held her hand over Gigi's until it, too, was covered in red. "They already had reports from the damage done to the building," she told Harlow, her voice a hoarse whisper. "I told them she's been hurt by the falling stone."

Gigi let out a snort, then winced as pain shot

through her at the change in expression. "Good. I can sue."

"You'll never need to work again," Rainey said with a smile, though her eyes were full of tears. A deep crease formed between her brows as she looked at Harlow. "But you better explain yourself."

Harlow nodded, her own vision blurred. She wiped her eyes with the back of her hand. "Okay," she said. "Okay..."

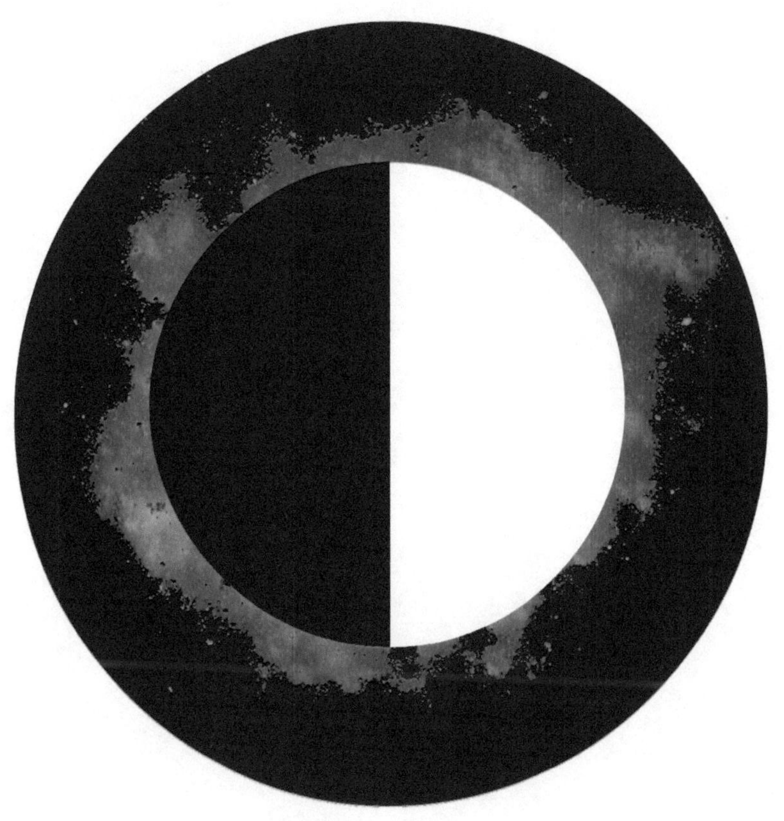

# THE GENERAL AND THE QUEEN

essa and Len were at the scene just as the red and blue lights faded from view. Len's hand squeezed Harlow's shoulder tightly as they watched the ambulance turn the corner, carrying her friends away to the hospital with injuries none of them could explain. Dessa nodded for them to move on and led the way down the sidewalk that had become crowded with students, all gawking and pointing to the sky. Gently, Len guided Harlow away from the broken building and the police putting up tape around the rubble.

They walked in silence for a long while until she found herself standing in front of their apartment building, looking up at the moon's reflection off the glass. At last, Dessa stood at Harlow's side. She slipped her hand into Harlow's and a warmth spread through, thawing the numbness that had settled into her bones. She let out a shaky breath, her shoulders slumped inward as the memories of the night flooded back into her.

"I should've seen it coming–"

But the squeeze of Dessa's hand silenced her, followed by Len's soft voice. "Let's go up. Take a shower. I'll have tea waiting for us when you get out, okay?"

Harlow nodded. She refused to let the sting of tears defeat her, to show that she was afraid. She held her head high, biting her lip to keep it from quivering, and together, they made their way into the safety of their home.

At least, it was safe for now.

CLEAN, warm, and finally able to relax her muscles after the long, scalding shower, Harlow sat on the couch with a cup of steaming tea in her hands. She held it close to her chest, inhaling the familiar scent of earthy chamomile and sweet honey.

Len never acted like a spell caster the way Dessa did. But Harlow was certain that there was magic in her food and drinks. She poured love and hope into everything she did. Her signature sweet nighttime tea was always full of protection and care. It never failed to lull her into a restful, dreamless sleep, even on her worst days.

Across the little coffee table, Len sat on the floor with her own mug held carefully in her hands. Beside her, Dessa lit another candle, whispering something quiet and calm under her breath. The space filled with more light as the flames before them flickered in a peaceful dance.

Harlow smiled gently. At least all these candles were the same vanilla scent she had bought on clearance, so long exposed to the open air that she was sure they wouldn't throw their smell too far. It wouldn't feel oppressive, just warm and calm and like she was in a home where a loving parent made cookies.

She curled up tighter. She just wanted to sink into the tea, let the scent of old vanilla envelope her like a cocoon.

But Carina broke the silence at last as she jumped up onto the arm rest of the couch like a shadow. "Did they see the Mechoida?"

Harlow nodded. She sipped her tea loudly.

The familiar clank of ceramic on wood startled her as Dessa set her mug down. "Are there cameras there?"

Harlow shook her head. "No, but good thinking."

Dessa smiled, though it was hard to tell if it was a smirk or a chuckle in the low light of the candles. She went on, "Gigi okay?"

Harlow took another long sip, savoring, for just a moment, the way the honey hit the sides of her tongue, the warmth of it running down into her core. "She is. Mostly. It could've been much worse." She sank deeper into the couch. "I shouldn't have hesitated."

Len held up a hand to pause her quickly. "It's not that," she said. "You're plenty decisive."

Dessa raised a brow in agreement. She let out a little snort.

"It worries me that they attacked like that, though," Len went on. "Why go after humans all of the sudden?"

Dessa shrugged. "Perhaps they're trying to wake others up? Maybe you like Gigi and Rainey so much because they're one of us?"

Harlow shook her head again. "I don't think that's it. I feel like... It felt personal."

"It *felt* personal and it *was* personal are two different things," Dessa said, her voice low, as if she was afraid to offend Harlow with her bluntness.

As if she hadn't said so much worse before and come out unscathed.

Dessa took a long sip of her tea. Her eyes were fixed on Harlow with an intensity she hadn't seen in a long time. "It's also possible they're simply testing the boundaries of their abilities. Throwing moonlight, trying their attacks more openly. They might be trying to see what they can get away with."

"She's right. We should consider all options," Carina agreed, though her tail thumped dully on the couch.

Len tapped her mug with her fingertips gently. "Do you suppose that it's more than that?"

Dessa's brows furrowed. "What do you mean?"

Len shrugged lightly. "First Fox, then the attacks tonight, one right after the other. It all *feels* like something." Her eyes flicked to Dessa. "Before you say it, I know it's different to feel it than it is to *be* true. But you have to admit, it does feel like things are leading to something. And quickly."

"It's all been leading to a war for as long as we've been here. Just like last time. They repeat the cycle," Carina said. She looked up at the group and her ear flicked. "We need to practice patience, even if the enemy doesn't."

Harlow leaned forward. "It's a war they want. And it's a war they'll have. But we'll win this time," she said. "We just need to up our own game."

"The battle for our own world destroyed it," Carina said. "Be careful to involve Earth so quickly."

Harlow emptied her lungs in one heavy sigh. Carina was right. As usual.

A loud vibrating spooked Harlow from her seat. She jumped to her feet, mug clutched tightly to her chest as she searched for the sound.

Her phone, face up with the display reading 'Aunt Always Answer' in lieu of a photo, lit up the screen.

Harlow's heart raced in her ribs. She looked up at the others with wide eyes.

"It was only a matter of time," Dessa hissed quickly. She gestured to the phone. "Well, go on then. Let's get this all over with and hear whatever insane idea she has this time."

"Easy for you to say. I'm the one she expects to carry out the insane ideas," Harlow shot back. She grabbed the phone, took in a deep breath, and answered.

"Come immediately," the voice on the other end said without any pleasantry beforehand.

"'Immediately' meaning...?" Harlow began. She looked down at her comfy pjs.

"Bring the bow and the shield."

Harlow looked at her friends, brows raised.

Len was already up, fixing her dress to look presentable.

The line hung up and Harlow sighed. "We'd better get going."

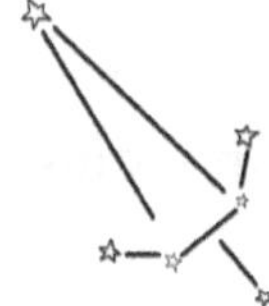

THERE WAS no place quite like her aunt's home. Though, calling it a *home* would be inaccurate. It was really more like the inside of a magazine Harlow had seen when they did interviews with celebrities. It was the kind of place that put fake apples in crystal bowls on counters to look like they ate real food and were down to earth, when really, everyone knew it was a facade.

It was stark, pristine, monochromatic in shades of pale blue from floor to high ceiling.

It had been a central location for her and her friends for years. A place to lie low. To be hidden in plain sight. But it never really felt like *home,* even when it was the only place she rested her head. Harlow had spent most of her time away at various trainings or on the roof.

She was certain her old room had been repurposed years ago. She never went in to look after she left.

The only good thing about the penthouse of the huge skyscraper was the view. At night, the lights of the city mirrored the starlight above and everything below looked small and clean. The floor to ceiling windows let it all in. The dark and the light and the space between.

From here, they could see the looming halfmoon sinking lower into the buildings as the night blended with the first hints of dawn.

Her aunt stood at the window. Her reflection in the large glass, slightly blurred and muted color, stared back at Harlow with an impassive expression. "They're getting bolder," she said at last, turning her head over her shoulder for a moment to catch Harlow's eyes. She sounded bored.

Beside her, Len's steady presence grounded her. She cast a quick side glance at Dessa who raised a brow back at her, urging her on.

"My friend was hurt," Harlow said at last. "It's not just 'bolder', they're hurting humans."

"Have you discovered how it managed to do so much damage?" The Queen asked as though she hadn't heard, or cared, about what Harlow had just said.

Dessa stepped forward. "I believe they are getting better at harnessing the moonlight. It seems some of them are able to wield it... almost like a missile. It's strong."

"An interesting theory. They have been known to do that." The Queen turned back to the window. "Before."

*Before.*

The word hung between them dangerously. The Queen rarely spoke about *before*.

Before they were reborn on Earth was a time of strife and destruction. Some of the memories of war were still just out of their grasp. How much, though, Harlow couldn't be sure. It sure as hell felt like most.

"How are we supposed to fight against them if they're throwing moonlight?" Len asked, her tone steady and strong.

The Queen hummed. She turned back to them with a small smile. "How do you fight something far away?"

Dessa cocked her head. "With precision."

"You draw them to you," the Queen corrected.

Dessa's jaw tightened.

"We will bring the fight to them from this point forward," the older woman went on. "Find and destroy as many as you can. We do not go one night without seeking them out until the full moon."

Len looked at Dessa for a moment before turning sternly back to the Queen. "Is it wise to seek a fight?"

"It's the only way," the Queen said. "If they have found a way to harness moonlight like this, far more terrible things are on the horizon. This war is escalating. We must bring it to them."

"I agree," Harlow said, begrudgingly. A flush of heat radiated through her cheeks as she felt Dessa's hard stare land on her. "We need to bring this to them, and before the full moon." She side-eyed Dessa for a moment, the weight of her disappointment heavy on Harlow's shoulders. But she couldn't dwell on that for now. "They hurt people close to me. They're a threat. We should draw them here. To the roof. Far away from anyone else and do our best to end it there."

"Agreed," the Queen said. "Leave one alive. Tell it to bring the others here. The rooftop the night before the full moon. They will come."

"You're sure?" Len whispered.

"Yes. The power of the moon seeks to corrupt all it touches. It will try to seep its light into you all. They will take the opportunity."

"You know this for sure? Leaving one alive is dangerous enough–" Dessa was cut off quickly.

"It would be better... if there were less before the full

moon." The Queen paused. She placed her hands behind her back gently, a tired motion. She sighed. "Carina should be with you going forward," her aunt said, changing the subject quickly. "All your guards should be."

"There's no reason for it." Harlow grimaced. She did her best to relax again, though she hated being questioned like this, hated being told what to do like a child. "I'm the sword."

Her aunt hummed. She moved along the wall, eyes lowered at the city as though she were surveying her own kingdom. "You are."

"Then you trust me to handle this."

"Yes."

*It wasn't a question.* Harlow's eyes narrowed. She bowed, slowly.

"Report back when you have more information."

A dismissal, curt and final. About as loving as her aunt ever sounded. 'Report back' was her 'get home safe'. At least, that's what Harlow always told herself.

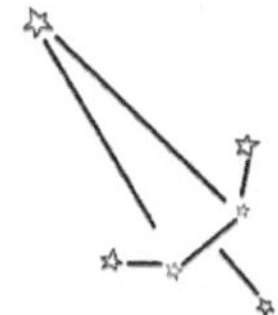

"I don't like this plan," Len said as soon as her feet hit the sidewalk. "It seems foolish and rash."

The city was empty. It was just before dawn, the pale pink light from the sun was beginning to touch the tops of the surrounding skyscrapers. Exhaustion mixed with a buzzing excitement inched its way through Harlow's body, warming her like the rising sun.

Dessa nodded. "Agreed. We can't just blunt force our way through things like this." She paused for a moment, waiting to see if Harlow would fight her on her dissent. When it was clear the other woman had not broken her stride, she went on. "Harlow, are you serious about leaving one alive? Having them on the roof is one thing. We can kind of contain them there, but have you forgotten how they're going to get there? They'll cut through a whole group of people if they have to."

Harlow shook her head. "It buys us time," she said. "It's a rough draft. It can change."

"Tell that to the Queen," Len grumbled.

"Not yet," Harlow said, confidence back in her voice. Each step farther from the building emboldened her. Freedom from the shadow of the building brightened her heart. "Look, sometimes the key to dealing with her is placating her. And besides, her plan *is* the best we have. For now."

"You're serious?" Dessa leaned down to catch Harlow's gaze. "You mean to defy her order?"

Harlow shrugged. "I don't mean to do anything but hunt them down for now."

Len tossed her head up to the sky. A small grin formed as the sunlight hit her silver hair, illuminating her brightly. "She said leave one alive. She failed to specify when."

Harlow's own smile widened. "See?"

Dessa rolled her eyes, though she tried to hide it by fixing a lock of hair behind her ear. "Fine. But no more running off on your own. From now on, we do this together. Deal?"

"Deal," Harlow lied.

In her pocket, her phone buzzed. A quick vibration that jolted the three of them from their thoughts.

Harlow fished it out. Rainey's name lit up her screen, the preview of a text flashed before the screen turned dark once again.

Her jaw clenched, fingers tightening around the phone. She wanted to know how Gigi was, but worry paralyzed her. She stopped in her tracks as fear, an unwelcome and unfamiliar emotion, raced through her.

It could be bad news. Terrible news.

"You should look," Len said.

Harlow sighed and opened the text before she gave into the impulse to hurl it far away from her.

Rainey: Hey, they're letting us go. I'm taking Gg home

thank the stars

She sent it before she had the chance to censor herself. She cringed at herself and her past expression. It probably sounded fake to Rainey. She typed quickly, trying to recover as they continued down the empty sidewalk.

is she okay?

Rainey: Yeah but we want to see you. You know. About the

Rainey: Thing we saw

okay. soon.

Rainey: Today

Harlow rolled her neck. She looked down the road and watched the shadows deepen as the sun continued its easy rise into the sky. She wanted to see them, check in and make sure they had everything they needed. But she also hated the idea of explaining what had happened to them.

Dessa put a gentle hand on her shoulder, catching her attention with a light squeeze. "Are they okay?"

"Yeah," Harlow said as she stuffed her phone away. "They are."

"Are *you* okay?"

Harlow shook her head. "Not really. But when am I ever?"

# CHAPTER 10

# IT WAS NEVER THE CAT

The mid morning came too quickly.

Harlow hadn't slept at all but time still passed in a series of rapid blinks. She tossed and turned the rest of the early morning, worrying about Gigi, worrying about her future, worrying about how she was supposed to outsmart the Queen, the Mechoida, and her friends.

She worried even more that she had less than two weeks to get a plan together before the final showdown.

Harlow was used to getting things done. How exactly they got done was always up in the air. She found the plan while she was in the middle of it. After all, her life had always been one of rapid change at the most inconvenient times. She couldn't stay one step ahead, so instead, she barreled forward, shoving her way past obstacles and vulnerability, leaving a trail of broken walls and hearts in her wake.

There was no fighting her nature now. No sense in agonizing over what she'd say to them, how she'd explain herself, or what lies she'd tell. She'd get through it the same as she always had. With a bloody nose and a laugh or two.

Still, she resented the nerves that crackled electric beneath her skin. It was daylight, but she wasn't safe. She couldn't count on the old rules.

Not anymore.

She spent the entire walk to Gigi's apartment looking over her shoulder, flinching at any sound other than her own feet on the pavement. She took several purposeful wrong turns, memorized the faces of everyone she passed. She kept this up until she was very, very late.

Harlow stood outside the door to Gigi's apartment with a bouquet of flowers that she had simultaneously thought were too expensive and would have spent double to obtain. They were stargazer lilies, Gigi's favorite.

Harlow remembered learning this fact one night of a million strange questions. She hadn't meant to file it away. In fact, she wasn't even sure why she knew it.

The memory was vague. It felt familiar yet foreign, like fumbling for the light switch in the dark and touching something unexpected. Everything got strange in her mind after the Mechoida attacked. The moment it turned toward Gigi, the corruption had taken hold, obscuring and warping any memory that had once been filled with joy.

She could only hope that it would brighten back up eventually and she would be able to look back on her memories of her night job with the same fondness she once did. And hopefully it wouldn't take long.

She looked down at the flowers and frowned. At least, she was *pretty sure* these were her favorites.

In her other hand, she gripped the bottle of wine tighter. Three cards: a 'get well soon' card, a 'sorry I missed your birthday' (they didn't have a 'sorry I lied and a monster mauled you' card), and a 'happy retirement' card wedged between her hand and the glass, making it difficult to keep her grip. For a faint moment, she worried that it'd all come crashing down and she'd be standing in a puddle of shattered glass, reeking of bottom-shelf pink wine.

But now, as the back of her neck began to bead with sweat under the direct sunlight, an intense and sudden flurry of nerves built up in her stomach that had nothing to do with the wine or the cards or even the flowers, which, now that she looked at them closer, maybe were *Rainey's* favorite...

No, despite being asked to come, she felt like she was intruding and it made her feel like a predator about the ask to spend time with prey.

It was her fault, even indirectly, that Gigi had been targeted. And she never wanted to put her or Rainey in that situation ever again. So she fought her urge to flee the city, fake her death, and begin wearing a mask like Batman at night. Instead, she had agreed to meet them and explain herself.

She owed it to them to stay.

And she supposed she owed it to herself to finish her degree...

If she managed to live long enough.

Just as she was trying to figure out the best way to knock with both hands full and precarious, the door creaked open.

Rainey smiled softly through the crack in the door. She

looked at Harlow from her shoes to her forehead, as if assessing it really was her. Puffy bags, dark under Rainey's eyes, and still reddened corners betrayed her long night full of tears and worry no matter what her smile tried to cover up. "Come in," Rainey said, making way for Harlow to pass.

Harlow gave the empty street another quick glance in both directions, then practically leaped inside, shutting the door behind her with a definitive, and somewhat rude, thud.

A sudden wave of vanilla hit her nose. A sense of calm and comfort enveloped her, as though the scent was a spell just for her. The small studio was packed with adorable, whimsical decor. Pink sheer curtains let in warm sunlight, lighting the space with an otherworldly glow. A huge bed was piled with plush pastel pillows, fuzzy animal stuffies, and heaps of chunky knit blankets.

Every inch of the space burst with blissful playfulness in the way only Gigi could make look good. Despite the clutter, it was clean and in a state of organized chaos. Like patterns and textures grouped together. Everything seemed to have a place to belong.

Rainey took the flowers and wine from Harlow gently, extracting the bottle with careful precision as Harlow's fingers clung to the three cards. She examined the bottle with one raised brow, letting the flowers fall in her other hand.

Harlow thrust the cards toward her, covering the wine label. No need for Rainey to notice that this was the budget friendly stuff, even if she was sure it was all either of them could afford. She shook the cards twice. "I... um," she started, a flush crossing over her nose. "I didn't know what to get."

"Shoes off," Rainey told Harlow dismissively as she looked over the three cards.

Harlow kicked off her sneakers, laces still knit, and wiggled her toes free. Her mismatched black and gray socks looked out of place among all the comforting plush pastels. Her frown deepened.

"I don't think I can have that with the pain meds," Gigi said from the couch that lined the foot of the bed. She was curled up under a pastel faux fur blanket, almost entirely hidden among all the bulky, soft fabrics. She turned to Harlow, her face bandaged on one side in white gauze.

Harlow winced at the sight of the bandages. She tried to play it off as she looked around the room, running a hand through her short hair. "Nice place," she said as casually as she could.

Gigi waved her hand as if she thought it was an

insult. "Yeah, girly girl has a girly apartment. Shocking. Front page news, really."

Rainey sat on the floor near a small coffee table, her legs crossed. "No, it really is nice," she said.

Harlow cautiously ventured further into the room with light steps, as though she was about to step on a Lego at any moment. For all its cuteness and soft textures, part of her felt as though she had entered a mouse trap. She took in a deep inhale, letting the sweet vanilla smell infiltrate her senses again. It calmed her quickly, though a lasting unease stuck with her.

"How are you feeling?" Harlow asked at last. She lingered beside them, not yet sure she should sit beside them.

Gigi sighed. "Not great. You see, I have two massive cuts on my face and I'm out of a job until they repair the observatory. Which will probably be long after graduation."

"I'm sorry..." Harlow didn't know what else to say. She was sorry, but that felt so dismissive, without the weight in her heart that accompanied those words. Her eyes scanned Gigi's face. She could see no malice there, though her expression was still impossible to gauge with the bandages hiding all subtly. She took another careful step closer. If Gigi had been injured in any other way, what would she say? At last, she went with surface level interest. "Did you need stitches?"

"Glue, actually," Gigi said confidently. "I'm going to tell everyone I jumped into a tiger enclosure to save a toddler and fought it off with my bare hands. The tiger, not the toddler." She didn't pause for either of them to catch her quip, instead, she merely tilted one side of her lip up and kept going. "Maybe I'll use some shimmery golden eyeliner in the scars once they're all healed up. Kintsugi my own face."

Rainey looked at Harlow and shrugged.

Harlow let out a long breath in return. She had been worried that Gigi would have deep scars, that she'd never forgive her, that this was the death of any semblance of friendship that had been fostered between them. That maybe she'd have to dodge items thrown at her head, or insults to her ego.

Instead, Gigi seemed surprisingly at ease.

Gratitude and guilt blended in Harlow's heart, a swirl of bitter and sweet. She did consider these people her friends. At least, she was closer to them than any other human. Yet, Gigi's jovial attitude and laid-back reaction confounded her. It was so unexpected that Harlow realized she didn't *really* know them at all.

Rainey leaned forward, both elbows on the low

coffee table to prop herself up. "I like that idea," she told Gigi. "But hopefully it won't scar much."

Gigi burrowed lower into the giant blanket. "It's just a body," she said wistfully. "But contrary to belief, beauty can also have brains. And I want to use mine." Her eyes shifted to Harlow with an intensity that sent a chill down Harlow's back. "So the prevailing rumor is that a meteor hit the observatory. Very ironic."

Rainey sighed. "The good news is, Professor Sato called me. Well, the bad news is, she said that she has no idea when it'll be repaired. In the meantime, she's going to see if she can get us two weeks' pay."

"Goody," Gigi said. "I'll tell that to the landlord. Maybe if I cry, he'll take pity on me."

"It's not nothing," Rainey countered. "Better than nothing."

"You could still sue? Split the money three ways?" Harlow said, a genuine smile crossing her lips. Without thinking, she took a seat across from Rainey, and for a moment, ease settled into her body. It felt natural to sit beside them and talk about wild plans and silly ideas, even outside of work.

Gigi shook her head. "No, no. No sidetracking the conversation. And, no offense, Harlow, I love you and stuff but we'd split it two ways because I'm *starting to suspect* that you got us into this mess."

Harlow looked down at her hands. She had never had to explain this to anyone before. Not really. Dessa and Len had already had enough context through their own memories. All she had to do was fill in some gaps here and there where she could. She had left much of it to her aunt back then, too. It was easier that way. Her aunt had all the memories of their past, up until the very end.

With them, she didn't have to dive into her own missing past. They simply accepted that there were huge gaps in knowledge and understanding because they lived it.

But this?

She had no idea where to even start explaining things to someone who, just a day before, had no idea about any of it. If they hadn't seen it all with their own eyes, she was sure that any talk of this would have them calling the psychology department to be studied.

Harlow tapped the table with light fingers. She focused her gaze on the grain of the wood, the way it moved in wavy lines, weaving and blending in with one other. Where one began and one ended was hard to find, but she traced the lines anyway until she heard her voice shake as the words poured out. "What you saw was a Mechoida. They're like me. Which is to say, not from here. From Earth. Except, back then, they harnessed moonlight. It makes them dangerous. The moon is strong…" She looked up at Gigi, trying to understand her reaction. Her face, the half she could see, was focused, but there was no confusion there, as if she understood exactly what Harlow was saying. "They've never gone after humans before… I don't know what happened. But they're changing. Fast."

Rainey leaned closer. "Why do you say 'humans' like…"

"You're not one," Gigi finished for her.

Harlow took in a deep breath until her lungs stung. She let it out slowly through her nose. "I am," she said. "I am human… Mostly. I was reborn here after the war on my home. So were some of my friends. Well, a lot of us, actually. Our planet was destroyed, and a spell was cast to send us all here. Most of us don't know who we were, though I'm sure they feel different in a way they can't explain." She looked up again, both her friends leaned in closer. She went on. "When we wake up to who we are, who we were, there's a change. I don't know how it works all in all. Some of our old life comes back. Sometimes that includes magic. Or, I guess you could call it magic."

The room was quiet.

Harlow watched specs of dust in the air catch the light, sparkle, then fade in a gently swirling cloud. She went on. "The Mechoida are like us. But they don't use the starlight. They use moonlight. It's more powerful. And forbidden. It corrupts everything it touches, in the end."

"You used the starlight to make the sword?" Rainey asked.

Harlow nodded. "We're all from another planet. Far away from here... Some of us can harness starlight. It's rare. Rarer than transforming with moonlight."

"How–?" Gigi started, but her hand went to her cheek. She sucked in a loud breath.

Harlow went on, trying to get Gigi's mind off the pain, "I'm told that there are gods who gifted us this power. A God of Stars and a God of Moons in a constant battle for the light since the beginning." She looked down at her hands. What she was about to say was blasphemous, though she knew they wouldn't understand the gravity of it at all. She summoned her courage. "But I'm not so sure. That could just be an old myth. I don't think I believe in them."

Rainey and Gigi settled in. Both looked ready to hear more.

For nearly half an hour, Harlow explained the history of her old world. Of the magic that it contained, the world war, and the extinction of their planet. She talked about the gods and their corruption. About her friends who stayed by her side through it all, and the cat-like guardians who studied their whole long lives to learn how to use the moonlight so it would delay the contamination.

She talked until her voice started to ache.

When she was done and she was certain that there was no room for questions, she waited, eyes back to the grain of the wood, careful to keep still though all she wanted to do was burst free of her spot and run far, far away.

Rainey let out a small huff, breaking the stillness between them. "So this whole time, we've been blaming your cat when it was really giant moon magic monsters..? Do we owe the cat an apology?"

Gigi nodded. "The craziest part of this story is that we actually believed that you had a vicious cat that clawed at you all the time." She turned to Rainey. "We might be idiots."

Harlow snorted, a lightness filled her at last.

"Is there a way we can help?" Rainey asked.

"We have a lot of free time now that our night shift is on pause," Gigi added.

It felt free to have it all laid bare but as she looked at them, in all her entirety, the smallest twinge shot through her heart. She knew it couldn't last. There was still the deadline, the danger, the uncertainty of it all.

They knew what they had found themselves in, but they didn't *understand*. How could they? It was still her job to protect humans. Even the ones who didn't think they needed protecting. Maybe especially them.

Harlow shook her head. "You saw how dangerous they are." She stood up, so fast that Rainey flinched. "I'm really sorry, Gigi. You have to know that I didn't think something like that could ever happen."

"It's fine." Gigi smiled. Then winced.

It wasn't 'fine'. Nothing about this was. It was a disaster attached to a rocket ship and everyone Harlow knew was grounded in the exhaust flames. She shouldn't have let her guard down. But now, she had fulfilled her duty as a friend. She told the truth and let it out. If she had to throw stones at them to keep them safe, she would do just that. She only hoped it didn't come down to that.

"Try to stay inside at night," Harlow said quietly, her gaze fixed on the floor. "You're safe in the daytime and during the new moon. I really am sorry." She turned to leave, ignoring Rainey's protest as she slipped on her shoes and walked out into the bright sunlight.

She didn't have the luxury of friends.

She had monsters to fight.

# CHAPTER 11

# THE BEST DEFENSE

The light through her bedroom window illuminated Harlow's living room in a golden orange glow. The sun was beginning its rapid descent, ushering in long shadows and a sense of purpose that hid in the spaces where the darkness fell. Soon, the shadows would fade into the surrounding night and action would fill the emptiness like starlight.

Harlow laced up her boots with steady fingers just as Carina entered the dwindling beam of light. The cat looked up at Harlow, then shook her head.

"So soon?" Carina asked.

Harlow flashed her a confident grin. "I have my orders. Eliminate as many as possible."

"And leave one alive."

Harlow sighed. She leaned back in a low squat and pressed a hand to her forehead. "Yeah," she said at last. "Easier said than done. But that means no more nights off. Especially if there's no observatory work."

Carina's tail flicked up, a little question mark.

Harlow rolled her eyes, but a small puff left her lips as she chuckled lightly. "You're worried about bills?"

Carina cocked her head. "I've become accustomed to a certain standard of food. I like the good stuff."

"You sure I can't convince you to go back to the dry kibble?"

Carina hissed. "If I had to live a whole lifetime studying the art and science of resisting the corruption of an ancient Moonlight God only to be reborn *again* as a four-legged animal, the least you could do–"

Harlow raised her hands, cutting Carina off. "I surrender. I'll find another gig, alright? A gas station or something has got to be hiring night work." She looked up at the ceiling. "Or... maybe I'll *rob* the gas stations."

The cat huffed, dismissing Harlow's musings on turning to a life of crime as if Harlow was simply complaining about the weather. Carina's eyes made their way down to Harlow's boots, then back up. "Well, if you're insisting on going out tonight, let's not waste the moonlight."

Harlow nodded. She let out a little groan as she rose slowly to her feet again. "Come on."

Harlow and Carina stepped out into the twilight to find Len and Dessa, dressed in black workout clothes, standing on the sidewalk.

Len had her arms crossed over her chest as her eyes fell on Carina and Harlow. Her hair was pulled back in a loose ponytail, uncharacteristically away from her face, and her expression stern.

Dessa, wearing a black tennis dress and notably no jewelry, stood beside her, looking even more petite by comparison. She shifted her weight from one leg to the other, her hand finding her waist. "Thanks for the invite," Dessa said dryly.

"You didn't get my carrier pigeon?" Harlow asked with a raised brow.

Len's eyes narrowed. "Or your evite. How strange."

Carina darted between Harlow's legs. She trotted to the other two and looked up at them as a group of people passed by. She meowed loudly.

"Vela and Ara are off on the other side of the city," Dessa told the cat. "We thought we'd divide and conquer."

Carina gave a little nod, then took off down the street.

"I didn't think it was wise to split up," Len said softly. "But it might be necessary." She turned, then gestured for them to follow.

Harlow and Dessa cast quick side glances at each other, neither knowing quite how to respond. Len was right, as usual. But then, their best chances of getting ahead of things was to find as many as possible.

The two caught up to Len and a calm silence settled between them.

Night fell over the city as they walked deeper into the downtown.

Lights from the giant buildings began to turn on. Streetlights shined down the familiar glow and neon business signs flickered on in business windows. The sidewalk was busy, but they knew all the right places to be, every darkened alleyway and side street empty of people where the shadows took hold and monsters lurked.

Still, as their silent march continued, Harlow grew increasingly concerned that this would be an empty night out. She half considered ducking into a bar and complaining about their classes. At least it would pass the time and be somewhat entertaining. But she knew that the others would never go for it.

Besides, without Dessa's spells around their necks, it was very possible that they might draw the monsters in. The Mechoida always seemed to find her when she went off on her own.

"Is this all you do? Wander aimlessly looking for a fight?" Dessa asked after what felt like hours of aimless wandering in easy silence.

"The best defense is a good offense." Harlow turned a corner and they found themselves trapped in a dead-end alley, darkened and away from the busier road.

"That... doesn't make a ton of sense," Len said.

Dessa looked up at the brick buildings surrounding either side of them, so high their roofs seemed to blend in with the sky. She tucked a lock of hair behind her ear and cast a quick glance at Harlow. "Lost?"

Harlow shrugged. "They usually find me," she said honestly. She looked up at the night sky. At least the stars were shining.

Dessa huffed. "Maybe they're too scared with the three of us here?"

Len's brows furrowed. She turned back toward the way they came. "Perhaps there aren't many more left." Her voice was quiet, wistful, as though she wanted to believe it.

"Doubtful. We just haven't found them."

"Look, if I have to be out hunting and also worrying

about entertaining you two–" Harlow started, her hands waving, exasperated.

Dessa glared at her, silencing any protest. "Enough."

Len nodded. "We can call this a practice," she said. "You know, team building."

"I wonder if the cats are having better luck," Dessa said with a sigh.

Harlow led the way out of the alley. "Let's call it."

"Not so fast." Dessa hurried to her side. "This night isn't a total loss." She pointed to the late night noodle bar across the street, a hot pink neon bowl with electric yellow noodles dangling above in wavy lines. "I'm starving. And we need to talk about Fox. No more stalling."

"And go over our pitches for Jensen," Len added. "The finalized pitch is due tomorrow."

Harlow's head fell. She completely forgot about their pitch meeting.

"Fate of the world, final articles," Dessa said, weighing the imaginary options in her hands. One fell dramatically lower than the other. "Can't get a degree if the world ends."

"Some semblance of normalcy would be nice after... everything this week," Len countered.

Harlow's stomach growled loudly. "Eat first, talk later."

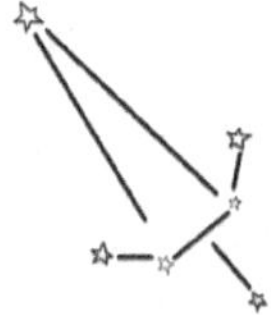

THE NOODLE SHOP WAS DARK, illuminated only by badly strewn string lights, colorful signage advertising a variety of drinks, and a few half burned out lightbulbs over the counter. It was crowded, as it was most nights, full of downtown workers still in their professional attire and a few university students who had managed to find their way off campus. The low din of conversations around them blended together beneath the loud electronic music blaring from the overhead speakers.

The three huddled together in a corner booth, each with their own half eaten bowls and mostly finished beers in front of them.

Dessa trailed her pointer finger around the rim of her cup lazily, gazing into the last of the bubbles slowly popping in the last sips. "What's in Your Cup? Why the latest addition to campus lied about their ties to a big coffee chain."

Harlow's palms hit the table. "Nooooo, don't ruin Espresso Yourself for me! Is that your pitch?"

Dessa laughed. She clinked her nails along the glass. "No, that's not really it. I just wanted to see your face," she said, though there was no malice in her tone. Her smile brightened as Harlow's hand found her forehead. Dessa went on, "I already wrote out three full pitches a week ago. You can steal one, if you want."

Len shook her head, the corner of one side of her mouth tilted up, amused. "I'd rather turn in my own, but I do need to run them by someone. They might be trash."

"Nothing you could ever do would be trash," Harlow said. Her gaze flicked back to Dessa. "Unlike some of us. For real, is Espresso Yourself shady?"

Dessa waved her away. "No, not at all." She clinked her glass against Len's in solidarity. "But before we hear any of your article ideas–"

"Fox, right," Harlow cut her off. She pulled her phone from her pocket and stared at the screen. "I'll ask him to meet us tomorrow."

"Not us," Dessa corrected. "I want to see his face when he sees me and Len. Unexpectedly."

Len shrugged. "That could tell us something about him."

Harlow set her phone down. She had never had a problem holding back the truth before. But, somehow, it felt particularly duplicitous to lie to Fox about a meetup. Like she would be using her influence to her benefit. Using his affection, however misguided, against him.

She had never had anyone tell her they loved her. Though it surprised her, even scared her a little, she didn't want to let it go. It felt as though his words were wilting in her grasp as she considered it.

Her friends were right.

But that didn't make it any easier.

Harlow opened her phone before she could talk herself out of it. This was no time for second guesses. She typed out her message and sent it quickly, shoving her phone beneath the table before either of her friends had a chance to see what she wrote.

"Alright," she said. "Done. Now hit me with your pitches, Len."

"And remember, it's not cheating if I give it to you." Dessa rose from her seat on quiet feet, her empty glass in hand. "Refill?"

"So many," Harlow said.

"Are my pitch ideas that bad?" Len feigned indignation.

On her lap, Harlow's phone buzzed. Without looking, she pressed the side button until she felt the little vibration as it powered off.

She was a warrior. A crafter sof starlight. A reborn princess with a duty to protect this Earth – a tiny blue planet in a tiny galaxy in a vast and vibrant universe.

In the end, her classes didn't matter. But Len and Dessa *did*.

Even if a part of her could not care less what her professors thought of her or if she finished her degree with flying colors or by the skin of her teeth, she knew that her friends felt differently. These things mattered to them... usually. Like now, though the weight of the world was on their shoulders, Len was worried about her pitch, the one thing within her control.

Harlow had done her part to save the world for the night. Now, it was time to save her friend's grade.

That is, if she could talk Len out of writing yet another article on the woeful lack of safety initiatives on campus. Unequivocally, their professors had told her that it wasn't going to happen no matter how much she dug into it. Budgets and resources and whatnot. Complex solutions to uncomplicated problems.

Len never let it go.

"Where the budget goes: Why greed is failing our most vulnerable students," Len said once Dessa was out of earshot. She glanced around the restaurant quickly, then leaned in, silver hair spilling over her shoulder as she did. "If each dean took a small pay cut, it'd be doable to get more emergency call boxes up all over campus. I ran the numbers."

Warmth spread through Harlow's chest. It was a

curious mix of a little anger, a little disappointment, a little pride. It swelled up until she had to breathe it out in one long sigh. "Maybe you could sneak it in as an op-ed," Harlow said at last.

Len leaned back in her booth.

Jensen would never approve the angle. After all, she liked her job.

But that didn't mean Len ever gave up.

Dessa bounded back to the table with three glasses wedged between her hands. Despite the quick, high steps, she managed to not spill a single drop. Where she got her grace, Harlow would never understand. Even as she set them down and squeezed in close to Len, looking up at her with the most innocent smile, Harlow had to admire her ability to gracefully enter a conversation as though she had never left. "What about you try a different approach?" Dessa suggested as she nudged the beer closer to Len. "Tell Jensen you're doing a piece on the observatory disaster, but bring the budgeting into it from that lens?"

Harlow held up a hand. "Hang on now, we *want* the observatory fixed."

Dessa rolled her eyes, though her expression was still playful. "Of course," she said, then took a long drink. "Budgeting then leads to the lights on campus.

Lights on the campus then leads to safety. You're picking it up."

Harlow pulled her own glass closer. "That's a stretch."

"It's a long game."

Len sighed. "It always is."

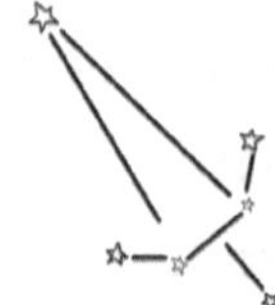

THEY LEFT the restaurant at closing, buying just enough drinks to keep their booth and not get kicked out.

The night air was cool, the city quieter as people found their way home before another work day ahead. It was late, and they were still no closer to getting a pitch Len was happy with, or a plan to tackle their monster problem.

Harlow turned her phone back on at last, checking her messages with her phone angled just slightly away from Dessa.

Enough, it seemed, for her to not see the screen. And enough for her to take notice. Dessa raised a single brow at her, then her gaze lowered to Harlow's phone. "What'd he say?" she asked, cautiously.

Harlow nodded. "He's good to meet up."

"With us or you?" Dessa pushed deeper.

"Me," Harlow said, her tone biting harder than she wanted. "I didn't say anything about you. Just that I had more questions."

Len nodded thoughtfully, looking up into the stars. "That's for the best," she said, as if understanding the dilemma Harlow was in. "I'm curious about him." The last part sounded like a lifeline, thrown to Harlow to keep her afloat in the conversation.

Harlow did her best to fake a smile as she put her phone back in the thigh pocket of her leggings. "Yeah, me too," she said quietly. "But the more important question is, are you going to take one of Dessa's pitches?"

"I have three," Dessa reminded them. "Because someone's got to carry this team across the finish line."

Len's fingers interlaced behind her back. She stretched as they picked up their pace in the dark. "Can you drag me instead?"

# CHAPTER 12

# KNOWLEDGE
# IS POWER

There had been no time to breathe. Harlow was just glad she had managed to shower despite the onslaught of chaos that had been thrust into her life. It felt good to be at least a little put together, though her hair was wild about her face, overrun with inconsistent waves that she didn't have the energy to tame.

She was up at dawn, a pink fizzy energy drink in hand, pacing her tiny kitchen like a caged tiger moments away from springing up on an unsuspecting tourist who got too close to the glass.

Any moment now, Len and Dessa would be knocking on her door so they could walk to their classes together and prepare for pitch day. She'd have to pretend that the class was important, for their sake, at least. She'd have to pretend that she wasn't being eaten alive with nerves about meeting again with Fox. And she'd have to pretend that it wasn't weird to see him standing beside Dessa after he had told her he *loved* her.

She took a long sip from the can, savoring the feeling of bubbles pop along her tongue, the tangy flavor of bright berries before the chemical aftertaste hit. It was something to focus on other than her recent mistakes...

Well, he *had loved* her.

The memory came crashing back down on her. She felt the weight of it, heavy on her head.

"Well, this is new," Carina said, appearing on the high countertop as if by silent teleportation.

Harlow finished her drink in one big gulp. "What?" she asked with an accidental burp. She wiped her lip with the back of her hand and leaned on the counter beside the cat.

"You being worried," Carina said. She pressed her

forehead to the back of Harlow's arm lovingly. "It's almost refreshing."

Harlow rubbed behind Carina's ear, the soft fur on her hand calming her heart rate like magic. "I'm not worried."

Carina purred at the touch. "Sure."

Harlow hung her head. She wasn't so convinced that 'worried' was the right word. Or even anxious. She was eager to get it over with. To *do something* so she didn't feel like she was just waiting around for everyone else to make their moves. She wanted to feel like she had control over something. Even if it was as simple as not burping up her energy drink.

She cringed at herself as another bubble escaped her throat. "Yuck."

"I don't know why you drink that poison," Carina said as she jumped down from the counter.

"Human bodies need sleep, unfortunately," Harlow said. She pushed herself to a full stand and stretched out her arms overhead.

"Then caffeine won't substitute. You're going to burn yourself out before the end of the big battle."

"If I can help it, there's won't need to be one–"

"They're here," Carina cut her off just as the sound of a small rasp at the door announced her friends' presence.

Harlow sucked in a deep breath. She pulled her shoulders back and grabbed her satchel from the floor.

"See you in the park," her cat called after her as she hurried to the door.

There was no escaping Carina's nosy nature. She'd come to meet Fox and there was nothing anyone could do to stop her.

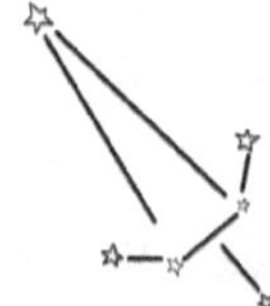

HARLOW WAS certain this was a horrible idea. Unfortunately, she didn't see any other option. She felt as though every idea recently had been a horrible one with no clear right direction, but with many clear wrongs.

Even Jensen had vetoed her pitch. Not that she particularly cared at the current moment. Still, the nagging feeling that she just could not make the correct choice settled deep in her bones.

It was a beautiful day. University students were outside, enjoying the fresh air as they made their way to class or the mall. Most were talking happily to their group, or simply looking down at their phones, head-phones in, and gentle smiles.

Everyone around them seemed as though they were happy to be out and moving. By comparison, she and the others looked glum. They stood still, waiting with frowns carved into their faces. As she and her friends stood beneath a large oak tree, shaded in shadow despite the bright sunlight overhead, a chill raced up her arms.

Harlow wished that she had forethought to run to the corner store for another energy drink. At least then she'd have something to do with her hands, even if she was pretty sure that this kind of tiredness, deep in her muscles, was something no amount of caffeine could fix.

Her eyes scanned the park and beside her, she clocked Dessa squaring her shoulders. Anxiety radiated from her friends, so evidently that she could almost feel it radiate from them.

Or, perhaps, it was her own beating heart she was aware of, clouding her perception of everything. She wasn't used to this feeling. She hated it.

At her feet, Carina pressed her fuzzy forehead into Harlow's calf. She meowed lightly, a reminder to stay strong, stay the course, and not let her mind wander too much to the worst-case scenario.

Harlow's gaze moved about the park again just as Fox turned the corner from behind a building. His eyes softened as they landed on Harlow, though his expression soured when he spotted Len and Dessa beside her. The quick frown replaced his easy smile so quickly, Harlow wondered if she had only imagined the smile in the first place.

He froze as if he had just stumbled upon predators.

Harlow waved him forward and from the corner of her gaze, she noticed Dessa's posture straighten again, bristling as Fox slowly walked closer.

His eyes moved from Harlow, to Dessa, to Len with an analytical stare as he approached with cautious, graceful steps. Even in his uncertainty, Harlow was surprised with the poise he exhibited. He walked forward with confidence until he was in front of them, tall, head held high though his jaw tightened.

Dessa wasted no time. She held her hand out with a bright, fake smile. "I'm Odessa."

Fox took her hand in his and Dessa shook it firmly twice.

"Helena," Len said, her voice hard and cold. Her hand remained at her side.

Fox's eyes traveled between the two. He lingered on Len's outfit, a flowing purple dress that must have reminded him of what they wore before. Back when they were royalty in crystal halls. The muscles in his jaw relaxed, the crease in his brow disappeared, though his eyes widened when he looked back into Len's intense stare. "The shield..." he murmured, then focused back on Dessa. "And the bow." His fingers twitched. "You found each other. Of course."

Several gold earrings jingled lightly as Dessa's head tilted. She was studying him, hiding her scrutiny with a charming smile that widened when his eyes fell on her. "We have *only* found each other. You're the first we've met who has woken up without... turning."

Fox rubbed the back of his head, his grin relaxed again. "It's lonely," he said, relief in his voice. "My whole life, it was like I was in a fog. When I realized why, the fog lifted. But then I found myself alone."

Harlow wondered if it would have been better to not remember. If the pain of knowing he was alone in this was worse than the discomfort of feeling out of place with no real reason. She wanted to ask him but the question stayed trapped in her chest. This wasn't why they were here. She couldn't entertain that train of thought for now.

Len looked down at Ara. The sleek cat rubbed her head along the bottom of her dress. "No companion?"

Fox shook his head. "I didn't have one. Even then."

"No?"

"No, most of us didn't. Don't you remember?"

Harlow stepped forward. "We don't. Not like you."

Fox bent down to get a closer look at the cats, resting his forearms on his knees. "You were all bigger then," he said gently as he raised his hand, slow and careful toward them. One finger extended for them to sniff. "Even when you weren't harnessing moonlight."

Vela raised a bushy tail into a little question mark as her neck extended toward him.

Fox let out a little laugh. "Strange to be on a planet with so much harmony between species, then coming here where we're all so separate. I didn't have a guardian then, but I did always wish..." He sighed, then lowered his hand to rest on his knee. "I take it you don't trust me, that's why we're meeting like this. Then, you are all here for answers? I'm happy to give them." Fox looked down at his feet. "I heard about what happened at the observatory." His eyes found Harlow's and his brows creased as he rose back up to his feet. "Is your friend okay?"

"She is." Harlow nodded. "How did you–"

"It was all over the school paper," he explained. "And the news, too. Though they didn't release your names."

"That would be terrible journalistic practices," Len said.

Fox nodded with a little snort. "Right, that makes sense. They just said people were injured." He looked at

Harlow, the same intense look that made it seem as though his vision had tunneled on her. "I was worried about you before, but now…"

Harlow's stomach fluttered under his stare. It was the way he looked at her, as though they were entirely alone, even with her friends standing beside her. He was singly focused now, unblinking, as if they had both been turned to stone.

The world quieted. Under the shadow of the tree, the people around them blurred, the sound of birds, the chatter of people, and the rustle of leaves faded. Harlow watched the amber of his eyes illuminate as they caught the light. The corners of his lips turned up.

"What do you know about what's been happening?" Len asked.

Fox blinked, and as if the spell had broken, he breathed again, eyes moving to her. "What do you mean?"

"Why are they suddenly getting stronger?" Len's voice lowered.

Fox shook his head. "It's not that they're stronger. It's that they're getting bolder. Something *is* happening."

"The way it did before?" Len asked.

"I don't know…" His shoulders pulled back, he looked up into the branches above. "I am just in the dark as you all are. At least, with what's been going on here."

Dessa put a hand on her hip, her bangles clinking loudly. "Do you remember how it happened before?"

"Most of it, I think."

"Have any attacked you since you woke up?" Dessa pressed further.

Fox reached into the collar of his plain black shirt. He pulled a necklace, a thin leather cord, from beneath and held out the little bag dangled from the end. His smile brightened. "You taught me this spell. Back then," he said, looking at Dessa.

"I don't remember you." Her eyes narrowed on the spell bag.

"I understand... And I didn't expect you to." He placed the spell back into his shirt gently. A slow, careful movement. "Has the Queen awakened yet? I worry..." His pause lingered between them, filling the open air with tension. He opened his mouth to speak, but nothing came out.

At Harlow's feet, Carina sat, her tail flicked. "Why are you asking about our Queen?"

Fox smiled at her, seemingly amused rather than startled that a cat had just spoken to him. "I don't have all the answers," he told her. "But I do think she holds a key piece to this. I worry that what happened back home is going to repeat here. I worry... that she'll hurt people."

"You were a soldier." Len said, a question phrased like a statement, as though she was litigating in a courtroom rather than speaking to a stranger in a park.

Fox nodded again. He took her bluntness with the same grace Harlow had seen before. "I was."

"Then you know what kind of leader she is. She would never harm her own," Len said.

Fox's jaw tightened. A crack in his marble, a moment of weakness.

"We just want information," Harlow explained, trying her best to sound calm. Her eyes locked on his, careful to avoid looking as though she was studying the subtle changes in his expression. "And I thought, since you have more of your memories back, you could help us."

"I said I'd tell you anything you want to know. I meant it."

"How can we defeat these monsters?" Dessa was quick to test him. "If you remember the war before, what were we doing differently that we aren't doing now?"

"How do we win this time?" Len added.

Fox's eyes landed on his shoes. "There's no

*winning,*" he said. "The war destroyed the planet. Everyone died."

Dessa folded her arms across her chest. "Then, what?"

"I have to believe that this time will be different. That somehow, *we* can make things right," he said. "We've been given an opportunity to redo this. To make better choices founded in knowledge instead of fear. But the Queen... she was fearful. I can only imagine she still is."

"You don't trust her?" Len asked, her tone direct, stare hard.

Fox looked up, but his eyes found Harlow. "I don't," he said, as if only to her.

"You served her," Len said.

"I served the princess. From the beginning. To the end."

*The end.*

Harlow could feel the pain in his voice. A small part of her heart shattered at the thought of the destruction of their home so long ago. She didn't remember much of it but she could imagine. The terror of the ground beneath them splintering, the impossible brightness of starlight falling from the sky, the horrible cries of every living thing on a planet unable to fight any longer.

The silence at the end of all things...

Harlow's eyes fell to the grass beneath her boots. She focused on the dancing shadows and patches of sunlight filtered down from above. "To the end," Harlow heard herself whisper as she looked back up at last.

Fox's eyes narrowed. "Until the very end." He held his head higher. "And beyond. I found you in this lifetime, on a different planet, didn't I?"

Harlow couldn't think about that now. Not here, not with Dessa close. "Why don't you trust her?" Harlow asked quickly.

"She withheld knowledge," Fox said. "And I didn't like the way she..." His eyes bounced to Dessa, then back to Harlow. "I didn't like the way she ruled. She used secrets like a blindfold and information like a weapon. Everyone should have access to knowledge. She fought to keep it from her people."

A long silence fell over them. Above, the breeze blew the leaves in a quiet murmur, as though they were talking for them.

Harlow held her breath.

"I agree," Dessa said at last.

Len leaned around Harlow to get a good look at her. Her lips were drawn into a tight line. "What do you mean?"

"Knowledge *is* power. The Queen wields it like

starlight," Dessa said with a small shrug, as though she was talking about the changing weather and not something border lining treasonous. "Think of how she's kept things from us – since the start. She always has more information but we only ever get it when it benefits her."

Len grumbled in response, a casual disagreement.

But Harlow's blood turned to ice. She had no idea that Dessa had felt this way. She hated that Dessa had dropped it here, like this, in front of everyone. All she wanted was to talk to her, ask her for more details. How long had she felt like this? How long would she have kept it to herself had Fox not brought it out? Didn't she trust *her*?

Fox put his hands in his pockets and waited as Harlow processed Dessa's words. He caught her eyes at last and the corners of his eyes crinkled gently.

Harlow let out a heavy sigh. She was tired of talking. She needed to move. Her legs tingled at the thought of just walking away.

"Dessa!" a clear voice called from the other side of the little park.

A young man from their class waved at them, a big, silly smile on his face.

Harlow huffed. She crossed her arms over her chest, though part of her was grateful for the distraction. She watched as he bounded up to them, golden curls bouncing in the sunlight with every step.

When he reached their little group, he glanced around at each of them. Probably trying to remember their names, Harlow assumed. She was too prickly for most people to approach. Len was always too serious. Dessa was the one who made friends with everyone, and usually dragged the others along for their socialization time. She was smart, kind, and most of all charming. Harlow had never seen her not be eager to help her classmates and TAs alike.

He gave Harlow another once over.

In his defense, Harlow couldn't remember his name either.

"How'd the pitch go?" he asked the group, clearly avoiding calling any of the others by name, though his eyes lingered on Fox a little longer. "Oh my gosh," he gasped. "Am I interrupting something? Who's this?" His tone was light, flirtatious even.

Dessa smiled, her whole posture changing in an instant to carefree and calm. "This is Fox," she said, extending her hand to him in a sweeping motion. "And, this is Lou."

"Journalism?" Lou asked.

"Physics," Fox answered.

Lou's face soured dramatically. "God, I could never."

"Well," Fox said with a smile, "we need everyone in the world."

Lou let out a light laugh. "Too true." He looked down, at last noticing the cats. "Whoa, these yours?"

Dessa waved them away and the cats scattered, each in a different direction. "We feed the strays," she lied with ease. "Pitch went well. Jensen loved mine."

Len's shoulders slumped. "Mine, not so much."

"Mine either," Lou said. "What a hard ass."

Fox smiled at Harlow, the two of them on the outskirts of the conversation didn't seem to bother him much at all. In fact, he looked as though he preferred it, as if they were sharing their own side conversation. Though, Harlow wasn't so sure she was exactly privy to what his smile was trying to convey.

"We're getting pizza," Dessa said to Harlow, pulling her back into the group discussion. "You coming?"

Harlow shook her head. "I need to walk around a bit," she said.

Dessa smiled, a knowing expression that set Harlow back into a state of ease. Though her quick shift to a dangerous flash of suspicion at Fox knocked her off balance yet again.

"I'll get her home safely," Fox promised. He shrugged at Harlow, hands still in his pockets. "If that's okay with you."

Harlow nodded.

Dessa cast Len a sideways glance. "Fine."

As if she needed a babysitter and wasn't a full adult, a princess, a general capable of complex strategy.

"Your lunch is on me," Lou said, obvious to the tension between them. He looped an elbow under Dessa's. "I need help on mine or I'll drop out."

Dessa nudged his shoulder with her own. "A beer too, don't cheap out on me."

"I would never!" Lou protested as he led her and Len away.

Harlow looked up at Fox once the others were out of sight. "I can take care of myself," she said.

"Of course," Fox agreed. "I just want your company, if you'll have me."

A flush burned at the tips of Harlow's ears. She shook her hair to be sure they were fully covered. She gave him one quick nod and started walking, for once, with no clear objective in mind.

# CHAPTER 13

# THE FIRST STAR

Time moved strangely with Fox. Sometimes, it felt as though hours had gone by when it had only been a glance, or like now, their walk around the downtown and back to Harlow's apartment had taken longer than she could have ever anticipated.

They had been walking in a comfortable silence, the sounds of the city filling in gaps where their conversation ought to go. Though there were a thousand questions vying for attention in her mind. But only one kept clambering to the top, scratching to escape.

Twilight lit the streets in gold and pink, glittering off the tall buildings like starlight on gentle ocean waves. On the horizon, where orange met brilliant blue, the first star sparkled against the swiftly falling night. Harlow felt the urge to reach for it, to pull its magic from the sky, feel it fill her bones and blood with power.

To call a sword.

Harlow stopped at the intersection where her apartment building stood. The light was green, the street empty, but she didn't move forward. At her side, Fox looked down at her. "I can leave you here, if you'd like," he said quietly.

Harlow shook her head. She stared up at the brick and glass building. She didn't want to go inside, to a place that she could hardly call home because it wasn't. Not really. None of this was and Harlow was beginning to think it never would.

She backed away slowly.

Fox stood still, his head turned to follow her.

"Come with me." Harlow gestured for him and in a single long stride, he fell into sync with her steps.

"Where are we going?"

"The photography center."

Fox looked forward as a few people passed them. "Won't it be closed?"

Harlow glanced up at him, flashing a half-smile. "I have my ways."

Fox let out a light laugh. "Reminds me of before. You're going to get me in trouble again."

Harlow's smile grew, her cheeks reddened. "Did that happen a lot?"

"I was always ready for more." He nodded to the left as they reached the corner where the sidewalk led back into the heart of the university grounds. He turned, the tips of his fingers brushing along her lower back as he guided her with him.

Heat flared across Harlow's skin at his gentle touch. Her stomach flipped, but she kept her footing and followed him just as his hand slipped back into his pocket.

"Where–?"

"Shortcut," he said as though he hadn't noticed the electric shock of their touch, or the effect it had on her.

Maybe he hadn't at all.

Harlow took a deep breath to steady the flutter in her core, the quick beating of her heart. It was just a touch. Innocuous and friendly. Nothing more.

She busied herself watching the sky growing darker, ignoring the burning in her hand that longed to reach out for his. Just as she decided she was done trying to figure out why her body reacted this way, how strange it was to feel like she had known this stranger for a life-time, they found themselves through the little park, and standing in front of the small photography gallery building.

It looked out of place among the taller, newer structures, but it was nestled in comfortably, cozy despite not fitting in. It had a little house-like front with an A-frame roof covered in tiles long bleached a pale yellow by the hot summers. The old wood, kept well maintained and a simple stained brown, showed that it was still loved, despite its age. It was because of its uniqueness, the way it quietly waited, hidden yet so visible once someone noticed it, that Harlow had first been drawn to it years ago.

It was also because of its age, and thus its old locks, that it proved easy to sneak in after hours. Harlow had to admit, that part was an added bonus that helped her fondness for the building blossom.

She had spent countless nights there, alone among the old black and white photographs of landscapes and trees, lost in a forest of shadow and light. It was a safe place. A hideaway when everything else felt too big, even to her. She prided herself on never backing down from a fight. But some days it was just hard to search one out, or hard to admit that she had nearly been bested.

On nights like those, she found herself here.

The sky above was darkening swiftly. The yellow lights along the walking path flickered to life farther down the sidewalk. But here, it was still dark. The university had strict lighting requirements due to their old, out-of-date observatory. And though the professors had lost the battle with the surrounding city on stricter lighting laws, they held firm on the campus grounds.

It gave the university a surreal feel. An oasis of quiet among new, loud, bright technology in a rapidly changing world. Harlow always wondered if she flew over the city at night if the little square mile would look like a piece of the world had been cut free or if the radiance of the surrounding light made it easy to see, like a child playing peek-a-boo.

Under the pale shine of the half moon, Harlow nodded for Fox to follow her to the small alleyway between the photography center and the massive building beside it.

She looked up at a narrow window along the side of the center, nestled between the bricks.

Harlow smiled.

"Need a boost?" Fox asked.

Harlow's grin grew wider. There was something so familiar about the way he asked. He didn't ask what she was doing, why she stopped. He didn't look at her like she was crazy, or ask if this was a bad idea. He was completely unbothered by her implication that she was about to break into a building. Completely ready to offer help when he saw that the window was just a little too high for her to reach, too small for him to fit through. "I've done this before," she said, though as the words left her mouth, a sting like a quick electric shock hit her in the heart.

She had, with Dessa and Len.

Years ago.

The night they had broken in to look at art, but all Harlow could keep her eyes on was Dessa, radiant in the faint glow from a far window. Beautiful, with her dark hair blending into the shadows...

Harlow shook the thought from her mind. She needed to move.

She took a quick breath into the bottom of her lungs, then launched herself at the wall, kicking off it quickly, fingers grasping the ledge with her left hand as her right fumbled out a small knife from her pocket. She unhitched the lock with the blade, then looked down at Fox and flashed a wink.

Fox laughed, looking up at her with admiration in his eyes. "Is this goodbye?"

Harlow wiggled through the window, feet first. "Come around the back door, I'll let you in."

Fox nodded and made his way out of sight down the dark alley.

Harlow landed on her feet silently. The dark bathroom was empty, as it always was after hours. She hurried through the cluttered office and out into the main room where the walls of massive photographs hung.

Fox was waiting for her when she opened the door with a smile and a single white flower.

"How did you–?"

Fox nodded to the rose bush behind him and shrugged. "I was feeling impulsive."

"What about the bees?" Harlow raised a brow.

"They'll survive," Fox whispered. He held the rose out to her, thorns already cleaned from the stem.

Harlow took it, her hand grazing over his as she did. She moved for him to come in, ignoring the rush of warmth that raced down her spine.

Fox crossed the threshold with a single, confident step.

The door closed with a soft click, covering them in darkness.

Harlow watched his outline survey the room slowly.

She tracked his subtle movements as she circled him, the rose raised close to her chest like armor. If he noticed her caution, the way she watched him like a shark, he hid it well. "Need a light?" she asked at last.

Fox shook his head, raising a single brow at her. "Do you?"

"I guess we can all see in the dark better than the average person," Harlow whispered. She wasn't even truly sure if what they were counted as *people*. They were, and they weren't. The differences were subtle. Faster healing, stronger, better vision, but whatever anatomy made them different, she didn't really understand.

She wasn't sure her aunt did either. Though now, doubt crept into the empty spaces in her mind.

Fox stepped deeper into the room. He went directly to a large photograph of a waterfall. He stared at it, eyes scanning over the details captured on the paper, like he had never seen anything so magnificent before. His lips parted in awe.

Soundlessly, Harlow stood beside him. "This is one of my favorites."

"It's beautiful," Fox murmured, his eyes still stuck to the image, unable to pull away. "There's much beauty to be found here."

Harlow glanced at him from the corner of her eye. "Do you remember our home planet?"

Fox nodded. "We didn't have waterfalls. Or giant redwoods. No bees or roses." He paused for a moment, the silence settling between them comfortably. Once again, if he noticed her looking at him, he pretended not to. He simply seemed content in their silence, happy to be lost in the photograph. Until, at last, he asked, "What do you remember?"

"I remember the purple sky," Harlow said.

"It turned yellow at dawn."

"I remember the sounds of the waves."

"We could see the ocean from your window."

"I remember the sky full of stars."

"Then they all went out."

Harlow turned to him at last. He was still studying the photograph, though a slight frown marred his face.

He tore his eyes away and looked down at her, his frown gone, replaced with a tranquil up tilt as if he had forgotten his last words already. "We did have cats, though. Or something like them. They were bigger there, and we could all speak with them... I'm glad Carina kept the form most comfortable to her here."

"She's glad for it too, though she wishes she could talk to everyone. And was bigger. Really, she wishes it was back the way it used to be. Though... she doesn't remember much either," Harlow admitted.

"Do you remember me at all?" Fox's hand lifted slowly, fingertips finding the outer petal of the white rose still in Harlow's hand. With great care, his fingers traced the rose, down the stem, to Harlow's hand where they curled around hers.

Harlow's heart began to thud in her chest, at the touch, at the way he looked at her, at the memory she was certain was there but couldn't quite grasp. Before she could think of any of the other burning questions she had for him, and before he could pull her closer, she blurted out: "Why did you tell me you loved me?"

Fox's eyes rounded in the dark, the question catching him off guard. "Because I did," he said simply.

"Did I love you back?" she asked.

"Very much. But perhaps not as much as I loved you," he added the last part with a laugh, as though he was telling an amusing story. "We were happier then. Before it was all destroyed."

Harlow was afraid that would be his answer. Afraid, even more, that it was true. "I wish I remembered you..."

"So do I."

Harlow sighed out, anger in her tensed up muscles releasing into exhaustion with her breath. "Why can't I remember? The Queen didn't approve? What happened to us?" The questions piled on top of each other, burying her beneath their weight.

Fox merely smiled, his hand lifting from hers to brush aside her blue and pink hair from her cheek. "Do you want to remember?"

"Yes."

Fox stepped back.

His absence was immediate. A cold emptiness rushed through her.

"I'm afraid so much of what you have been taught is misinformation meant to keep you in darkness. Harlow, I can help you find the light. You just need to ask. Do you want me to help you?"

A tingle prickled at her scalp. It crept down her temples and along her spine.

Somehow, this conversation felt like one they had a hundred times. She had seen it in her dreams. Felt it in her chest. Lived it once before. She knew this. But this time, it would be different. This time, she would be better. She could keep her friends. Keep the planet safe. This time–

"Yes." The word was so faint on her breath she wasn't sure she had said it at all.

But Fox held out his hand, and as she took it, she knew that he had heard her perfectly. That her 'yes' was more than an answer. It was a promise.

He led her to the photograph in the corner, a black and white moment captured in time. A forever silent aspen forest where the leaves stayed frozen and the grass never grew. White bark, scarred with black markings, reached up in scattered rows farther than the top of the image could show. There was no sky. No end.

"I love this Earth." His fingers lanced in hers.

"I want to keep it safe," Harlow said.

"We will. Together."

"How? How can I remember?"

"Knowledge," he said.

Harlow's eyes stung as she gazed with him into the empty woods. She loved it too. She didn't want to be a part of the destruction of another world. Her other hand tightened into a fist around the rose, stripped of thorns, as the memory of Gigi's scream pierced her heart. Her pulse raced at the thought of her friends still staying by her side through it all.

Humans had such a profound beauty to them, despite their many flaws.

The woods seemed empty until you sat still long enough and began to notice that it was teeming with life, quiet and small.

Even the deserts were bright in the darkness, when all the animals came out from their dens and hideaways, ready to greet the night.

She thought of the cities full of people living their

best and worst days. Of weeds cracking through cement. Of birds that made homes in the crevices of roofs. The lights that reflected the stars.

She wouldn't let this world be destroyed.

No matter what it took.

# CHAPTER 14

# THE NIGHT

Harlow flopped onto her bed with a loud groan as soon as she made it into her room. Her night with Fox had ended in a blur. She had been exhausted, tired to her core. He walked her home in silence and left her with a smile and nod before disappearing down the street.

Knowledge.

Harlow knew it was dangerous. She could keep trying alone. Keep her friends free of it to protect them.

It would be hard. But she'd done hard things before. Kept hard secrets.

Before she could think any more about it, she found herself falling into a dreamless sleep.

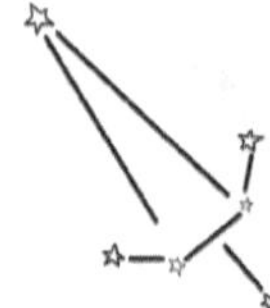

THE NEXT FEW days passed quickly.

Harlow spent her daylight hours trying to appease Len and remind Dessa that she was more than capable of doing her own schoolwork and organization, thank you very much. Their nights were spent wandering the city, looking to pick fights that had suspiciously run dry.

She dodged questions here and there from both the Queen and her friends about what she had been up to otherwise.

Now, they all lay on the floor of Harlow's apartment, star-fishing and complaining about due dates and money now that Harlow was out of work. She did her best to play along, though all she was thinking about was when she could next meet up with Fox to discuss how exactly he planned to help her with her missing memories.

Harlow's phone buzzed, blissfully pulling her from

her racing thoughts. She picked it up quickly, unable to keep herself from gasping as she read the text.

"What?" Dessa cried, rolling over onto her stomach. She snatched the phone from Harlow's hand.

"Hey!"

Dessa waved her off. Her eyes grew wide as she told Len, "Rainey... from the observatory?"

Harlow nodded, making a weak attempt to get her phone back.

Dessa pulled it closer to her, scooting back out of Harlow's reach. "'Gigi made you a costume to fight monsters'?" Dessa read the text aloud.

"What?" Len asked, suddenly more invested in the drama between the two. "A costume?"

The phone buzzed again and Dessa was quick to read the follow-up message. "'Come over and we'll make sure it fits and works.'" She looked at Harlow.

"Works? What does that mean?" Len asked.

"No idea," Harlow said honestly. "I'm surprised she's well enough to do anything, to be honest. Or that she even wants to still see me after what happened..." The last part was added as an afterthought, but it was the truth.

"Please," Dessa scoffed. "What space nerd wouldn't want to be involved in a reincarnated alien battle for Earth?"

"Says the nerd," Len said. "It took you forever to admit any of it and it was happening *to you*."

Dessa read the next text, ignoring Len. "'So when are you coming over? I also made a big batch of pasta. And some training tools that I think will help.'" She paused, the phone vibrated loudly in her hand again. "'I'm just going to keep texting until you answer.'" She tossed the phone back to Harlow. "Wow," she said. "How'd you get so lucky to have both them and us?"

"I must have been amazing in a past life." Harlow shrugged.

Len snorted. "You better answer her. I think she's serious when she says she'll just keep at it."

Harlow typed quickly. She looked up at her friends. "Want to come?"

"And see your amazing costume? Absolutely!" Dessa nearly jumped her feet. "Now?"

Len fell back on her side. "Give them a moment," she said.

"No." Harlow rose to her feet. "They're good now."

"That was fast." Len pushed herself up onto her elbows.

"Gigi moves at the speed of light," Harlow explained, groaning a little as she rose from the floor. The lack of sleep was starting to catch up to her. "But she's still chronically late. She says it's a curse."

Len's smile grew, though if she was amused at the idea of Gigi's curse or giving Harlow a sympathy grin, Harlow couldn't be sure.

"I'll lead the way," Harlow said. "It's not far."

"Leave a note for the cats?" Len suggested.

"They'll be out 'till dawn anyway," Dessa said.

Harlow grabbed her keys, tucking them into her crossbody running bag. She paused at the door, her hand still on the knob. "Wait, can they read...?"

Dessa waved again. "Honestly, Harlow."

"Let's go," Len cut in before either of them could get another word in.

GIGI'S APARTMENT was just as Harlow remembered it. Small, colorfully decorated, a little cluttered, smelling deliciously of cookies and honey. Rainey instructed them to take off their shoes at the door, completely unfazed at the other two showing up in tow. She smiled at them kindly, introduced herself, and explained that there was enough spaghetti for all of them, so long as they didn't mind that it was gluten-free.

Len's gaze moved about the apartment with a

steady stare. When they landed on Gigi, still curled up in bed where Harlow had last left her, Len's eyes softened. "You must be Gigi," she said, her voice uncharacteristically warm.

"What gave it away?" Gigi asked, grinning then grimacing at the movement. Her hand went to the clean, pastel pink gauze on her face. She ran her hand down it, checking for any lapses in its hold.

"Well, that," Len said. She and Dessa moved deeper into the room with cautious steps.

Gigi pulled back her blanket as she scooted to the end of the bed. "Are you guys... you know... privy to the nighttime happenings on campus?"

"Unfortunately, we're the reason there's nighttime happenings," Len said.

Dessa jumped in quickly. "She means we're reincarnated aliens too. Not that we're moon monsters." She lowered her hands. "Wait, how much of it do you know?"

Rainey was busy in the kitchenette. She poured a few glasses of sparkling water into mason jars. "I think a good chunk of it," she said over her shoulder.

Harlow took a seat at the little couch at the foot of the bed, cautiously sitting on the very edge as if Gigi was about to scold her away. She glanced at her, but the other woman seemed happy, if anything, that Harlow had made herself at home.

Rainey set the cups on the coffee table. "Hydrate. It's lemon, hope that's okay."

Dessa sat at Harlow's feet. She took a cup for herself and handed one up to Harlow. "Hydrate for what?" She eyed the cup.

Rainey smiled. "Well, I may have created a..."

"MMA2000," Gigi finished for her. "Moonlight Monster Automaton."

"2000?" Len asked with a raised brow.

"It sounded cooler." Gigi shrugged. "MMA just sounds like those dumb cage matches."

"Dumb? It's a legitimate sport! Put me in a–" Harlow started.

Rainey set her cup down, a loud clank that silenced Harlow's protest. She was clearly in no mood to argue those little things that had kept them entertained all night back in the observatory. She looked at Harlow with the same maternal glance that meant *shut up right now.* Harlow knew better than to keep arguing. "It's a mechanical training monster," Rainey explained. "It's kind of finicky because it was Frankensteined together on a tight timeline, but we can test it out tonight, if you're up for it."

"And, if the costume works, I'll get to work on

making some for you guys, too," Gigi said. She looked up and down Dessa's small frame, then to Len's tall stature. "I'll need measurements though."

Dessa took a small sip. "Costumes, you say? Like... are they cute?"

"Look around," Gigi said with a wide sweep of her arm. "Of course they'll be cute. And functional, I hope. I got the idea when I thought Harlow's cat was mauling her."

"Well, when we *thought* she was mauling her," Rainey corrected.

"Right," Gigi said brightly. "A lightweight, breathable material that moves well with the body but is harder to penetrate. It was tricky, but I think I've got it."

At last, Len sat beside Dessa, finally comfortable enough to let her guard down just a little. She clanged her glass against Dessa's gently, a silent cheers to whatever chaos was to come.

Dessa's smile only grew. "And you both worked in the observatory?"

"We're Janes of all-trades," Rainey said. She stretched her hands behind her back. "Alright, come on. Drink up and then we'll head over to the gym."

"You stashed the MMA2000 in the apartment community gym?" Len asked. She took another long drink. "Won't there be people?"

Gigi laughed, though her volume was more contained that Harlow had ever heard it. "Oh, Helena. Len. Sweet, very tall child."

Len's eyes narrowed, her cheeks flushed an undeniable shade of pink.

Rainey leaned forward on the coffee table. "This apartment is mostly full of very stressed, very unhappy, architecture students who didn't realize their major is mostly math and it's midterms. There won't be anyone in there."

"It's a fishbowl, though," Gigi added quickly. "So maybe a few frantic people walk by and think we are using some fancy new workout equipment? We should still be able to talk freely there. It's a big room. Lots of space."

"They do sunrise yoga on Saturdays," Rainey added, as though it were terribly important.

Len pulled her long silver hair back into a low ponytail.

Dessa's rings shimmered in the warm light of several lamps as she tucked her dark hair behind her ears.

Harlow rolled her neck. "Alright," she said. "Let's see this costume."

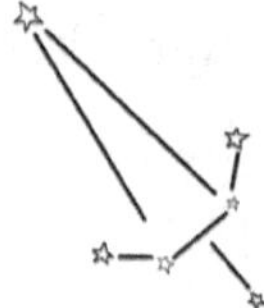

THE GROUP STOOD IN THE, as promised, empty gym. It was large, high ceilings lined with white ceiling fans bolted to the metal rafters, with a comically spacious mat floor space. A few pieces of brand new workout equipment were shoved to the edges of the floor to ceiling glass windows. From the looks of them, they had been there a while, neglected to bake in the sunlight that magnified through the windows.

It was dark outside. Their reflections looked back at them, faint in the low glow of string lights strewn over a cobblestone courtyard battling for dominance over the bright overhead fluorescents.

"Hang tight," Rainey said as she flicked off one of the light switches by the door. Half the lights turned off, and the space felt infinitely more welcoming without all the harsh shadows. Outside was more visible now, and Harlow breathed a quiet sigh of relief that she could better observe whoever walked by.

Rainey hurried to the side of the gym, to a mini-hallway that Harlow hadn't noticed before. From the shadows, she wheeled out a huge, eight foot tall metal monster.

Harlow and the others squinted at it, trying to figure out what exactly it was. Her best guess was some kind of metal scaffolding covered in fabric. A mechanical bull attached to the scaffold, a series of violent, sharp looking arms jostled as it was brought out before them.

Rainey set it in the middle of the room with a huff.

Harlow kicked herself for not offering to help move it. She had been too amazed, and horrified, by the thing.

"You weren't kidding about the Frankenstein monster reference," Dessa said. She crept closer to it, lowering at her waist to get a better look at how it was all attached to one another. "You do the wiring your-self?" she asked Rainey.

The other woman nodded, pride clear on her face. "It was the best I could do in the time crunch." She pulled out a huge box, a remote control of sorts, by the joystick on top. "Should still work to test out the mate-rial in the fabric and maybe get a good workout. The movements won't be the exact same as the one we saw that night, of course. But you can call this a variant."

Gigi shook out a ball of fabric before her, a bright pink and blue shimmering bodysuit with a little frill skirt attachment.

Harlow crossed her arms. It was cute. Kind of. On someone else. "No black... or?"

Gigi gasped with exaggerated offense. "A thank you

would do." She held it higher. "And look, I made it a little more feminine." Her hand held up the skirt, lifting it up to expose a series of pockets. "Hidden pockets, of course. Now if anyone gets a photo of you fighting monsters, you won't have a lumpy butt. I think of everything."

Len nudged Harlow with her shoulder.

"Thank–" Harlow started.

"I am a genius, it's true. No need to get all sentimental." Gigi held the outfit out further for her. "Should be cut proof. *Not* stab proof. But the monster seemed to mostly do a lot of clawing, not biting. Just like your cat, so we thought."

Harlow took the outfit from her with a smile. Up close, the fabric really was lovely. A sparkle about the material made it look infused with magic. The skirt was, she had to admit, cute. And a little genius.

Rainey pointed to the small hallway where she had stashed her metal monstrosity. "Bathrooms down there," she said.

Harlow left the group behind to change. The solid click of the stall door locking snapped her into sharp focus. Everything that had happened between her and her friends, both groups, felt like a dream that she was only just now waking from.

They were here, caring for her, for each other in

their own small and big ways. It was strange and lovely to see them all in one room, getting along as though they were old friends. She examined the outfit in front of her more closely. It made sense that they'd get along. In all her life she'd had so few friends, there must have been something in common with all of them.

Except, she thought, one.

Harlow removed her old black leggings and pullover, then searched for her phone among the pile. The screen lit up and her thumbs tapped the keyboard quickly.

when can we meet again?

The answer came almost immediately. Her ears reddened as she read it.

Whenever you ask

tomorrow?

Buy you a sugar coffee?

something stronger?

At night?

Harlow threw her head back. She let out a small groan. She was being stupid. But she couldn't ignore the flicker in her stomach that rose up into her chest like bubbles. Or the draw of knowing more.

should I be worried?

Not around me.

I'll text you later

Looking forward to it. Be safe.

Harlow shook out her tingling limbs. She hopped on the balls of her feet, back and forth a few times to loosen up her joints and let out any lingering tension there.

"Harlow?" Gigi called as the door to the bathroom creaked open. "Does it not fit? I kind of went with approximations."

Harlow shook her head. She smiled so her voice sounded calm. "I was busy inspecting the material. It looks great. I'll be out soon."

The door closed with a sad little thud.

Harlow slipped the bodysuit on quickly, stuffing her arms through the long sleeves. She was excited to discover that there were little holes for her thumbs to slip through that helped to hold it all in place, and provide coverage over most of her hand. She felt along the sides, to the miniskirt and pockets, and down the leggings.

It was surprisingly comfortable. Stretchy, seemingly breathable, and, she hoped, cut proof.

Harlow opened her stall door, her bundle of black in her hands. She did her best not to look in the mirror, but as soon as she passed it, she found herself leaning back, standing on her tip toes to see as much of the outfit as possible.

Harlow smiled at herself. Then scowled.

Damn it. Gigi knew what she was doing. It did look great.

Harlow crept out of the bathroom, holding her still warm bundle of old clothes close to her chest. She thought it looked great in the moment before, but now, standing in front of all her friends, she felt a little silly.

Gigi motioned for her to twirl. "Let's see it."

Harlow shook her head. "It looks great, okay?" She threw her clothes onto the floor and held her hands out wide.

"Harlow!" Dessa and Len both gasped, their eyes wide and Harlow realized that neither of them had probably ever seen her in a skirt or dress before. She had never had time for things like that. Never let herself worry about fashion. She had her wild hair color, and that was about as self expressive as she ever got. As she looked down at herself, the pretty pink and blues like mermaid scales, the skirt flared out around her hips to bring shape to her silhouette, she wished she had made more time.

She shook her head. No time. Not yet. "Yeah, yeah. But let's see if it works." She had no doubt, but she needed to change the subject. Quick.

Gigi put a hand to her heart while Rainey set up a base at the corner of the gym, her large remote resting on her lap as she nestled in between two ellipticals.

"Let's see if *this* works," Rainey said, looking up from her lap with worry creasing her brows. "We all might want to back up a bit..."

# BY ANY
# OTHER MEANS

The MMA2000 was hastily built. That much was evident. But it was also dangerously effective.

The mechanical bull attachment, nearly the length of a full person, rumbled and flailed about, waving metal arms with sharp attachments wildly through the air. It sliced up, down, jerking left then right, then back up again in unpredictable movements.

Harlow ducked and dodged as best she could. She

was light on her feet, agile, despite her tall stature. She moved easily, though, a bead of sweat dripped down her temple. They hadn't been testing the murder machine long, but Harlow's inability to anticipate its next direction and her constant readjustment, jumping, and weaving had already begun to tire her out.

She stopped a moment, glancing behind her to see Rainey, smiling maniacally in the corner like a supervillain.

At her side, Gigi held up her phone, taking notes. "Would you say your sweat is being whisked away, or is it sticky in the suit?"

Harlow breathed out, a long, tired sigh. "I'm fine," she said between heavy breathing.

"Would you describe your butt as 'swampy' or 'airy'?" Len called back. Her face was serious, but beside her, the other women snickered.

Harlow's eyes narrowed. "Not going to lie, it's pretty... dry." She ducked a metal arm with a dull knife welded at the end.

"If you think of anything else to help," Rainey said, clicking a button on the remote quickly as the machine pivoted to an up and down slicing motion, "let us know."

Harlow jumped as an arm swept her feet. "Are either of you" –she hopped back, narrowly avoiding the back end of the mechanical bull– "secretly good at neuroscience?" A metal arm swung down and she spun to her side. "Make us a helmet to retrieve past life memories?"

"Harlow," Gigi said as though she was scolding a child. "We're not *that* good. I just took some fashion design classes. I can make you look *really cute* in a helmet, though."

"Are you missing a lot of memories from... your home before?" Rainey asked, still busy working the large remote.

Harlow dodged back with an unexpected yelp.

"Many. It's part of our issue with ending this war here. We don't remember how it ended before," Len, blissfully, answered for her.

"You could try therapy?" Gigi shrugged.

Len laughed. "Tried that for my anxiety. It worked well."

"Yeah, I guess it'd be hard to explain what the goal is... What about those past life regressions?" Gigi was typing furiously into her phone now.

Harlow jumped, then rolled when another arm came down, this time, faster.

"I tried that. Total hoax," Dessa said with a wave of her hand. "He kept trying to lead me toward being Queen Elizabeth the First."

Gigi looked up from her phone, her shoulders slumped. "Well, then I'm out of ideas."

"Watch out!" Rainey called, a toothy grin still plastered on her face.

Harlow turned back just in time for the mechanical arm, with a saw attached, to slice at her abdomen. She held her forearm in front of her to take the worst of the damage, but the mechanical arm's force was too strong. It knocked her arm away, slicing across her stomach.

Harlow fell back, hitting the ground with a hard thud, her breath knocked from her lungs.

"Harlow!" Dessa cried. She was at Harlow's side in a flash. She scooped Harlow's shoulders up in her arm, her free hand moving hair from her forehead as she scanned down Harlow's body in search of injury.

Harlow coughed. Her lungs stung with the force of the hit. Her arm was going to have a bad bruise. At least, for a little while. But as she pushed herself up onto her elbows and looked down, she realized why Dessa had so suddenly stopped fretting over her.

The bodysuit was undamaged. Not a scratch or a hint of fraying fabric.

"It works," she choked out, turning her head over her shoulder to catch Gigi taking diligent notes on her phone that Harlow had to imagine amounted to 'suit impervious to swinging saw'.

Beside Gigi, Len's shoulders relaxed.

"We'll take two more," Dessa said, her fingertips squeezing Harlow's shoulders gently.

Gigi nodded, looking Len up and down. "I'll get measurements."

"If you can make Len's sturdier, she's the shield. And mine with more stretch?" Dessa added loudly. "I need to move to make sure this one doesn't get into too much trouble barreling through things." She looked down at Harlow with a little wink.

Harlow flushed. She was right, but she seethed with how accurate Dessa always was.

"You're sure it's not too much?" Len asked.

"She loves it," Rainey said, the remote finally out of her hands.

"You worry a lot, huh?" Gigi asked Len. It was blunt, but kind, chipper and earnest in the way that only Gigi could manage.

Len snorted, crossing her arms over her chest. With a slight cock of her head, she said, "Well, I am the shield."

"Worrying is what Len does best," Dessa added quickly, before either human could ask follow up about what it meant to be 'the shield'. She released Harlow at last and sat up straighter. "We can't compensate much yet..."

"Help save the university from giant monsters? I'm pretty sure it's worth it." Gigi shifted her weight to one foot, a hand came to her waist, a casual stance as though the words she just said were a quote from a movie rather than her real life.

How Gigi and Rainey had been so willing to help them was a mystery Harlow wasn't sure she'd ever solve. It had taken the shield and bow longer to come to terms with their new reality, and they had been younger, more willing to accept that the world was not as it seemed.

Gigi went on, "Besides, it gives me something to focus on while I wait for my attorney to get back to me about the settlement."

Harlow sat up fully at last, free of Dessa's arms and the gnawing guilt that her touch left behind. "Attorney?"

Gigi laughed. "Just my mom's girlfriend. But she's good at what she does. I thought I'd shoot my shot and see if I could get us all a little something to tide us over while we're without work."

Rainey propped up onto her knees. "The 'meteor' might have been an 'act of god' but the shoddy, old wiring sure wasn't."

Gigi pointed at Rainey with a wink. "Exactly."

Harlow sighed. Extra money would be nice. Carina

had made it abundantly clear that she was not willing to go back to the discount kibble. And she was sure her aunt would be little help in keeping them afloat. Harlow let her head fall, the warmth of Dessa's embrace still lingered on her back. She didn't need to worry about that now, either the money or the way she felt secure, if only for the briefest moment as Dessa held her close, looking her over with concern.

Her moment of rest didn't last long.

"Not to alarm anyone," Len said quietly. Her eyes were glued to her phone. "Don't look right away, but there's this woman out there that's been watching us for several minutes now." Her gaze flicked up, then back down at her phone and she pretended to be preoccupied with it.

Rainey stood and moved closer to Gigi nervously. "Maybe she just is weirded out by the machine in here?"

"MMA2000," Gigi corrected, her tone was anxious despite the smile she wore.

Len put her phone in her pocket and nodded subtly to the direction of the woman outside. She moved to pretend to inspect the MMA2000 as Harlow rose to her feet, moving the other way so she could catch a glimpse of the woman without looking like she was trying.

There was, in fact, a young woman outside. She was standing in the shadows at the edge of the sting lights in the little courtyard. Her arms hung loosely at her sides, her posture tired – with shoulders slumped and head low. Her eyes, however, were fixed on the group. She didn't move at all when Harlow made eye contact with her, didn't blink, didn't look away.

"Creepy," Gigi whispered. "Maybe she's, like, on something...?"

Harlow took in a long breath.

The woman jerked forward, as though she had been pushed from behind. With unsteady feet, she stumbled forward but her sight never left them. And there was no one else with her.

"What–"

The woman's eyes began to glow, a deep purple.

Harlow swore under her breath. She held out a hand to stop Dessa from coming any closer. "Stay here," she ordered the group and broke out into a run across the empty gym.

"Like hell," Dessa cried after her.

The door to the apartment gym didn't have time to slam shut before Dessa was through it, following Harlow closely like a shadow in the low light.

Harlow stopped at the other end of the courtyard as the woman in front of them began to burn blue and purple. Her mouth opened and where teeth and tongue should have been, was merely an empty abyss, void of color and texture.

"Do you know who you are?" It was Len's voice behind Harlow, bold and bright.

A chill ran down Harlow's spine when the woman jerked forward, one hand extended toward them, claws already forming where her fingers had once been.

Harlow's arm was up to the sky before she could concern herself with watching the transformation happen in real time. She had never seen a Mechoida shift – in fact, she rarely ever thought of them in their earthly forms at all. But there was no time for that.

Starlight flooded into Harlow's hand, taking shape of her sword.

The woman, now half monster, turned on her heel and raced down the narrow corridor that led to a shadowy walkway between the buildings.

"Where is she going?" Len cried, shield already formed beside Harlow.

"It's a trap." Dessa pulled her bow, shimmering arrow ready to launch.

The Mechoida turned a corner and out of sight.

"Damn," Dessa hissed. She tucked her bow close to her hip.

Harlow's grip on her sword tightened. Trap or not,

she couldn't risk it hurting anyone else. She took off after it, her friends' protests echoing behind her.

When Harlow turned the corner, the Mechoida was standing still, its back to her as if frozen in space and time.

The swirl of moonlight around its massive body radiated out, illuminating the darkened walkway with an eerie, ominous glow.

Harlow raised her sword.

"Wait!"

Harlow's muscles strained as the sword hovered, about to strike. She turned over her shoulder a moment to see her friends, Dessa with her arrow nocked and Len with her shield protecting Gigi and Rainey.

What were they doing here?

Harlow's heart was racing in her throat. She wanted to tell them they were stupid, to tell them all to back away, to keep them safe.

Her sword came down.

The Mechoida bellowed, a loud sound of agony as moonlight poured from the cut in its massive back.

"Stop, Harlow!" Gigi called from behind Len's shield. "Stop! She's a person!"

Harlow's eyes narrowed at the gash in the Mechoida's back. Her jaw clenched. Hatred, anger, a righteous fury tore through her body. These things hurt her friends. They hurt her. They wanted her dead. They wanted this Earth. They destroyed her home.

An arrow flew past Harlow's cheek, hitting the moonlight creature in the arm. It burst brightly, then disappeared as swiftly as it had come.

The Mechoida stumbled now, silent. It fell to its knees, then collapsed onto the ground. Silver wisps of moonlight floated delicately back into the sky like the last of campfire smoke. The woman was human again.

And bleeding.

Harlow blinked, hard.

Dessa and Len were at her side in an instant. Len's shield was still up, now in front of Harlow.

Harlow shook her head. She couldn't process what she had just seen. What she had felt. She had never experienced anything like it. She watched the red seep into the sidewalk, slower than it should. At least all of them were fast healers...

Harlow's knees went weak, but she pushed past Len's shield anyway as she released the sword back into starlight. She knelt beside the woman now as fear took over where anger had been. Her hands were shaking.

Len crouched beside her, ripping free her own jacket with quick efficiency. She tied a quick knot with the sleeve fabric onto the woman's arm and pressed the rest of it to her back with firm pressure. Harlow noticed the sweat on her brow as she worked, the way her breathing came in shallow.

At the other end of the corridor, Rainey and Gigi clustered together.

"Is she...?" Gigi asked quietly.

Dessa took over for Len, pressing her full weight to stop the bleeding. "She's alive," she called back.

The woman was stomach down on the ground, hair splayed across her face. But she was breathing steadily.

"She'll be alright," Harlow said quietly. She wasn't sure Gigi or Rainey could hear her. She could barely hear her own thoughts over the drumming in her ears.

"Alright?" Dessa snapped back. "Harlow, she's a Mechoida. She didn't even seem aware of her actions. She's not *alright*. She has to..." Dessa's pressure lightened slightly.

Len forced her aside with her shoulder. "I'll take over."

Dessa's body tensed, her fingers curled into fists.

The sound of footsteps running toward them broke their stand off. Rainey pointed to her phone. "The ambulance is on its way."

Dessa's stare hardened. "What if she transforms again in the hospital?"

The woman took in a long, deep breath. Through

her light hair, Harlow saw her eye blink open slowly. She groaned, then coughed.

"Do you know where you are?" Len asked.

The woman blinked. Her eyes glimmered the same deep purple of the night sky.

Harlow was on her feet, yanking Dessa up and behind her. "Get back!"

Len's hands rose, slowly from the crumbled fabric of her jacket just as the moonlight took hold of the woman's limbs.

The ground cleared of blood in her glow, as though it were never there at all.

Harlow grabbed Len by her elbow. She hoisted her up roughly, using her full weight to get Len to her feet.

The woman, half Mechoida, half human now, stumbled up. She turned to the group, her face a snarl. She was all snout and shadow now. She squared her shoulders, rising to her full, massive height.

"I'm finishing this," Dessa said. She pulled her bow from the sky.

The Mechoida laughed.

Harlow's blood ran cold. It was messing with her just like before. The only question was: why? She reached up for her sword.

Its laughter only grew, a guttering, horrible sound.

Then, it flew down the alley with long strides, out of their sight before she could process it.

Dessa threw her bow to the ground. It shattered into silver and gold sparks, then vanished as quickly as the monster had.

Behind them, Harlow heard Rainey sigh. "This is going to be hard to explain to the EMTs."

Harlow wanted to scream, but it caught in her throat. They had made enough noise and chaos here to call plenty of attention to themselves without her adding a frustrated screech. She grabbed Dessa's hand, then Len's, and pulled them along with her as she ran back to the gym with the humans close behind.

Harlow let them go as soon as she reached the door. She threw it open with a deafening bang and raced into the bathroom. Harlow peeled herself free of the body-suit, and threw her workout clothes back on, not worrying about them being inside out, or backwards, or any other sign of her hurry.

She was out into the main gym before anyone had a chance to follow her. Harlow's heart pumped violently in her ribs. She grabbed the base of the MMA2000 and heaved it back into the little hallway by the bathrooms. She hadn't noticed it before, she'd have to hope the medical team was just as obvious.

"What'd you tell them?" Dessa asked Rainey while Len rushed to help Harlow push it further.

"That there was a woman injured, a big cut in the courtyard," Rainey said. Her eyes were wide, but her expression was otherwise blank. She stared at nothing as Harlow finally stashed the giant machine.

"You could tell them it was Harlow, that she refused medical treatment," Len said. "We'll be long gone before they get here."

"No." Dessa pulled an arm around her stomach. She squinted past the glass into the dark courtyard. "The Mechoida know we're close with humans now. They knew they live here."

Len's head fell. She clearly hadn't considered that leaving the humans alone was a huge risk. Her jaw tightened.

"I'm on it," Harlow said. She rested her back across the saw arm.

"Don't!" Both Gigi and Rainey shouted as Harlow pressed into the saw and fell down.

Pain shot through Harlow's back, but she didn't have time to process it. It would heal, no one would know anything supernatural had happened here, that's all that mattered right now.

Dessa cut a thin wire of a rowing machine in the

corner with a knife she pulled from her side. The wire snapped, zipping up violently.

"Where did you get–?" Rainey asked through her hands. Her face shifted between Harlow and Dessa and now Len, who was busy opening the door for Harlow.

Dessa winked. "A woman can't be out at night without protection."

"You use STARLIGHT!" Rainey cried.

Dessa smiled. "The cord snapped, it flung up and hit her in the back, alright?" she said with raised hands. "I'll get Len. She'll stay in here with you. I doubt the Mechoida will be back tonight. And I doubt the EMTs will want your statement."

Harlow, despite her pain, beamed with a strange sense of pride and admiration watching Dessa work. She slipped out the door, with Len's help, but Dessa was quick to follow.

"I got her," Dessa said gently. She slipped her own arm between Len's and Harlow's, keeping her weight countered so Harlow could lean on her as they walked to the middle of the courtyard. "Keep an eye on the humans. Calm them down," she told Len.

Len nodded as the red and blue flashing lights crested the rooftop.

Overhead, the gibbous moon shone down on them, the shadow like a mocking smile.

# CHAPTER 16

# VICES, SLICES, AND PARADISES

arlow's cut was not so deep that she needed treatment. She and Dessa staunchly refused to be taken to the hospital for a tetanus shot. She assured them that she'd be fine and had an urgent care facility down the street if she really needed to go.

They left with the warning that she needed to tell the apartment management about the state of the equipment right away.

Harlow had simply laughed as they walked back the way they came, clearly in more urgent need elsewhere.

Dessa smacked Harlow's arm with the back of her hand once they disappeared from sight. "Idiot!"

Harlow stifled her laugh, it caught in her chest and settled there, uncomfortably. "Sorry–"

"I had that shot," Dessa scolded.

Harlow's head hung, the back of her neck in a low stretch as she felt her back begin to stitch itself back together. "We'd make a good team if you just listened to what I don't say." Her half-smile flashed up at Dessa, trying to lighten the mood. "That was fast thinking in there." Her head tilted to the fishbowl windows where Len was calmly speaking with a traumatized looking Rainey.

Gigi was sitting down, her eyes closed as if in a meditative state.

Dessa let out a frustrated grunt. She threw her hands up in the air as if trying to be free of Harlow, to once and for all toss her to the sky and watch her float away. "I–you–really–" Her words stopped each time she tried. Her shoulders heaved a moment as she collected herself. "We need to figure out what to do with your friends. The Mechoida know where they live now. I'll make spell bags but..."

Harlow watched Gigi's eyes open slowly, the way they scanned the reflection, searching for answers that none of them could give.

The door to the gym opened and Dessa took a step back from Harlow.

"Gigi is going to stay with Rainey while we figure this out," Len said as she approached them. If she noticed any strangeness between them, she played it well.

"I'll get right to work making the spell bags," Dessa said. "I can give them to a third party on campus. Make sure nothing follows them to Rainey's home."

Len nodded. A long pause followed as the trio watched the two humans. Each seemed defeated in their own way.

It was hard to watch. All the joy and pride of helping them before was gone, replaced with the burden of knowledge that they couldn't give back.

"And the newly transformed Mechoida..?" Len said at last.

Dessa curled one arm around her waist. "It seems like she transformed against her will, didn't it?" When no one answered, she let her arm drop. Her stance firmed into the ground. "But also that she was baiting us. A hive mind, maybe?"

Harlow looked up at the moon. It was so bright she had to squint to make out the craters and shadows. The Mechoida used the power of moonlight. Moonlight made them bigger. Stronger. More monsters than anything. But what if instead of a hive mind, Harlow thought as her blood chilled down her arms, they were able to access all their memories with it?

She transformed without realizing it was going to happen, judging by the slowness of it. But then, why was she there, staring at them in the first place? Why had she run when she saw them? Fought when she got them alone?

What is she remembered..?

At her side, Dessa's eyes narrowed. "What?"

Harlow shook her head. "Just strange," she murmured.

"'Strange' is when you misplace your keys, turn the whole place upside down, and then find them somewhere obvious," Len said. "This is…"

"A very bad sign of things to come," Dessa said. "We need to change our strategy."

"And the Queen?" Len offered.

Harlow's back bristled. She laced her fingers together, trying to keep them from forming fists. "We keep this close. For now."

"Is that an order?" Dessa challenged with a raised brow.

A sting in Harlow's eyes pierced her painfully. Tears, she realized just before it was too late. She blinked and looked up at the stars to keep them from falling. "It's a request," she said at last.

"Granted. Damn, don't take me seriously all of the sudden," Dessa said as she leaned in closer to the two of them with a smile. She clasped her hands on their shoulders and gave the two taller women a light shake. "We're in this together. The three of us."

The corners of Len's eyes crinkled with a small, but genuine smile.

"Step one is making sure we all get home safely," Dessa went on. She dropped her hands and the instant her touch was gone, Harlow's heart sank. "Step two is showing up on time to class. I'll bring coffee. Three, we figure out what the hell is going on."

Len let out a small laugh. "You forgot sleep," she said. "*That's* step two."

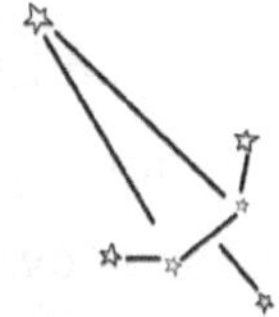

When Harlow arrived home, it was nearly morning. Rainey had texted her that she and Gigi arrived safely at her home, and that, for all their fear, Gigi was already sketching out new outfits for Len and Dessa.

Harlow had replied with a thank you and a sorry. Though, she wasn't really sure what was for what. Thank you for helping them in the first place. Thank you for being a friend. Thank you for not cutting her off entirely even though Harlow had, in their eyes, almost killed a person in front of them. Sorry she had.

Harlow took a long shower, blasting angry music from her phone so loud she was sure she'd get a complaint in the morning from her neighbors. But she didn't care right now. All she wanted was to drown out the voice in her head that reminded her she had hurt a person that night. That she hurt people every time she went out looking for a fight. Sure, they wanted her dead too, but... Harlow had never seen one transform.

It was easier when they looked like monsters. When they attacked her with brutality. When she didn't have to think about the human cost.

Her phone dinged twice on the floor beside the tub, cutting the music into choppy segments.

Harlow pulled back the shower curtain with steady hands and through the steam, she read Fox's name on the screen. Her heart sped up. She had told him she made it home safely. She hadn't really been sure why at the time. Now, clean, and clear-headed, she regretted it a little.

Still, the concern that radiated from the words on the screen warmed her in a way she couldn't describe. She didn't want him to worry. But he was.

For her.

Harlow was used to concern packaged in humor. Her human friends did it with her caffeine consumption, her food choices, her strange and stupidly explained scratches. Her other friends had long given up on expressing their discomfort with her choices. Instead, they too, relied on teasing her.

Her aunt had never once been concerned with anything other than her ability to perform and succeed.

She leaned over the fiberglass tub and quickly wrote him back.

all good

explain tomorrow

Let me know if you need anything before. I'm here

Harlow had half a mind to tell him to bring her

favorite energy drink and to go breakfast. Instead, she flipped her phone over and let the water wash over her until she heard a song she hated.

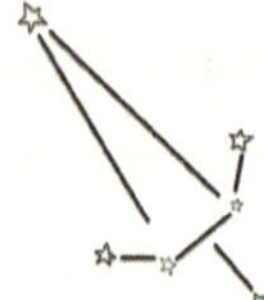

THE NEXT DAY passed in a blur. A sleep deprived, frustrated blur.

No matter how she turned over the night in her mind, she couldn't shake the feeling that something was deeply wrong. That she had made the wrong choices. She wasn't used to overthinking. Or even being tired, really.

If this was how most people felt most of the time, she wasn't sure why everyone always gave her so much grief for her caffeine consumption.

It was noon when she decided to call it quits for the day. She disappeared from campus and texted Len and Dessa that she wouldn't be making it to class and not to worry, she was just going to nap.

She set an alarm and fell asleep before she could overthink.

Harlow dreamed of a beach, idyllic waves and warm sand. A place she had never been but always wanted to go. The ocean was calm and clear, the palm trees swayed gently in the salty breeze, casting cool shadows over her face as she stared up into the cerulean sky...

HER ALARM WAS BLARING from her phone but it was Carina's paw pressing on her cheek that woke her from a deep sleep. She blinked a few times as the cat came into clearer focus through a sleepy haze.

"Feeling sick?" Carina asked after Harlow silenced her phone.

Harlow sat up slowly, stretching her arms up until her shoulders popped.

Carina grimaced at the sound.

"No. Just so annoyed I had to sleep." Harlow yawned.

Carina jumped off the bed, tail swishing through the air. "That sounds right. Annoyed at what?"

Harlow rolled her neck, clearing away the last of the sleep that lingered there. "Everything."

"And, what is the alarm for?" Carina asked.

Harlow's stomach flipped. She sat up straighter. "I'm meeting Fox," she said honestly.

"At night?" Carina cocked her head to the window where the stars were shining.

"Yeah," Harlow said. She combed through her hair with her fingers and inspected her reflection in the glass.

It would have to do.

Not that it mattered.

It wasn't a date...

Right?

Harlow shook her head, her hair tousled lightly around her chin, reactivating the waves so it didn't look *too much* like she just woke up.

"Are you and the cats going out again tonight?" Harlow did her best to redirect the subject back on Carina. "I think you guys have more than earned a rest."

Carina's tail flicked once more. "We are taking a well-earned night off, yes."

"Rebellious," Harlow teased. "I like to see it."

Carina scampered out of the bedroom with light feet. "Don't tell the Queen we skipped a night and I won't tell her you're meeting with an undisclosed past life... friend."

"Friend, yeah," Harlow said, too quickly, but the cat was already out of the room, away to lounge on her favorite spot on the back of the couch. "It's a deal!" She called, louder.

Harlow put the TV on for Carina and slipped out of the apartment.

Why the space cat, who transformed into a mighty warrior with the power of moonlight, enjoyed trash programming, Harlow would never understand.

Perhaps everyone had their vices.

At least hers was silly.

# CHAPTER 17

# THE SPEAKEASY

ox was standing at the corner of the intersection where he had told her to meet him. He was looking out into the bustling nightlife around him, still as a statue, and just as impressive looking. He stood out, tall and confident, among the crowd though he wore the same business fit as the rest of the downtown night crowd.

This part of town was always busy, even on weekdays. It was mostly people getting out of work late, meeting up for drinks and dates, or ducking into a restaurant for a quick bite before heading home. The streetlights were dimmer here, but the restaurants and bars that lined the lower levels of the street burned brightly through their large windows.

It was crowded, loud, and frustrating to get a table anywhere here.

But just as Harlow began to grow wary of the plan, as if sensing her, Fox swiftly turned his gaze toward her, a sudden smile lit up his face when he made eye contact with her.

Harlow couldn't help but smile back, though she lowered her head to avoid him noticing the flush that burned in her cheeks as she made her way closer.

"So I'm not sure if you're new here," she said, "but this part of downtown is actually kind of trendy."

Fox's smile widened, dimples in one cheek forming. He pulled one hand from his pocket and gestured for her to come closer as he turned on his heel. "I have a place in mind," he said as his fingers laced through hers with practiced ease. "Follow me."

Harlow's breath hitched in her throat. The warmth of his hand radiated through her. She was grateful he was a pace ahead, leading the way through the sea of people so he wouldn't notice her face and ears reddening.

She followed, hand in hand as a strange feeling ate

its way through her. It wasn't guilt, or fear... but something close to it. It mixed with excitement, hope, and joy into a cocktail that she wished she could spit out.

And that she craved more of.

Fox gave her hand a little squeeze, then he let go as they arrived at a little bookstore she had passed a hundred times, but never ventured into.

It was an unassuming storefront. Gold lettering on the window shimmered in the light of the surrounding restaurants. It was only wide enough for two rows of bookshelves lining the brick walls, and a little round desk in the middle where the register and a very bored looking old man sat, a worn book in his hand, raised up so half of his face was obscured.

Harlow raised a brow at Fox. "I'm not much of a reader," she said.

"You just haven't found the right book then," Fox said with a sly grin. He opened the door for her and a little bell above chimed as she stepped through.

The man at the desk brought the book down a little to see them past the pages. He looked at Harlow's hair like she was an alien.

Then again, Harlow thought, she was.

Kind of.

But when Fox stepped in after her and put a firm hand on her shoulder, the man's eyes softened.

A tall man in good clothes could go anywhere.

It was unfair.

"Can I help you find something?" The old man's voice was worn as his hands that, at last, lowered the book.

Fox let his hand fall and slip back into a pocket with a kind of nonchalance Harlow couldn't help but envy. He took a few steps toward, then tapped the desk with his long fingers three times. "I'm looking for a specific book."

"Aren't we all?" The old man glanced down at the desk where Fox's hand lingered. "Do you remember the title?"

"I don't," Fox said. "But it's a pirate book. Blue cover."

"We have it in stock."

"Excellent."

The old man rose from his seat with a little groan. He shuffled to the back of the store where a wall to ceiling bookshelf with neglected looking books stood. He pulled a blue book, and a secret door swung in, revealing a set of narrow stairs. "Enjoy your evening," the man said as he moved aside for them.

Harlow hurried to follow Fox down, curious as to what exactly she'd find.

After a short descent, the basement opened up to a

large, dim room. Exposed brick and floating metal shelves lined with books covered the walls. Plush couches and low tables with candlelight were mostly empty, though the few people already seated were too wrapped up in conversation to notice them.

Quiet, soft jazz played over speakers Harlow couldn't see. The sound of crushed ice in a metal cocktail shaker cut through from a large backlit bar where a man with a looped handlebar mustache and a black vest busied himself.

"If you'd still like to try a book, there's plenty here," Fox said, tossing his head to the shelves.

"I'd rather just talk," Harlow said, trying to look less impressed than she was at her surroundings. She had never been to a place quite like this, a hidden speakeasy where people looked like they had transported themselves from another time and place.

She looked down at her outfit and felt terribly underdressed. At least she had the forethought to put on semi-nice jeans instead of leggings. Though her plain white tee shirt called more attention than she wanted in the low light of the underground bar.

She was away from starlight...

"How'd you find this place?" Harlow asked at last.

Fox led them to a couch in the far corner. He sat down on the edge, leaving plenty of space for Harlow.

"On accident, actually. I came into the bookstore one day and tapped the counter and asked for a book recommendation."

"And, they let you in with just that?"

Fox laughed. "The woman at the counter took pity on me, I think. There's supposed to be a different color book a night and you're supposed to be in the know. But it always starts with tapping three times. She must have thought I was stumbling my way in."

Harlow let out a snort. "And did you ever get that book rec?"

Fox tossed his head to the bar. "From the bartender that night. Terrible book. I don't even remember the name of it."

"That bad, huh?"

Fox nodded. "What are you having?"

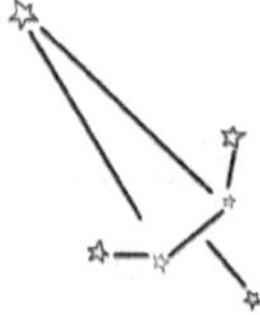

THEIR DRINKS IN HAND, the two sat side by side on the couch as candlelight flickered shadows between them.

Fox ran his thumb along the side of his short glass, cutting a line through the condensation slowly. He was quiet for a long while, a contemplative expression etched into his face. When at last he spoke, his voice was low, a deep rumble as though it came from the depths of his chest, "You're hurt."

Harlow side eyed him, her drink half way to her lips. She set it down with a definitive clank on the dark wood table in front of them. "What do you mean?"

Fox turned to her and his eyes ran down her slowly. "The way you are walking today... You're hurting. Was it something that happened last night?"

Harlow took in a long breath.

Her back had been aching dully all day as her body worked hard to stitch the last of her skin together into the scarless seams. It wasn't enough that she thought anyone would notice.

He was observant, she had to give him that. Or, she was bad at hiding things.

"Yes," she said. "It was my own choice, though."

"To injure yourself?" Fox's eyes widened as if he couldn't believe what he heard. His lips quirked up, though, a level of amusement at her word choice.

"Yeah. Long story."

"I have time."

"I don't." Harlow picked up her glass with swift precision. She took a long sip and clinked her nails along the rim, grounding herself in the glass's cold condensation, in the light *ting ting ting* of her tapping.

She sighed, trying to let out the tension slowly building in her core, letting go of the incredible warmth of his closeness as he put an arm along the back of the couch, encircling her. "Things are changing so quickly. I need to access my old memories soon to help us turn the tides…" Her heart beat faster. "You said you could help."

Fox leaned back, just enough for her to feel his absence.

From the other side of the room, a small group stood up to leave, exchanging long goodbyes with carefree smiles. He watched them with intensity, silent until they disappeared up the stairs.

"Do you know the old stories of the gods?"

A crease formed between Harlow's brows. "I don't believe in the gods," she said honestly, as though compelled to speak the truth. Her voice was firm and resolved. Her back straightened as a burst of adrenaline shot through her limbs.

"Neither do I," Fox said with a light laugh. "I believe in the power of the light, that's all."

Harlow waited, eyes narrowing.

"I don't know if I can help you. Not directly, at least." He was still smiling, as if waiting for the punch-line of a joke. "I was lucky to get my memories back, it seems."

Harlow deflated. Nothing about this was funny. Annoyance flared through her.

Fox went on before she could argue, "But I think your guard can help you."

"How?"

Fox leaned his forearms onto his knees and cast her a playful glance. "They have studied both sides of the light, haven't they? Magic is potent, but it's stronger with moonlight."

"You're suggesting using the power of the moon-light?" Harlow couldn't process the words she had spoken, how quickly she had said them.

Fox shrugged, his casual and kind smile lit his face in the dim candlelight that danced across his skin. "It might be worth asking," he said at last.

Harlow drew back.

Fox caught her gaze. "No one gets to tell us what to do. Except us," he said.

Harlow downed the rest of her drink, it nearly shattered when it hit the table. "I'm sick of people telling me what to do."

"Of course you are." He tilted his head in closer.

The thudding in Harlow's chest accelerated. She flushed at the closeness, the way his eyes moved across her face like he was trying to memorize her. The tips of her fingers buzzed with electricity. All she wanted to do was reach out and grab hold of him, pull him into her arms and taste his lips...

"You're a princess. A warrior. A leader of armies. You give orders, not take them."

Heart racing, insides on fire, Harlow moved closer to him. With determined hands, she laced her fingers behind his neck. His eyes burned into hers at the touch but let her pull his head down closer. His skin was soft, the exhilarating smell of fresh cedar and warm bourbon surrounded her and all she could think about was the desperate wanting of *more*.

Heart racing, and mind clear, she let her body move on its own.

Her forehead rested on his and she closed her eyes, feeling the heat of his breath on her neck as his hands found her waist, gentle and firm. She waited agonizing moments, stilling herself until his breathing was steady and she could no longer stand the tingling in her lips, the overwhelming need to know what it would feel like...

Harlow pulled his chin up at last. And kissed him.

Fox groaned against her lips, an electric pulse raced through her body at the sound. Every limb burned, her muscles tensed – the same feeling of pulling starlight down, the same warmth and power and strength.

Harlow let go, half expecting the underground bar to be filled with shimmering stars.

But it was dark. Low music still played. No one seemed to have even noticed them in the corner. What had felt like a momentous moment, a treasonous touch, the start of something massive, was only theirs.

Fox's hands left her waist, fingertips trailing her skin beneath the hem of her tee shirt as he let go.

Harlow sat back, searching his face for any sign of his state of mind. Was he angry? Did he care? Did he still love her? She almost apologized as all her thoughts saturated her mind, but the intensity of his gaze, the subtle flush in his face in the dark, his lips parted still, stopped her from saying anything else.

He cupped her cheek in his palm as though she were a precious, delicate thing he was afraid would disappear in his hands. "Come back to me," he murmured gently.

Harlow's chest tightened. A vice on her lungs squeezed so hard she thought she might scream unless she was back in his arms. Harlow's lips found his again and the same familiar spark ignited in her core.

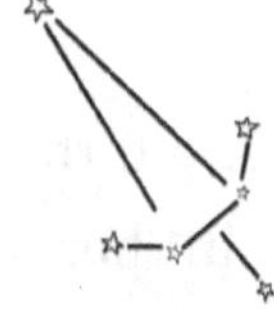

Fox walked her home with his usual demeanor, as though nothing had changed between them. And, she supposed, for him, nothing had. He had already told her they were together before. He had already told her that he loved her. He had loved her then, and loved her now... Though she couldn't be sure the reason for either.

For him, their moment of connection beneath the little bookstore, however fleeting it was, must have felt like coming home.

As she cast him a long look, watching his serene smile, his head held high, and shoulders strong, envy crawled through her bones. She wished she could be so certain of her past that she could be secure in her present. But instead, she felt like she were living in a dream-like state.

For her, the two of them walking together in the dark was as natural and powerful as being beneath the starlight. And as terrifying and vulnerable as being under the same moon.

She focused her stare on their matching steps in perfect sync with one another despite his taller stature. She counted the cracks in the sidewalk. She told herself to breathe.

The complexity of it all, the sheer vastness of the two truths she held in her chest began to burn painfully in her ribs, as if the words she wished to say were being branded into her heart instead of coming free from her throat. But what they were, even she didn't know.

His feet stopped, and so did hers.

Harlow looked up at her apartment building.

Home so soon. And yet...

Fox's hand slipped into hers, replacing her thoughts with warmth. He lifted her hand to his lips and pressed a gentle kiss on her fingers.

"Goodnight," he murmured, his lips grazing along her hand before he rose at last. "Stay safe." His fingertips fell from her hand as he turned back the way they had come.

He didn't look back.

HARLOW SAT on the scratchy carpet floor of her apartment looking out the window. She was tired. Exhausted, actually. But she couldn't sleep no matter how she tried. The whole night felt like a dream. She was so certain that at any moment, she'd be sitting up in bed, gasping for air...

Carina pranced to her side, flicking her tail in a little

question mark as she approached. She looked up at Harlow. "Take a melatonin."

Harlow snorted.

Carina sat silently beside her for a long moment, looking up at the stars with her through the gaps in the buildings. "What's wrong?"

Harlow curled her legs up to her chest. She rested her chin on her knees. For the first time in a very long time, she felt small. "I need to access my old memories," she whispered.

Carina cocked her head. "You have them."

"All of them." Harlow fell back, landing hard on her back with her arms spread wide. "There's something wrong. And I'm worried I'm missing something. Something from the past that can help us." *I'm missing Fox,* she wanted to add. Instead, she put her hand, the one he had kissed gently at the door, over her mouth. She growled through her fingers. "There has to be a way... some magic we're not thinking of."

Carina was still for a few moments. Then, her tail thumped dully on the floor. "Perhaps," she said quietly.

"With moonlight?" Harlow curled up around the cat.

"Perhaps," Carina repeated.

"You know how, don't you?" Harlow asked as she stroked Carina's fur. She felt comfort in the touch, the soft fur, and heat radiating from her. Carina was grounding, a steady force when everything else was adrift on a turbulent sea.

Carina bristled, but leaned into Harlow's touch nonetheless. "It's too risky."

"It's risky to keep going the way we are now, too, isn't it?"

"I can train you," Carina countered. "I can teach you how to keep yourself safe. Or safer... from the corruption of the moon's influence. We used to study the way for decades before we ever harnessed the moonlight."

Harlow rolled back over, staring up at the ceiling. "I'm afraid there's not enough time."

"There's always time."

"Until there isn't." Harlow closed her eyes. "The Mechoida are getting braver. Stronger. More of them will wake up. And when we do, it'll be–"

"A planet destroying event," Carina cut her off.

Harlow nodded. Her eyes drifted to the table where the single white rose with wilted tips of its delicate petals rested in a glass pink cup. "Can you help me?"

"Harnessing the power of the moon can destroy you."

"Not doing so can destroy the world."

Carina closed her eyes slowly. When they finally

opened, she was looking up at the moon. "I will channel for you," she said. "It's my duty."

"I can't ask that–"

"You're not," she interrupted again. Her resolve was clear. "I have trained two lifetimes for this. And..." Carina's pause lingered in the air between them.

Harlow's heart beat dully in her chest, a rhythmic sound reminding her that with each beat, time passed toward some unforeseen outcome, a battle or a slaughter, a peace at last or a planet destroyer.

She waited.

"And more than that," Carina said, "I am your friend. If you think this is the way, then I'll help you."

"Thank you..." Harlow breathed. Her heart expanded in her chest, and yet her anxiety pumped through her along with the gratitude and love.

Carina cast a glance at Harlow. "But we're bringing the others in, too."

Harlow nodded. She had figured as much.

"No matter what we find in your past," Carina said. "I know they'll stand with you."

Harlow wasn't so sure. Len would. Probably. But Dessa? Dessa always knew best and damn anyone who got between her and a goal. And Harlow still hadn't been able to find out what Dessa's goal was. She has indicated that she distrusted the Queen. Alluded to the only way out being quick and brutal. But Dessa was always several steps ahead of everyone.

If she didn't anticipate this move, Harlow wasn't so sure she'd stick around for the outcome.

Still, Harlow had no idea what this kind of magic would do. She was sure that Carina would need Vela and Ara. Or, at least, want them there to share the load. It was unfair to ask her not to bring them in when there was so much at stake

"We can try to share the load," Harlow said at last. "If we harness the moon's light, maybe you and the others could all pitch in. It'd be less on you and less on me?"

Carina's ear twitched. "Possible," she said. "You're sure about this?"

Harlow nodded. "Positive."

"How about after a power nap?" Carina said.

Harlow's vision began to blur, her eyelids heavy. Now that the plan was set, the only thing left to do was rest. "After a power nap..." The words drifted off with her consciousness.

# THE SUN-FILLED NIGHT

The rooftop was empty as it always was. From the top of the five story building, Harlow could see the damaged observatory, the grassy mall, the pathways leading through the university grounds like veins in a living creature. All connected, yet scattered upon first look. The stars were shining brightly overhead, the moon was nearly full.

Since Harlow had discovered the roof's easy access years ago by impulsively opening a door at the end of a hall and climbing a set of old stairs, the group had used this spot as a place to feel closer to the sky. A secret place to call their own after nights battling Mechoida. They found themselves here after leaving bad parties. During the chaotic stress of finals week in their under-graduate years.

It seemed like a good place to meet. Somewhere secluded but accessible. Somewhere familiar and safe.

Harlow, Dessa, and Len all stood there now, as they had so many times before. But this time, instead of smiling and laughing over whatever happened in their latest disastrous escapade, they each carried a heavy weight on their shoulders, worry etched into their faces.

Harlow had told them their plan with as little detail as possible. Hell, even she didn't really know the details. All she knew was that Carina told her it *might* work but that the moonlight was too dangerous to be sure or test it before.

No one had said anything when she was finished. For a long time, they all just stood and stared at noth-ing, no one wanting to speak first.

"This is a cataclysmically bad idea," Len said at last. At her sides, her fingers curled. Her stare hardened. "But I'm in."

"Me too," Ara said at her heels. The cat arched her

back, running her body along Len's leg until her long tail wrapped around her calf.

"Are you serious?" Dessa scoffed. She folded her arms around her waist, eyes rolling. "I'm still on team 'cataclysmic'."

"What could make you change to team 'reckless but necessary'?" Harlow asked sheepishly.

Dessa looked away, dark hair falling into her eyes. "I don't know. We need more information..."

"This is the way to get it," Harlow said. "We need to shine more light on the past. We've been trying other methods for years. We've exhausted everything... This is just another way."

Len nodded. "Perhaps the only way."

Dessa's grip on her body tightened before, at last, she let go, arms falling to her side in defeat. "You're going to do it anyway," she said, staring hard at Harlow. "I better be here to make sure the plan doesn't totally go to shit."

Harlow smiled. Relief washed through her and for the first time that night, her body relaxed; the muscles in her jaw loosened, her shoulders lowered.

If Dessa was there, things would be okay.

If Dessa believed, she'd be alright.

Dessa bit her lower lip for a moment, considering

the plan. "You do understand that this is a theoretical situation based on very little evidence," Dessa said.

"Right."

"There's no guarantee this will work at all," Dessa went on.

"I have to try."

Dessa sighed. "Fine." She let out a little huff, clearly exasperated by Harlow's inability to budge. "But only if you let me put a protection charm on you."

Harlow nodded. She wasn't sure how it would help, but Dessa and her spells never seemed to fail. "Alright."

Dessa approached her slowly. With her face illuminated in the pale light of the moon and the distant warmth of twinkling city lights, she looked ethereal. For a moment, Harlow swore she saw her as she once was... But she looked up at Harlow with the same eyes, human as ever. A crease formed between her brows as she caught Harlow's stare. So much worry...

All Harlow wanted to do was reach out and hold her. To tell her that it would be okay and that she was strong enough for this. But instead, she lowered her head and closed her eyes as Dessa removed a golden locket from her own neck and placed it gently over Harlow's head.

"Rosemary for shielding. Thyme for courage," she whispered the ingredients of the locket to Harlow. "Not that you need that."

Harlow's eyes fluttered open as she felt the weight of the charm rest coldly on her sternum. She smiled at Dessa who gazed back at her with a wicked expression.

"And fennel," Dessa added. "For your fuckery."

Harlow snorted.

Len put a strong hand on Harlow's shoulder. She smiled at Dessa. "How'd you know?"

Dessa shrugged. "I get a call in the middle of the night telling me to meet Harlow on a roof? I assume fuckery."

Carina moved between them with silent steps. "Let's do this. Harlow, sit."

Harlow sat down between her friends. She rested her hands on her knees and looked up at them with a big, fake smile.

In a bright flash of sparkling light, the three cats transformed. Their bodies expanded, swirling moon-dust filled their shapes. Pale pink light cascaded outward from their limbs like a glowing mist around them. Purple, pupilless eyes found Harlow.

"The moon reveals pathways in the darkest nights. These paths can lead us to truths we may not be able to carry," Carina's voice spoke clearly, though her mouth did not move.

Harlow's heart began to drum loudly in her chest. Anxiety prickled her bones with the burning desire to move and fight and run. She did her best to stay still, grounding herself in the concrete below. "I understand," she said at last.

"I will help her carry them," Len said, her voice clear and bold. She sat beside Harlow with decisive ease. Her arm wrapped around Harlow's shoulders in a strong embrace.

Harlow's eyes widened. She shook her head. "No–"

"And I will, too," Dessa said. She sat on Harlow's other side, her hand slipping into Harlow's. She tilted her head up and smiled at her with a tenderness Harlow hadn't seen in her before.

"Some choices cannot be rescinded," Ara said at their sides, above, and below all at once.

"Consequences cannot be undone," Vela whispered, her massive head low to look into their eyes.

"I understand," Dessa said. She gave Harlow's hand a squeeze. "Where Harlow goes, I go."

"We'll find out together." Len held Harlow's shoulder tighter.

Carina and the other guards circled the group, their paws lifting from the ground effortlessly as bright moonlight danced between them. Moonlight filled the spaces between them, brilliant color, bursting with life.

They spoke in unison, their voices loud and clear,

"With the light borrowed from stars, light the path to your past. These willing hearts journey with her. Borrowed, bettered, brightened. Light the way."

A beam of light hit Harlow square in the chest.

She fell back.

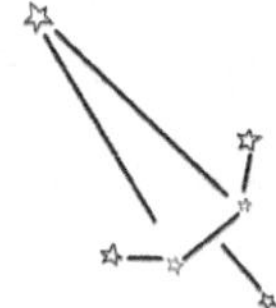

HARLOW SCRAMBLED to her knees as a cloud of dust spiraled around her. She coughed, choking on dirt and smoke that stung her lungs like fingers reaching down her throat to strangle her.

A sudden dread filled her. Muscles tensed. Heart raced. Fear mixed with anger and pain. A pain so piercing that she could no longer think clearly.

And she was alone...

*No. Not alone.*

Through the cover of pink and purple swirling smoke, the silhouette of the Queen stalked toward her. She was walking slowly, purposeful steps that sounded like gunfire in Harlow's ears. At last, she broke through the haze, coming into sudden, vivid focus.

A sword of starlight shifted in the Queen's tight

grasp as she clenched her fingers around the hilt. Her eyes were fixed on Harlow, a detached ferocity in her gaze.

The Queen was looking at her, but Harlow wasn't sure she was truly seeing her. Not as she was. Not *who* she was. Not as family, her daughter, her general, her princess. She looked at Harlow the way a beast stared down another that wandered too close to their territory.

She was ready to kill.

But not in defense.

Ready to kill because she could.

Because it was easy.

But it couldn't be.

Harlow would never hurt her. She wasn't dangerous. She wasn't too close. She blinked away tears, the terrible stinging in her eyes ripped at her sight.

Betrayal settled in like stones in Harlow's heart, weighing her down until she sank down low to the floor.

"Why are you doing this?" Harlow tried to ask but her voice was stuck in her throat, burning her up from the inside.

This was her.

But it wasn't.

It was her aunt.

But it wasn't.

This was the past. On a planet far away. A place she called home and yet remembered so little of.

The space around them was smoldering. Brilliant blue flames gnawed at the walls and crawled through the large shattered windows. Stonework made of a shimmering crystal-like material reflected the fires brightly, illuminating Harlow's warped reflection back to her.

She stared back at herself with terror-filled eyes. She was bloodied. Her bright hair was long, flowing around her as though she were in space, weightless... though her bones felt so very heavy... She tried to stand up despite the pain in her chest, the pain in her limbs. She stumbled forward, hands finding the floor as she pushed up as hard as she could. She was fighting to keep herself upright.

Fighting for her life.

She looked up.

Her aunt held the sword high.

"My sword!" This time, her voice was clear. She held her arm out, fingers reaching for the starlight within the shimmering blade. It pulled away from her, retreating as if repulsed.

The harder she scrambled for it, the more bright

blood bursting from her side, the harder it retreated into the Queen's grasp.

Harlow held a hand to her ribs where hot liquid poured from her. She had to stop this... the bleeding, the fire, the deadly battle.

"*You* were the sword," the Queen said, her voice laced with a viciousness Harlow had never heard before. A god dealing judgment.

The Queen held the sword high, her face impassive in the firelight. "I must do what is right. You are our destruction."

Terror surged through Harlow's veins, hardening every muscle. She sprang up on shaking legs, her side burned as the movement ripped her open.

The hard blow of the blade came down around her, blinding her with pain.

And thrusting her into darkness.

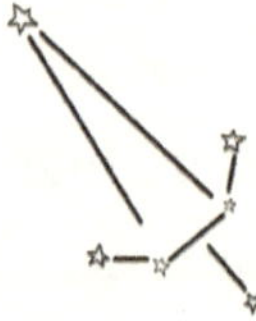

HARLOW GASPED FOR AIR, her hands held around her neck to stop the bleeding where the sword came down. Her heart pounding her energy out of her body, betraying her.

She was dying.

She didn't want to die.

There was so much left to do.

She didn't want to die.

*"Harlow!"* Dessa's voice called her back from the brink, just as her consciousness began to darken.

She felt her friends' arms around her, pulling her up from the hard ground. And as she opened her eyes to the clear starry sky, felt the cool prickle of the night air, she realized that she was back.

She was safe.

She was home.

Harlow kept her hand on her throat as she curled into their embrace. Her body shook, finally freeing itself of all the terror and the horror she had felt just moments ago. She let a choking sob bubble up from deep within her, clearing the way for her to speak. "She killed me!" The words came out in spurts, in time with the strong beating of her heart, still fearful in her chest. "She killed me."

"We saw," Dessa breathed into Harlow's hair. She pulled her closer into her small frame as Len squeezed them both tighter. "We were with you."

"I wasn't there to protect you," Len whispered. "I'm sorry."

Dessa shook her head into Harlow's neck. "What happened?"

Carina, still in her moon-filled form, looked down at them. "This is troubling."

The other two cats nodded in agreement.

"There is much to consider," Vela said calmly. She trotted farther from them, then shimmered back to her small house cat body. She looked up at the stars and went on, "The planet looked like it was already on the verge of destruction. Why would she need to kill you?"

"Breathe," Len said, though it came out like a command. She gave Harlow's shoulder a firm shake. "Breathe in. You're alive."

Harlow's fingers unclenched at last, half moon cuts bloomed in her palms as she relaxed. She took in a shaking breath until she couldn't fill her lungs any more.

"And out," Len said.

Harlow let out the breath in one loud huff. She dried her face with the back of her hand as shame tore through her. She had been crying. She was wet with tears and snot. "Ugh..." She cursed her body for letting her down. For exposing the fear for what it was. Primal.

And shattering.

Dessa pressed the locket to Harlow's chest. "We're here, Harlow."

Len looked at it with a raised brow. "There's not enough fennel in the world," she said quietly.

Harlow snorted. She rubbed her nose with her sleeve as the other two cats reverted back in front of them.

At the horizon, the sky began to fade into a lighter shade of blue.

# CHAPTER 19

# THE PLAN, OR LACK THEREOF

The realization was, as Carina had warned, a half-lit path. The moon stole light to illuminate the way and kept the rest in dark shadow.

Harlow couldn't act surprised that the moon's magic had only shown her the moment of her death and left out the context. Where were her shield and bow? Where were the guardians who were supposed to stay by their sides?

Harlow's mind spiraled on itself.

Her aunt had never particularly been warm with her. Harlow always ascribed this to having raised her under the hard conditions that governed their lives on Earth. It was hard to be a parent, unexpectedly. Harder still to be one when you were responsible for the fate of the entire planet. Given everything, Harlow always figured she didn't have it all too bad. So... surely she hadn't *meant* to murder her?

"What the fuck happened?" Harlow broke the silence.

The words sounded as stupid out loud as it did her heart.

At this, Len had side-eyed her. "Well, you got murdered in the most foul fashion."

They sat in Harlow's apartment, all snuggled into her bed with a cup of coffee or tea clutched to their chest. None of them had slept, though, Harlow suspected that was for the best. She didn't want to imagine the dreams that would infiltrate her mind once her eyes closed.

She needed to stay awake for now.

Harlow sipped her coffee loudly. "Do we call Fox?" she asked at last. At the words leaving her lips, she wished she could pull them back.

Dessa's eyes narrowed. She stared into the green tea

in her hands, legs curling up closer to her body. "Why wouldn't he just tell you what happened? What's his goal here?"

Len shrugged. "Would any of us have believed him if he did?"

Dessa sighed. "No," she admitted begrudgingly.

Len pressed the thick blanket around Dessa's feet, warming her with a little squeeze. "Let's consider, then, that Harlow trusts him."

Dessa grumbled to herself, slurping her tea loudly to cover whatever harsh words had left her mouth.

"I do trust him," Harlow said quietly.

Carina's ear flicked.

"But..." Harlow stopped herself. She wasn't sure she was ready to admit yet that he had told her he loved her – she especially wasn't ready to admit that she knew, in her heart, that back then she had loved him too. That they had kissed in an underground bar and that it felt natural and normal.

Her eyes found Dessa's, and a flash of heat flared across her cheeks. She had loved Dessa, too.

She *loved* Dessa, too.

Harlow burrowed herself closer to Len beneath the blanket. Len was solid, calm. Her shield – even when she hated to admit she needed one. She settled into Len's shoulder. "Okay, what do we think we should do?"

Len wrapped a protective arm around Harlow. She breathed in so deep that Harlow rose with her, prompting her to take her own long breath.

It was going to be... what it was going to be.

Harlow couldn't convince herself that it would all be okay just yet. They were spiraling toward something, a meteor that couldn't change its course. At least they could try to determine where it would crash.

Dessa leaned forward, the mattress shifting beneath her. "We have to be clever. The Queen won't admit to anything if we confront her head on with questions."

"Right," Harlow agreed.

"So this is where we come in," Dessa went on. "We can't have you going in there, sword waving around like a lunatic."

Len snorted. "Word choice."

Dessa rolled her eyes, though her smile won, brightening her face like sunlight. With her, the mood of the room shifted to one of calm, even a faint joy, despite their circumstances. "Pun not intended. I'm so clever sometimes I don't even realize it."

Harlow smiled back. "You are smarter than you know," she whispered.

"Which is saying something because you're very much a know-it-all," Len said, though her voice was kind.

"Well, I know a lot."

"Do you know how to get information out of the Queen?" Len asked.

"*That* may take a bit of strategizing," Dessa conceded. She set her cup of tea on the floor, leaning her entire body off the bed. She retrieved one of Harlow's notebooks from underneath the pile of clean laundry. "Pen?"

Harlow nodded to the messy desk and Dessa sighed.

"I'll get it," Ara said from across the room. She hurried to the desk, retrieving the pen with her mouth.

The faint sound of the pen scratching against the pages filled the air as Dessa began to scribble wildly across the notebook. She glanced up at Harlow and smiled. "Want to add to the brain dump?"

Harlow nodded on Len's shoulder. "Yeah, just add 'murdered by my own sword by my own family... equals question mark question mark'. That should suffice."

"Really? That's all you're thinking about?" Dessa's tone was serious, though her eyes shined as her grin broadened.

"Yep," Harlow lied. "That'll about do it."

Dessa went back to her writing. In big bold letters, Harlow read the middle of the page: 'Stay alive'.

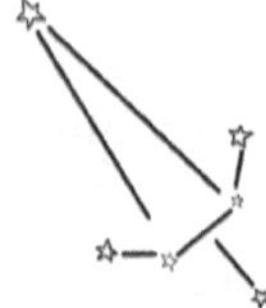

IT WAS MID-MORNING. Light filtered through the curtains in a soft golden glow, illuminating a halo around Dessa's head as she sat in Harlow's desk, having cleared it of the papers and mugs and various trinkets that Harlow had accumulated over the year.

Harlow's eyes were closed, but she refused to sleep. Every time she caught herself settling deeper into Len's shoulder, or her consciousness beginning to fade, her eyes snapped open wide, and she stared into the beam of light until she was awake enough to carry on.

Len, however, was fast asleep, her head leaned back against the wall, quiet little snores humming from her nose like white noise.

Len, however, was fast asleep, her head leaned back against the wall, quiet little snores humming from her nose like white noise.

Dessa stretched. Her hands lifting up over her head, her baggy crop top exposing her ribs.

Harlow bit her lip and closed her eyes, savoring the familiar stinging sensation as though it were a wicked form of penance. She had no right at all to look at Dessa.

Though she had broken no vow between them, she still felt like a traitor.

Their past in this human life had always been marred by their previous one. A complicated mix of emotions they couldn't name or identify the origins of lingered in Harlow's heart, especially in seemingly insignificant moments like this.

A single kiss, stupidly shared in an old photography gallery when they thought Len wasn't looking. One kiss, stolen in the dark, was all it took to make their easy friendship complicated.

And immaturity. If she was being honest, immaturity got in the way back then. Most of it had been Harlow thinking she was mature enough to handle complex emotions. She had grown up fast. Fast enough to think she was a healthy adult. Too fast to actually know what that meant. She had been immature back then. Easily frustrated, angry, impossible to work with... It was no wonder their kiss had ended there and never repeated.

Harlow pretended it was fine ever since. Like it didn't matter. Like she didn't care. Like her heart wasn't broken.

At least Dessa always seemed fine. She had kissed her, smiled as though she had *finally* felt genuine joy, and then the night after, she had taken it back, citing it being too risky to jeopardize their friendship. Dessa valued her *too much* to compromise their relationship. And that was for the best.

Harlow knew she was right.

Mostly.

It hurt still, years later in that small aching way that was sometimes easy to forget, and surprisingly painful when she suddenly remembered it was there.

"Okay, here's the plan!" Dessa spun the chair toward the bed.

Len snapped up, thrusting Harlow off her with a grunt. "Plan, right–"

"Ow!" Harlow exaggeratedly rubbed the back of her head.

Dessa ignored them both with practiced authority. "We need to debrief with the Queen tonight. It's almost the full moon, and we need a better understanding of *her* plan. I'll do the talking, you two shut up."

Harlow's brows rose. "That's the plan? You just *be smart* and we don't open our big dumb mouths?"

Len glanced at her phone. "No offense, Dessa, but it took you two hours to come up with that?"

Dessa smirked. "Almost three, actually. And no, that's not all. We're bringing the Queen into this century." She held up her own phone, a text from Rainey prominently displayed on the screen.

Harlow squinted, leaning closer.

Dessa turned her phone around quickly. "I'll do the talking, you guys do the shutting up, Rainey's got the spy wear."

"The what now?" Len asked.

"Look," Dessa explained, "we can't do this on our own. What we've been doing, including dabbling in forbidden, and potentially dangerous magic, isn't working. I figured Rainey seems techie."

"I'm still surprised by how…" Harlow murmured under her breath. She had been working with them for so long but Rainey had only mentioned her hobbies in passing. Most of the evenings were taken up with chatter about the silliest things.

Dessa ignored her. "She agreed to help us out with a hidden camera. You know, those tiny ones?"

"We're going to nanny cam the Queen?" Len's voice was higher pitched than Harlow had ever heard it.

She put a hand on Len's shoulder. "I'll handle it. You guys don't even need to know about it."

Len breathed in until her chest puffed out. She sighed it out. "Alright," she said at last. "But we need to be sure Rainey and Gigi are safe, too."

"Way ahead of you," Dessa said. "Rainey is dropping it off with a friend, and we're meeting them at Espresso Yourself."

"She just happened to have one lying around?" Len asked, moving on to the more pressing concerns, it seemed.

Dessa laughed. "Yeah, apparently she's modifying her doorbell camera. She said it shouldn't be too hard." She turned to her phone on the desk, swiped at it a few times, then glanced up. "But Gigi is insisting we provide our measurements in exchange."

Harlow snorted.

"Relentless, those two," Dessa agreed.

"I'll bake some cookies, too," Len said, rising from the bed with a little groan.

"I'll scrape up some money together to cover the cost of the doorbell." Harlow reached out for Len's hand. She pulled Harlow up with a quick motion.

"From where?" Dessa looked around the cluttered room.

Harlow shrugged. She hadn't thought that far ahead.

"Let's stick to cookies for now," Len said with a yawn. "We'll focus on repayment after we save the world."

# CHAPTER 20

# A STORM OF STARS

The little camera was hidden among big fake jewels on the front of what clearly looked like one of Gigi's handbags. Harlow had to admit, it was a bit hard to tell what it was among the clusters of bright and black sparkle.

Rainey's friend, a sweet-looking woman with graying hair despite her youthful appearance, gave it to them without question and excitedly took the home-made sugar cookies and an envelope with measurements and twenty-two dollars.

Bag looped around Dessa's shoulder, and stomachs turning with anxiety, the group stood now at the bottom of the large building as an orange glow washed over the city. Shadows stretched out long, enveloping them in a crisp darkness.

They looked up, but none of them made a move to take another step closer.

At last, Harlow flashed her friends a half-smile. She took a few steps toward the large front doors, busy with people coming and going. She waved for them to follow. "Come on, then, let's see if we're any good at this spy business."

"I can guarantee we are not," Len grumbled.

Dessa took Len's hand, then followed after Harlow. "Are you going to be alright seeing her, after..." She trailed off, her words fizzling away as they entered the building and were met with the low hum of music and conversations.

Harlow squared her shoulders, her smile only grew as she made her way through the lobby. "I'm the sword."

Though she felt more like a letter opener. Like a plastic thing molded into the shape of a great sword. A small novelty that got lost into a desk drawer, forgotten, dull, and useless.

She glanced back at her friends. Both seemed preoccupied with their own worries to notice that Harlow was bluffing. That is, until Dessa's eyes flicked up to hers.

Harlow tossed her head back. "Good thing my instructions were to be quiet." She hoped her tone was jovial, silly, even.

"Yep. Just let me talk today, if you can help it."

HARLOW'S HEART was in her throat as the door opened. She wasn't sure what she would feel at seeing her aunt, the woman who had raised her, in front of her after learning what she had the night before. She took in a deep breath through her nose so no one would notice her anxiety as it prickled up the back of her neck.

She tried to imagine what it would look like...

The Queen had two ways of greeting them.

She would either be staring out the window, surveying her kingdom and would hardly glance at them as they entered, or she'd be sitting on the couch, a glass of wine in her hand and a penetrating stare so intense, it'd stop them in their tracks.

This evening was neither.

They walked into the penthouse and found nothing waiting for them.

The large room was empty but for their own reflections staring at them in the massive windows.

Dessa's eyes scanned the room quickly.

Harlow put a hand out, stopping either her or Len from moving forward as she craned her head to get a better vantage.

Len leaned down. "She was expecting us, right?"

Harlow's hand lowered. The three cautiously ventured deeper into the room.

Dessa placed her bag along the long kitchen counter, tucked away by the wall, as Harlow glanced toward the top of the window, looking for starlight.

It was still twilight... It couldn't be that a monster had come to find her. The Queen must have just–

"Kill count." The Queen's voice boomed through the room. She appeared from the hallway, meticulously put together as always, though there was a disorientation about her that made Harlow recoil slightly.

She couldn't place what felt off, except that, maybe she was shocked to see her from a different angle suddenly. Or she was surprised at how easy it felt to be conflicted rather than angry with her. Her emotions turned over in her heart. Too much for her mind to rationalize.

"Zero," Dessa answered. "We had one. It was close."

"It got away?" The Queen made her way to the kitchen, barely glancing at them as she passed.

"It did," Dessa said. "We watched it transform in front of us. It seemed new."

The Queen only hummed in response.

Dessa cast a quick side glance at Harlow as the Queen filled her cup from an open bottle. She stood taller. "I think they're waking more of them up. We should postpone the battle."

Len's eyes widened.

The Queen snapped her attention to Dessa. "You are questioning me?"

Dessa smiled faintly. "Not at all," she said kindly. "Merely suggesting that as more of them awaken to their–"

"If they are growing in numbers, all the more reason to take them all out in one single swoop," the Queen cut her off. She looked at Harlow. "What do you think?"

Harlow itched to look to Dessa, to gauge if she was supposed to answer or wait for a cue. But she knew her aunt would see the shift in her eye. She couldn't risk it. "I agree."

That felt safe.

Dessa went on, "We need more information. How are they waking others up? Can we stop that process?"

The Queen huffed.

It was the most exasperated Harlow had ever seen her. She couldn't reconcile this version with the one in her vision, the one from her childhood, even the one from a few days ago.

Harlow looked more closely at the Queen, trying to sort out a clue. She seemed so... human. The glass of wine at her lips. The faint wrinkles around her eyes and across her forehead. Years of worry etched into her face. Her fingers gripping the glass looked like the branch of a tree. Her shoulders were slightly slumped inward. Harlow almost felt bad...

Almost.

"What more information do you need?" The Queen asked.

"We need to know more about our past so we can understand the future," Dessa said. She was bold and bright. It sounded like something she would say no matter the circumstances. "How did they recruit others to their cause back then? Perhaps if we know that, we can piece together what's happening now."

A drop of sweat raced down Harlow's spine.

The Queen's glass clinked against the counter as she set it down with a scowl.

Harlow's heart skipped a beat. Her muscles tensed.

"You don't need anything from me except guidance," she said, tone back to the usual commanding sound despite her previous outburst. Or, as much of an outburst as she *could* have.

"But if–"

"The Mechoida are strong. They will only grow stronger as their plague spreads. We will eliminate them before they infect everything else around them." The Queen's tone was stern, her jaw clenched as her eyes found each of theirs.

When they landed on Harlow, a chill shot up her limbs. Her fingers instinctively twitched for starlight.

Fear.

Harlow realized, painfully, that it was fear that ripped through her veins.

"Go do your job." The Queen waved them off as she took a long sip of her wine. "Come back the night before the full moon. I want to know if I will need to do this myself."

Len bowed her head.

Dessa did the same, but added a little curtsey, her back foot dragging out to get even lower.

Harlow's jar clenched. But she did her best to tilt her head as her heart beat faster in her chest.

As the three found their way out, the Queen called after them, "And don't forget your purse."

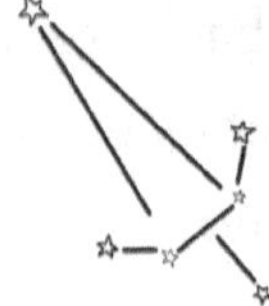

ONCE FREE OF THE BUILDING, with the starlight overhead in the swiftly darkening sky, Dessa glanced down at the jeweled bag. "Well, it was a good try," she grumbled.

Len leaned over her shoulder, looking directly into the camera. "I doubt we would capture anything from this anyway," she told the bag. "She's not one to talk to herself or do anything incriminating in her own home. Too careful." She straightened up, ushering Harlow and Dessa into the flow of the people along the sidewalk. "Well, I liked the idea of getting more information. But I probably could have told you she would shut us down like that."

Dessa shrugged. She slung the bag over her shoulder, gold earrings jingling lightly. "I think I actually got a lot out of that interaction."

Harlow's heart was still loud in her ears. She shook her head, feeling the tickling of her hair along her cheek. She listened to the random conversations, trying hard to piece together the lives of the people around her. She wanted to distract herself from anything but the failed, seemingly half-hearted attempt at reconnaissance, the sad way they left empty-handed, and with a gaping hole in her chest.

"Oh yeah?" Len said, breaking Harlow's thoughts. "Do tell?"

"Well, for one," Dessa said with a bright smile, "we now know there's a deadline. One less arbitrary than it originally seemed. She's stubborn, but not thoughtless." She nudged Harlow's shoulder. "And we know she *really* doesn't want us having any information about the past."

"We *did* already know that," Len said.

Dessa raised a brow. "Yes, but did we know that Rainey also gave me a very small listening device that I put at the bottom of my shoe and then scraped into the rug when I did my little exit?"

Relief and pride swelled in Harlow's chest. It wasn't all for nothing after all.

"You did what?" Len gasped.

Dessa winked. "And, sure, I doubt we'll get anything from it, but you never know." She took hold of Harlow's elbow. "We need to figure out why she's in such a rush to end all of this."

"Perhaps she's worried about more damage to civilians?" Len prompted as someone on the sidewalk dodged her, then threw her a sour look.

Harlow glared at the person, but the moment was already gone, and Len didn't even seem to notice.

"Let's get something to eat. We can try to figure this out over a meal," Dessa said as they turned another corner. "What sounds good?"

"Rocks?" Harlow grumbled. At least, it felt as though she had eaten a handful of them. Heavy stones rested deep in her stomach and a slight nausea settled deep in her core.

"Burgers?" Len offered, ignoring Harlow's melodrama.

Dessa, at least, seemed sympathetic. Slightly. She smiled at Harlow but her eyes were gleaming with some kind of mischief. "Some place with milkshakes?"

There it was.

Harlow huffed. She hated the little superhero themed diner just off campus. It was tacky and overly cluttered and all the servers wore capes.

Dessa loved it there, though she assumed it was mostly because it annoyed Harlow so much. Otherwise, it was the opposite of everything Dessa was.

Len was already leading the way.

There was no stopping it once she got an idea in her head.

The feeling of ease that had been there moments ago was gone.

This night was doomed.

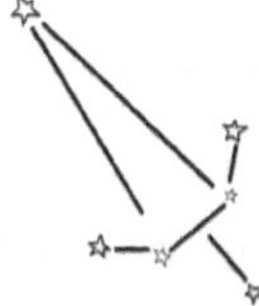

AT LEAST THE Hero's Journey did have excellent milkshakes, though Harlow would never admit it.

As predicted, the diner was crowded. It was too bright. Too loud. Too many bold colors and reflections bouncing off glass shadowboxes along the walls that held signed memorabilia and comic books that probably cost more than all of their rent.

She slouched over her demolished cheeseburger, blowing bubbles into the bottom of her narrow milkshake glass, half listening to Len and Dessa across the table talk about what they hoped the Queen would randomly say to herself while wandering her own home, or if she'd invite someone incriminating.

At the mention of her aunt having any friends or allies, the two laughed and waved their hands as if it was the silliest thing in the world.

Harlow, however, simply shrunk down further into the red vinyl booth, her thighs sticking slightly to the cheap fabric. She grimaced.

"Oh, come on," Dessa said through her laughter. "It would be funny to catch her on a date."

Harlow bit her straw, opening one side of her mouth to growl. "It would not."

Len scooped a few of her fries onto Harlow's plate. "Alright, so maybe covert operations aren't our speciality. But we do excel with battle plans. What's the plan of attack tonight? Are we going to go looking for a fight? Keep up the pretense that we're doing what she wants for now?"

"They seem to be finding us just fine," Dessa said. She took the half eaten top bun from Harlow and picked off the sesame seeds, popping them into her mouth one at a time like they were some kind of delicacy.

Harlow picked at the extra fries. She was starving. But everything except the milkshake tasted like ashes. Perhaps she was too tired to chew...

"What I really want to do is pick Fox's brain about the vision," Dessa said. "I think that has to come first. How does he play into all of this?"

Harlow's brows furrowed as a flush in her ears burned. She absolutely did not want to see Fox right now. And, more than anything, she wanted to run into him and feel his strong arms wrap around her as though he, alone, in this frail human form, could keep her safe. She wanted to pretend. For a moment.

And she didn't want Dessa anywhere near him, too.

She blew out a big bubble in her cup. It popped with a dull, wet sound.

"Can you tell him we'd like to meet tonight?" Dessa asked, waving her hand in front of Harlow's face. "And stop blowing bubbles, you child." She said the last part in jest, but all Harlow felt was the sting in her heart.

She sat up straight. "You think you'd cut me a little slack for once." The words tumbled out before she could stop them. A deep breath later, and she regretted even coming out to eat at all. Shame bit at her as Dessa pulled back slowly.

Len put a hand on Dessa's shoulder, her eyes kind. "I think tensions are high right now," she said softly. "We are all feeling a bit anxious, yes?"

Harlow glared down into her half-empty cup. She took in another long breath, unsticking her legs from the booth as she shifted uncomfortably under Len's stare. Her heart was still in her throat as she choked out a quiet, "I'm sorry."

Dessa sighed. "No, I'm sorry," she said. Her fingers laced together on the tabletop. "Listen, I'm mad at myself a bit. My plan was bungled and... I'm sorry I wasn't there for you. Back then."

Harlow looked up as Dessa went on, so quiet she could hardly hear her in the rumble of the diner.

"I saw how frightened you were without your sword... I hated seeing you like that. I can only imagine how it actually *felt*."

"Can I take any plates?"

"Moonlight!" Len cried, a hand over her chest as all three of them jumped in their seats.

The server, black cape and big smile on, seemed to manifest from nowhere, blissfully unaware of his blunder, or the swear that Len had dropped. "Still working?" he asked, his voice still the pleasant emptiness as before. He was looking out the window, mostly at his own reflection, it seemed.

Harlow's eyes were wide. She gestured broadly at the table. "Go away!"

"Alrighty," he said, still smiling as though Harlow had told him a joke that he had to pleasantly pretend he found amusing. "You pay the bill up front at the register when you're ready."

Harlow followed him all as he moved on to the other tables, equally disengaged with the rest of them, though no one else seemed as startled as they had. She pinched her brow. "How are we supposed to fight anything when a server dressed as Batman can sneak up on us?"

"At least Mechoida are huge," Len said with a snort. She eyed the bill on the table as though it was about to spring to life and attack them.

"Like I said, we need some help." Dessa pulled her phone from her pocket. "I'll check in on our superhero costumes and see if Rainey's heard anything on the bug."

"Don't pressure Gigi about it, though," Len said quickly. "She's already been through plenty."

"Please. I'm always charming and considerate. Unlike *some* people." She glanced up at the server as her thumbs tapped her screen with little soft clicks of her nails.

"Okay but actually I'm never coming back here again," Harlow said, heart still pounding from the surprise. "I'm serious. The milkshakes aren't *that* good. I'm boycotting."

Len finished her own shake in a few large sips as though Harlow was about to spring them all away immediately.

"Gigi said she's working on the outfits. Nothing but silence from the Queen so far, but that's good. It means she hasn't found the bug." Dessa's eyes flashed to Harlow. "You figure out if Fox is free."

Harlow eyed her own phone with trepidation. He had already texted her that he was still thinking about the night in the bookstore. Harlow's stomach dropped, but she smiled nonetheless. The bookstore... that was one way to put it... Harlow shoved the memories aside

and typed out the message before she could overthink
it.

> same

> i miss you i think

> unrelated, we need to talk

Ominous.

> about the moonlight

> meet at The Old Wall?

Of course, Harlow. When?

Harlow looked up at her friends. They were busy
gathering up the plates and napkins.

She wasn't finishing her milkshake. On principle.
She wasn't giving anyone the satisfaction of an
empty cup.

> tonight

I'll be there, princess.

Harlow stuffed her phone away and snatched the
bill with a grumble. She hated that nickname. But only
because, if she was being honest, the darkest part of her
wanted a different title.

"Let's get out of here," Harlow said, cutting off her own treasonous thoughts. "Fox is meeting us at The Old Wall."

# THE PLACE
# WITHOUT
# STARLIGHT

The night was still, despite the bustle of the city still awake just around the block. From there, on the high hill overlooking the cityscape, the stone wall shielded them from the noise below. The dark alleys were empty as people found their way into the bars and restaurants all alight with the yellow glow of streetlights.

The Old Wall was legendary.

While most of the city was modern and sleek, the wall here was made of gray, weathered stone. It separated the university grounds from the rest of the city, but only on the east side where things were older, quieter. No one who knew why the wall was erected ever shared it with the students. They had been left to rumor that it used to surround the whole campus, but had been demolished when the university expanded. Or that it was made to keep non-students out and that the whole place had originally been literally gatekeeping knowledge.

Or that it was made by aliens.

At least Harlow knew that one was untrue.

Still, it was a mostly abandoned place. Students came on graduation day to carve their names into the stone, a tradition that went back as far as the wall seemed to be old, judging by the long eroded etches that ticked all the way from the lowest stone to the highest, about forty feet up in the air on the city side.

On the university side, a hill crested up along the wall's path so that it was only four or so feet high. The names here were more modern, more easily read. Harlow always assumed that it was proof that generations got lazier with time. But, perhaps, they just got smarter. No one was climbing several stories for a silly tradition anymore, and that was probably a good thing.

At least, that's what Dessa had cried out to her as she scaled the wall on the city side after their undergraduate ceremony. Somewhere along the wall, on the tallest stone, Harlow had written their names with her pocketknife and drawn a little heart around them.

It seemed like a lifetime ago now.

But now, it was quiet, and dark. Now, it was as though the rest of the huge concrete city, the memories of simpler times, and worries that seemed so trivial now, were far away...

Fox was sitting on the ledge of the wall, long legs hanging over the edge with a casual disregard for gravity that Harlow had only seen in herself. From where he sat, it was a long, long fall to the bottom of the alleyway on the city side. At the sound of their steps, he turned his head over his shoulder, his smile lighting his face at the sight of Harlow in the dark moonlight.

His eyes scanned her face, lingering on the crease in her brow and the slight frown at the corners of her lips. His own expression transformed to concern, mirroring hers so quickly it was as though his smile had never been there at all. He swung his legs around to the other side where the wall and the hill connected. He rose to his feet, standing tall. Then his gaze found Dessa and Len at Harlow's sides.

Harlow led the way to him, her friends a few steps behind. If she pretended not to hear their footsteps, if she could cover her ears for only a moment, it would be as though it was just her and Fox. Like she was approaching him for a midnight stroll, hand in hand, and not to ask him hard questions about death and magic.

She stopped before she was quite at arms' length. She didn't want to be closer. Not now.

"You used the magic?" Fox asked quietly as her friends grew closer, his calm smile back.

Harlow nodded. Emotions she could not name rushed through her all at once. Her heart skipped, her hands clenched as the fear swelled up, overtaking everything else. She could smell the smoke. Hear the drumming of footsteps coming closer. Feel the blade come down on her.

The sting of tears pricked at the corners of her eyes as she held a hand to her neck.

He held out his arms to her, and though she wanted to run to him, to leap into his embrace, to sob and cry out that he had been right and that she was confused and afraid, she simply shook her head.

Fox's smile vanished. His hands fell.

Harlow looked back to her friends quickly. She didn't want to see the hurt on his face.

As Len and Dessa joined her side, Fox put his hands in his pockets. His eyes were still fixed on Harlow, though he asked the group, "What did you see?"

"The Queen killed me, didn't she?" Harlow asked.

Len took one step closer, putting herself between Harlow and Fox.

Fox flinched backward, pain clear on his face. His gaze lowered. "Yes," he said.

"Why didn't you tell us?" Dessa asked. It was a question with an obvious answer, but as Harlow's eyes shifted to her, she knew that Dessa had asked to get his reaction. She had always been smart enough to know when to play dumb.

"Would you have believed me if I told you?" His head tilted to Dessa, then Len. He waited until Len's shoulders relaxed before he looked back at Harlow. His eyes softened. "Would you?"

"No," Harlow said honestly.

She saw only his own candor in return. There was no malice there. No small twitch in his face, no flinch of his body to indicate he was anything less than honest with her. He simply looked... sad.

"I'm sorry," he said at last.

Harlow believed him. She was sorry too. More than

anything, she wanted those memories to leave her mind, for her to have been able to accept the truth without having to live it. She hated that this was the only way for her to learn the truth of what had happened to her. She had to see it for herself. *Feel* it for herself.

He was right. There was no other way.

She did always have to get her nose bloodied.

"You wanted us to find the answers ourselves," Len said. "But there are none. All we have is this one piece. Surely you can tell us more."

Dessa stepped forward and Harlow felt herself bristle. "Why did she do it? Why kill her?" Dessa demanded.

Fox's eyes locked on Harlow. The world around her faded slowly as though his eyes had cast a spell over her. "I never got that answer."His words lingered between the group, empty and cold as the vastness of space.

He finally tore his gaze from her and she let out a shaking breath. He looked to Len, then Dessa. "And neither did you. The Queen sent us all here almost immediately after. Everyone died by her magic as the planet broke itself apart."

Len recoiled. "I don't understand, though. I would never have left Harlow's side. I would have died before I let her come to harm. Where was I?"

Dessa nodded. "Same."

Harlow turned to them, her heart sinking beneath her ribs. "It was too late for me," she said. Harlow's mouth hung open, her hand went to it in an instant as if she had just spoken something vile. She had no idea where that came from. She just knew in her heart that it was true.

They hadn't left her. Not really. She was sure of it. But... it had been too late for her. She tried to rationalize her words, her mind spinning. "I'm sure you knew that you could do more good for more of us by being out there helping than dying by my side," she added. She held a hand out to Dessa who simply stared at it as though it was a trap. "You see the bigger picture."

"I wouldn't have left you," Dessa said through gritted teeth.

Harlow sighed, the pain of her own ignored bid hit her harder now that she had just done the same to Fox. She wrapped her arms around herself. "We're not getting anywhere. Let's walk," Harlow said at last. She started off before anyone could argue. The sound of her boots on the cobblestone sidewalk sounded like nails sealing her in a coffin.

Each step ached.

Behind her, the others followed behind closely, though Harlow noticed as she glanced back that each kept distance from each other. Even Len and Dessa seemed uncomfortable with each other now.

"We have to do whatever we can to prevent this from happening again here," Harlow said, loud enough for them to all hear. "Whatever mistakes we made then, we need to remedy them now. I can't have another planet's destruction on my heart." She stopped just short of a large overpass, the darkness within in stark contrast to where they stood, illuminated by moonlight.

"You won't," Fox's voice was bold behind her. "You didn't. This is all on *her*. Not you. *You* will be the key to save this world."

Dessa stood beside him. She crossed her arms over her chest and glanced up at him dismissively. "We will be, actually. She said 'we'."

Fox cocked a brow at her. "I heard."

Dessa smiled, brightly in the dark. "Of course."

Len stepped between them, towering over Dessa. "We need more information. There's just not enough–"

A growl from deep within the dark cut her off.

Under the overpass, the faint purple shimmer of a Mechoida glittered in the black.

*No. Not now.*

Harlow reached up, and called down the sword from starlight. It rained over her like embers, spinning itself around her as it quickly took shape.

Feeling the sudden weight in her hand, Harlow's grasp tightened around the heavy hilt.

She sprung forward into the dark.

"Harlow!" The voices of her friends echoed behind her.

Harlow swung her sword. The pale glow of the blade sliced a path of blazing light through the dark until it found the target: a massive monster with snarled snout and giant claws.

The Mechoida dodged her attack with ease. It growled, wide, empty mouth barred.

"I can't reach it!"

Harlow heard Dessa's voice in the dark.

"Go back!"

Len.

Harlow turned over one shoulder, her sword held high. They weren't here with her. They'd go back for starlight.

*Good.*

She could do this on her own. She wanted to do this on her own.

Harlow grabbed the hilt of her sword with both hands, raising it high to strike again, when she suddenly jolted forward, air knocked out of her lungs by the sudden force.

She gasped, but her breath wouldn't come.

Her sword clattered to the floor. Light, now disconnected from her, flickered for a moment, then went out as the sword disappeared in the dark.

She rose on unsteady feet, her arm out to call back the sword.

But it was too late. It was gone, and she was without starlight.

In the pitch black, pain suddenly bloomed through her as she coughed, trying to catch her breath.

A searing, burning rip tore through Harlow's back in the same space where her old wound had just healed.

She stumbled, then crumbled to her knees. The burning pain ran from her spine up to her scalp and down to her legs. It radiated out into every limb as the reality of what had happened came crashing into her.

There were two.

Two.

While she had been focused on the first, she had failed to see the other.

They never traveled in twos.

Never.

Harlow staggered forward on her hands and knees, pushing herself up off the gritty ground as best she could despite the cut in her back.

She needed to stand.

She needed starlight.

"Hatysa!" Fox's voice was clear behind her, cutting through the panic.

"Stay back!" She turned over her shoulder, but a hard shove in her back knocked down roughly before she could see him. A cry broke from her throat as she felt her body pressed roughly to the hard ground.

Harlow struggled beneath the weight of the monster's foot. She twisted her body, clawed at the ground, but she couldn't escape.

It was all over so quickly. One misstep. One moment of misjudgment. That was all it took.

And now she was done for.

A roar erupted through the tunnel, vibrating the stone walls and breaking Harlow's thoughts. She moved her head toward the sound, just as the monster's foot lifted.

She scrambled up to a squat but the cut on her back sent a shockwave of pain through her body and she fell forward. She took in a deep breath at last, squinting to see into the shadows at what had made the sound, what had distracted the monster from dealing a final blow.

In the dim glow of the monster's light, Harlow made out the shape of Fox, standing tall and brave.

Between the two Mechoida.

They towered over him, their massive bodies of swirling silver broader, stronger, faster. His hair was frayed, curls blew lightly around his head like a halo in the dark. She could make out the anger etched into his face as he stared up at them fiercely.

A chill washed over Harlow as fear set in where pain had been. She reached out to him and tried to scream, to tell him to run, but no words left her. She doubled over, a hoarse cough was all she managed.

"Leave her alone," Fox growled through gritted teeth. Harlow watched as he held his hands up, fists ready.

Was he planning to fight them bare-handed?

Harlow reached for him, a desperate attempt to try to stop him from coming any closer. She winced as her ribs burned with the effort.

She'd heal soon. But not soon enough.

He was one moment away from death.

And there was nothing she could do about it.

Harlow watched in horror as one of the monsters grabbed Fox by his arm, ripping open his shirt with its sharp claws as it lifted him up in a firm hold.

The other turned to the entrance of the tunnel at the sound of her friends shouting, though she couldn't make out their words in the chaos.

There must not be any starlight... or, perhaps, they were battling more outside. Either way, there was no one coming to save them. She'd have to fight her way through the pain, through the fear, through all of it to get to him. And once she got there, she'd have to find a way without starlight... but she couldn't think of that now. All she could think was that he couldn't die.

She couldn't let that happen.

Not when she still could stand.

The Mechoida held him up, its head tilted to get a better look at him in the dark. A hand went up.

Fox screamed.

But it wasn't pain, or fear. To Harlow's ears, it sounded like... anger.

A flash of bright silver and cool blue pierced the darkness and the cry grew louder.

Her eyes narrowed, trying to adjust to the flash of light then sudden, overwhelming darkness. She blinked, scrambling forward to try to get to Fox as spots of light echoed in her vision.

As they began to clear, Harlow's heart nearly stopped.

Three.

There were three now.

Harlow's eyes searched the ground for Fox's body, but it was too dark, too violent to make out anything clearly.

Except that there were three. And they were fighting each other.

Harlow gasped. She forced her legs to move, to carry her back away from the battle before her.

One grabbed hold of another, it bit deeply into its shoulder while the other tried tearing through the two with its claws.

Screeching, wailing sounds echoed through the short tunnel as they fought fiercely until, at last, one took hold of another, back feet slicing through its opponents middle as moonlight spilled out and, at last, the first Mechoida vanished like mist in sunlight.

The other turned its attention to the last one, its posture ready to pounce.

The other Mechoida cowered, shrunken down and backing away with slow, cautious steps.

Another growl tore through the night air, and the other monster turned down the tunnel and fled with the first following in close pursuit.

Harlow hurried forward to where they had been standing. There was no sign of the monster that had become moonlight. No sign of Fox.

The blood in Harlow's veins ran cold. Pinching, throbbing all throughout her muscles and skin vibrated through her as her human body worked to stitch itself together again. A numbing, throbbing ache battling with the dread that fixed itself to her bones.

The space was empty.

She turned to the other end of the tunnel as a burst of moonlight flashed, then vanished just as quickly.

Harlow hurried to the exit, her heart still pounding to the rhythm of her thoughts.

Not Fox.

Not Fox.

Not Fox.

Harlow stopped at the line where the shadow of the overpass met the light of the moon.

Fox stood, silhouetted by moonlight, bloodied by the battle. His eyes were still shining a glittering amber as they settled on her. He wiped his broken lip with the back of his hand.

And smiled.

# CHAPTER 22

# THE LIGHT WITHIN

"You're one of them?" Harlow's cry burst from her.

The stars were covered overhead, a thin haze of clouds reflecting back the light of the city. She pulled her knife from her boot instead.

A mix of pain and power surged through her body as she propelled herself out of the shadows, blade in her hand.

She stopped when she was inches from him, knife raised up toward his heart. Every muscle burned. Every fiber twitched to release the tension in her hand but she still stopped just as the tip of the blade pressed into his torn shirt.

Fox did not shrink before her. He squared his shoulders and looked down at her. A crease formed between his brows, though his eyes softened as she held up her other fist, bringing it up to protect her head. "Will you fight me without your starlight?" he asked, his voice quiet, laced with hurt and... betrayal.

He had no right.

"If I have to." Harlow's hand began to shake, the knife fell from his chest. She watched it drop to the ground, heard the dull clank of the metal bounce lifelessly on the stone. She could hardly stand...

"You don't," he said. He reached for her free hand slowly, as if afraid she'd break if he moved too fast.

Harlow's fists shot up to her cheeks. She took a step back to ground herself into the earth. "Don't touch me," she snarled.

"I'm not your enemy." Fox's hands lowered. "I won't hurt you."

Harlow's breath was sharp in her lungs, her heart was rapid beneath her ribs. She narrowed her eyes at him, studying his expression, searching for anything. Any meaning or reason. Any explanation for what had just happened.

Fox stared back at her, unafraid despite her ferocity. He let out a long exhale through parted lips. He tilted his chin to get a better look at her as she staggered back, on legs she could hardly feel. "You're safe now. I will keep you safe," his voice was a whisper, carried by the most gentle breeze.

The thin veil of clouds parted, drenching them in moonlight.

At last, Harlow lowered her hands, though the muscles in her arms were still tense, her legs still ready to run. "You're one of them." She hated how her voice came out a whimper, a betrayed whine.

"Yes," Fox said. "But I'm not like them. Some of us are different."

Behind her, Len and Dessa called out her name.

"Why–"

"You were once, too," Fox said, fingers grazing Harlow's arms until his hands held hers softly. He looked down at their interlaced fingers with a pained furrow in his brow. "I hoped that was what the moonlight would show you. But I guess your current conditioning is too strong."

"No." Harlow watched his thumb gently stroke her palm. She was numb. His touch was like air. A puff of smoke. She followed his touch, unsure if it was real at all.

"You still have the moonlight within you," he whispered. "You can feel it, can't you? The way you know things. You've seen the truth." He squeezed her hand. "You've known understanding beyond what others are capable of."

Harlow's body quivered, working hard to heal herself, working hard to stand upright, to not call starlight, to not run. "I wouldn't have…" she managed to say weakly, but the rest of her words fell away from her, disintegrating like crumbling stone.

Fox smiled. "You did. Because it's not what it seems, not what you've been taught. Why is the power only saved for some when it should be for all? That's why we–"

The sound of pounding feet broke them apart.

Harlow stumbled back, her hands burning where Fox had held them.

Fox looked past her, his head rising to his full height, strong and confident in the night.

Harlow watched his face begin to heal, faster than she ever had before. He stood taller, defiant, as Len and Dessa rushed to Harlow's side, their weapons glowing brightly in their grasps.

Len held her shield over Harlow. Her eyes scanned Fox up and down quickly, then moved about the shadows surrounding them. "They're gone?" she asked.

Dessa's bow was drawn, an arrow pointed back down the tunnel. "All of them?"

Fox nodded. "They're gone," he said, so quiet Harlow barely heard him over the sound of her pounding heart.

Anger bubbled up in Harlow's chest, threatening to spill out into a furious scream.

Len's eyes narrowed on Fox as the last of his broken skin mended in the silver light.

Dessa's stare followed. Her arrow lowered, but the bow remained steady in her hands. "You're hurt?"

It sounded like an accusation.

Fox put his hands in his pockets. He waited.

Harlow grabbed the knife from the ground. She looked up at the stars above. At the moon, nearly full. "There were two of them," she said at last. Her grip tightened on the knife's handle, squeezing until her knuckles hurt. "I was pinned. I didn't see that there were two."

Dessa's hold her bow relaxed. Her head tilted to catch Harlow's cold stare.

"Fox saved me."

"You used starlight? How?" Len asked.

Fox said nothing. He didn't shrink down, or look away.

"He used moonlight." The words spit out like poison from Harlow's mouth.

Dessa's aim was swift. In one quick motion, the bow drew up, her arm extended to pull back the arrow with all her force. She grimaced, her cheek pressed up to the glittering string. "Say the word, Harlow," she said, eyes fierce.

Len studied her stance, the shield expanded around Harlow, a spear manifested in her other hand. "Mechoida."

Where anger had been, a new wave of panic ignited in Harlow's body. She flipped her knife to face away from Fox, her other hand lowering Dessa's arrow. "No, it's not like that," she said, her tone shriller than she wished.

"I knew there was something wrong with you," Dessa's arrow was back to its position as soon as Harlow's hand lowered. "You've been lying to us from the start."

Fox waited. His eyes traveled from the tip of the arrow to Dessa's cold, calculated eyes. "I haven't lied," he said at last. "The Queen killed Hatysa. None of us were there to save her. You saw it. The moonlight isn't what you've been taught. The battle on our home wasn't between good and evil. It was light and dark. The moon is the true light."

"You're the enemy. You started this war. We're here to end it." Dessa's voice was a low growl in the darkness. "Tell me why I shouldn't finish this now, Harlow."

Harlow winced. A deep ache began to throb all over her body as her adrenaline began to weaken. "He saved me," Harlow spoke through the searing pain in her back. She gritted her teeth.

Len put a worried hand on Harlow's shoulder. Gentle, careful. Her spear was gone, but her shield still held strong.

Harlow pushed herself to stand taller. "The moonlight... it can do what we can't. Shine light on what was obscured. Help us when we can't reach the stars."

Dessa's arrow quivered, lowering slightly. She side eyed Harlow, keeping Fox well within her sight. "You're being heretical. You know the moon corrupts everything."

"Including me?" Harlow asked. Her hand held Dessa's forearm steady, though the simple movement caused her stomach to drop. Acid bubbled up into her throat. "I used moonlight to find answers. Maybe there are more?"

"We had the monks with us," Len said before Dessa could argue. "It wasn't just you. Or us."

Fox removed his hands from his pockets. He held

them up in surrender. "Why should the monks be the custodians of knowledge? Why can't it be for all?"

"They hurt our friends," Dessa snapped back. "They tried to kill Harlow just now. How is that 'knowledge'? They're beasts. Uncontrollable and dangerous."

"There are fractions just like any other group," Fox said. "Not all of us want revenge. I seek enlightenment. With the Queen finally gone, we can have a new age of understanding, of advancement. We will finally have a just leader. With Harlow on the throne–"

Harlow stumbled, her knees went weak and her balance tilted.

She wasn't healing fast enough. Her heart skipped. The pain was too great, her thoughts too scattered...

The last thing she heard was the sound of her friends' cries as Harlow fell into nothingness.

# A STRONGER MAGIC

The muffled sounds of familiar voices and the clinking of glasses pulled Harlow's awareness back from the empty. She could make out the sound of mugs and metal spoons stirring. She followed the low whispers of her friends, the biting remarks of Carina, trying to sort them into something that made sense. Their words were obscured by the haze that Harlow was still fighting her way out of, but the discussion sounded worried, and a little contentious, based on the tones and speech patterns.

Harlow's face contorted with effort as she forced her eyes open, willing her body to prop up onto her elbows.

She blinked into the dim light.

Morning sun filtered through the curtains of her room. She was in bed. Her room was tidied, and she was alone.

The sounds were clearer now, coming in through the open door.

They must be in the living space... Len must have cleaned her room.

Her body still ached, but it was dull and mild, as though she had simply slept in an odd position and not battled two monsters to the point of near death.

She rose higher, stretching her arms up overhead to work out the stiffness that had settled into her joints. A few pops echoed in her ears as her back straightened out at last and she took in a deep, satisfying breath.

"She's awake." It was Carina's voice, louder and clearer above the others.

Harlow swung her legs over the side of the bed, a small smile on her lips with the ease at which she was able to move with her usual swiftness. She made her way to the living room with light steps to find Len and

Dessa sitting on the couch, mugs of herbal tea and honey, from the smell of it, in their hands.

Each sat up a little taller as she entered the room. Both looked her over with worry deeply etched into their faces.

Carina, and the other two cats, were perched on the kitchen counter that overlooked the small space, their tails flicking dully on the surface.

"How long was I out?" Harlow asked, expecting the worst.

"A few hours," Len said. She set her mug down on the coffee table, rising quickly to her feet. "Tea?"

Harlow nodded as she scratched at her bedhead. "Just a few hours?"

Len was busy fiddling with the electric kettle in the kitchen. Her gaze averted as she scooped a spoonful of clover honey from a little plastic tub. "Not long." She inspected the boxes of tea, looking through the ingredients as her finger traced along the words. "Feel rested?"

Harlow caught Carina's narrowed stare. She looked away, ashamed, though, she wasn't really sure why. She turned to Dessa, who was blowing the steam up into her face, shielding her in a warm fog. "I do," Harlow said slowly, trying to read the room to no avail. Her fingers itched. "Why do I get the feeling that I'm in trouble..?"

Len's eyes shot up. "What makes you say that?"

Harlow flinched. "Nothing. Just... It's tense in here."

"Well, we used moonlight to heal you," Dessa said bluntly. She lowered her mug, but kept it close to her chest as if she was ready to launch it at Harlow if need be. "Seems to have worked."

Harlow's arms contracted around herself. She tried to remember what had happened the night before. So much. So much had gone wrong...

The gentle clink of the spoon against the ceramic sides brought Harlow's attention back to the present.

Len smiled kindly and slid the mug between the cats.

They shuffled a little, the movement allowing their bodies to do something other than sit and judge.

Ara scampered off to the sliding glass window by the couch. She pressed her head to the glass.

"You were badly injured," Carina explained as Harlow took her cup.

The space between them filled with warmth as the silver steam filtered into the air. The rich smell of wet earth, sweet honey, and crisp apple already working to heal the part of her that moonlight could not touch. The raw part of her emotions, chaotic, conflicted, and uncontrollable, began to feel less jagged as she breathed in deeply.

Carina's ear flicked. She straightened her posture on the counter. "You'll never guess where we got the idea to use the moon to heal you faster came from."

Harlow sank slowly to the floor. She set the mug down and then fell onto her back with a flat thud. "So you guys didn't kill him after I passed out?" She was only half joking.

Dessa sighed. "No, unfortunately. He helped us get you here." A long pause followed. She still didn't trust him, that much was clear.

But Harlow wasn't sure she did either.

"What are we going to do?" Harlow grumbled as she threw one arm over her eyes.

"Well, for one thing, we're *not* going to use moonlight anymore," Carina said.

"Agreed," Vela and Ara said, their voices harmonized from across the room.

"I heard that the other one thinks it's useful," Carina went on.

Harlow flinched at her refusal to speak his name. She tightened her hold on her head, then took in another long breath in through her nose, trying to recapture the feeling of calm the tea had brought her just a moment before.

"But we cannot continue to use it lightly," the cat

continued. "We studied lifetimes to learn how to control it."

"Only when necessary," Vela added.

"Or else it will control us," Ara said. "The moon corrupts. Always."

"Always?" Harlow heard herself ask.

"Always."

Harlow pushed herself back up, though the weight was heavy on her shoulders. She tucked her knees up to her chest and grabbed her mug with fingers that felt more like stiff claws. "The Queen... She wants us to call them all in a few days. Get the big battle over with. Why? What's the rush?"

Dessa's lips drew into a hard line. She took a sip of her tea to hide what looked like deep frustration as Len took the seat beside her with a small groan, as though it hurt to be still. "Rainey hasn't heard anything on the bug," she said.

"It would be nice if she was the think out loud type instead of the stoic, mysterious, brooding with a glass of wine type," Len said with a sigh. "We may still get lucky yet."

Harlow hummed, a noncommittal response.

"If she knows that others are waking up," Dessa said, "perhaps she's worried you'll meet Fox, sooner or later. He has *not* been subtle about wanting you as Queen."

"True," Len said. "That could put her in a time crunch."

Carina's tail thumped on the carpet. She cast a glance out the window, considering the possibilities.

Harlow was still stuck on the moonlight point. Her mind turned the thoughts, working them into something she could speak aloud. She wasn't sure how she felt about any of it, except stressed at the arbitrary deadline and mildly annoyed that she was still in the dark on all of it.

At last, she spoke, though she found the words to clothe her ideas as she said them. "I would be gone if it weren't for Fox. The moonlight has its uses. What if–"

"I've seen what happens when the untrained or ill-prepared use moonlight," Carina cut her off. "I remember then how it turned them, clouded their judgment and their morality. They sought power. Nothing more."

"But, what about the woman we saw before? She had just turned, it seemed. She looked confused..." Harlow tried to recall exactly what her expression had been, tried to replay the moments before and after as vividly as she could. Though it was only days before, it seemed like years away now.

Carina and the other cats exchanged a long look. "She looked disoriented?"

Len nodded. "It was strange. I've never seen anything like it."

Relief steadied Harlow's breath. She was grateful that Len had jumped in to corroborate her story when it was so vague now that she wasn't sure she could trust her own memories.

"Then," Dessa said quietly. "She wasn't newly turned. She had been using the moonlight for too long..."

"That's more likely," Carina said.

Vela moved from the window to Carina's side. She pressed a head to Carina's, then slinked around her, tail wrapped over the other cat's body. "Even we succumb to the corruption, in the end. Slowly, but inevitably, we too will slip away. It is the sacrifice of using the moonlight."

Harlow searched the palms of her hands as they rested in her lap. She studied the indents of each line, following them up to every finger, to the swollen knuckles from years of training, to the blunted nails, the calluses that peaked along her grip. Her body was already changed forever. What was the harm in asking just a little more for just a little longer?

As if reading her thoughts, Carina moved closer and

pressed a small paw to Harlow's thigh. "I'm grateful he saved your life," she said softly. "But I don't think it's wise to trust him."

Dessa pulled her legs up onto the couch. She was watching Harlow with an intense stare.

"Then what?" Harlow's tone was sharp, her jaw clenched. "We just go along with what the Queen wants until I end up no longer useful to her and she takes me out in this lifetime, too?"

Len held up a hand. "Of course not."

"We have a stronger magic, we should use it," Harlow said. Her fingers curled into fists.

"Then leave that to us," Carina said. "When the time comes."

A rumble in Harlow's throat stopped at her gritted teeth. She wanted to scream. Instead, she loosened her grip, and closed her eyes, trying to breathe through the flaring anger that welled up within her chest.

"We will need to confront her," Dessa said at last. "We'll do it together."

"Together. Because the real magic is the friends we made along the way," Len said, deadpan.

The room turned to her slowly, each with a parted mouth in disbelief.

"You did not just say that." Dessa shoved Len playfully with her shoulder.

"Whoa! The tea!" Len cried, balancing her tea aloft as her body jostled.

Despite herself, Harlow's laugh bubbled up and out her nose. She snorted, loudly, with the strange feeling that, although nothing had been resolved, things might just be on their way to becoming better.

# CHAPTER 24

# THE DEATH OF US

The problem with misinformation was that it was easier to spread than facts. The facts were often boring, complicated, and nuanced. Statistics needed to be checked and rechecked. Studies needed to be peer reviewed and scrutinized for a myriad of failings.

Meanwhile, sensational headlines didn't require much thought, especially if the biases of the consumer were being confirmed or validated. It didn't matter if it hurt or activated a fear response, that was still more comfortable to the brain than accepting it had been wrong, or that the betrayal was closer to home than they anticipated. No one liked to be made a fool. No one liked to feel stupid. And so, people clung to their safe beliefs, the twist of irony that doing so closed them off to the truth.

And once the misinformation was out there, it was hard to contradict. Even if someone logically understood that the news they received was inaccurate or false, the initial emotional response still trapped them in their distortion.

Harlow thought that building an entire class around misinformation, the media, and the public was stupid. And no amount of reasoning would change her mind.

It could have been an email summed up with: Do your due diligence. But even if you do, most of the time, people won't listen unless they already agreed with you.

The end.

No further discussion required.

Yet here they were, sitting under fluorescent lights, talking ad nauseam about the ethics of journalism like it was a survey course.

Harlow shifted in her seat, one leg bouncing rapidly like a rabbit warning its colony of a threat. She chewed her gum loudly. Anything to keep her actually sitting, vaguely pretending to listen to the small group talk about what their duty was to the general public when covering stories in science and technology.

Len and Dessa had been relegated to the other group of six and were having a lively debate about how to make scientific journalism more appealing to the average consumer. Big words were tossed around, along with what sounded like well researched examples.

Meanwhile, Harlow was put in the other group, left to feel like she was back in high school watching the smart kids from afar while the teacher put her with the rest of the students who were probably getting calls home about their lack of preparation.

In her defense, then and now, she was usually too busy hunting monsters to bother preparing presentations or doing homework.

She crossed her arms, dreaming about her next can of pink fizzy energy.

"Harlow?" Another student called, a bit too loud.

Harlow blinked, she leaned forward, arms resting on the ancient desk. "Yep?"

"Thoughts on the latest–"

"It's a propaganda piece thinly veiled as journalism," she said with a dismissive hand wave. "Right?"

The group all nodded, thoughtfully considering her fake opinion.

Harlow had found out long ago that if she said a few

buzz words with a certain level of authority, and then asked for people to agree with her, they did.

It got her out of a lot of trouble in her undergraduate school, even compelled a few teaching assistants to bump her mediocre grade up to something that looked more impressive on transcripts.

Still, it wasn't quite good enough to get her out of class. The best she could do was keep her head down and answer when people asked her opinion and hope she sounded like she was listening.

So far so good.

But her mind kept wandering to how their upcoming night was going to go. Looping thoughts of why her friends insisted on going to classes and acting like things were fine and normal when they were about to go head to head with a Queen of stars crept back in, no matter how hard she tried to focus. Images of Fox flashed alongside the looming dread, bringing with them stomach-turning nerves.

Her face drained of color, turning her cheeks to sheets of ice as the memory of Fox, bloodied yet calm, standing tall in the moonlight like an ancient god, filled her mind. Her shoulders slumped as the sinking feeling in her stomach turned to stone.

She was going to be sick...

The bell rang, loud and piercing through the side conversations.

The chair legs scraped across the linoleum as she rose quickly, her vision narrowing. "I gotta run," she announced to the little group. Her lips prickled as she took in a deep breath, steading herself on the desk.

From across the room, the professor rose from his seat. "Harlow?"

Dessa and Len were at her sides in an instant, holding her elbows up.

"I'm fine." Harlow breathed through the wave of panic. "Let's go."

Len looked up at the professor, raising a hand in apology as Dessa escorted Harlow out of the room.

The door clicked closed behind them. In the bright light of the hallway, Harlow felt like she could finally breathe, as if every breath before had been too shallow to matter. She filled her lungs, stretched her back until her ribs expanded, and she flashed a half-smile at Dessa.

"Do you think I can get out of small talk at the end of class every time if I pretend I'm about to faint?" Her tone was jovial, but she knew her cheeks were still colorless.

"Harlow!" Dessa whacked the back of her arm with her open hand. "What the hell?"

Harlow sighed out. She stood taller as Len slipped from the classroom. She cocked her head, trying to play the whole thing off. "If I hit up a vending machine will you guys attack me?"

Len's eyes narrowed. "No energy drink for you," she said.

"Besides," Dessa said, raising her phone with a little wiggle of her hand, "Gigi said she'll meet us in the cafe. She has the outfits ready."

"That was quick." Len's brows rose.

Dessa turned quickly as the door opened with a strained creak of the hinges. She was already halfway down the hall, not waiting for her friends to catch up.

Harlow smiled, trotting alongside Len with a newfound sense of strength in her body. Somehow, Gigi being quick to create something out of nothing made it seem like things were back to normal. For a moment. "She's efficient, but never on time," she told Len. She glanced over Dessa's shoulder as she typed back a message. "So if she said she'll be there in a half hour, I'd make it at least forty-five."

"You're chipper again," Dessa said.

Harlow shrugged. "I don't know what came over me back there," she lied as they exited the building, blinking into the afternoon sun.

"A side effect of the magic?" Len guessed.

Harlow shielded her eyes with an outstretched arm. She knew what it was, but she didn't want to talk about it now. She didn't want to talk about it ever. "No," she said, thankful for the bright sunlight washing out her pained expression. "I'm just still recovering, I think."

"Well, what can we do to help?" Dessa said as she dodged a group on the sidewalk. "We need to all be in fighting shape soon. Either to battle the Mechoida or... other adversaries."

Harlow shook her head. "I'll be fine. I always am." Her smile widened. "It's this class that'll be the death of me."

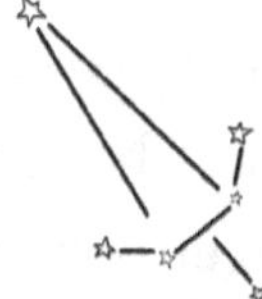

GIGI WAS LATE.

The group sat along the long table in the upstairs loft of Espresso Yourself with their lattes and pastries in a comfortable silence. It was surprisingly empty, though Harlow wasn't sure if that was usual for this time of day. She was always there from dawn to the mid morning, when everyone filed in a sleepy daze before their morning classes.

Dessa checked her phone, a crease in her forehead betraying her worry.

A loud stomping barreled up the stairs as Gigi hurried up, a big canvas bag slung across her chest and a splashing mug of coffee in her hands. Her hair was slicked back, tucked behind her ears with little glittering clips. She wore big false lashes, bright eyeshadow that sparkled in the overhead lights. Despite the hot pink bandage over her cheek, she looked immaculate as usual.

Rainey followed close behind, her own mug held precariously, though untainted in her hands.

"Sorry!" Gigi said as she sat down on the opposite bench with a loud huff. Her mug clanked on the table, spilling droplets of hot liquid over the sides.

Rainey took her place beside Gigi, though she set her mug down so gingerly it made no sound at all. Pleased that she had made it without spilling, she looked up at Harlow. "It really might be a curse," she said in a low tone. "That or the time-blindness is contagious."

"It's a curse!" Gigi declared with a huff. She slipped the canvas bag from over her head, already pulling the contents from the bag with quick movements. "Len, we have a nice lavender..." She pushed a bundle of light purple fabric towards her, then went back to fishing out the second, a jewel green color. "And, Dessa, I don't know. I got green vibes."

Dessa looked down at her forest green cardigan, layered over a cream shirt.

"You have an eye for this," Len said with a smile as she inspected her own outfit.

Gigi flushed at the compliment. "Well, you know. They all are made with the same cut proof material. I don't think I've mastered the breathability yet, but they do have pockets." She reached across the table to pull at the lavender fabric. "And Len, I modeled yours after the dresses you wear. It has a lot of... layers. But if that gets in the way, let me know. I can cut it down."

Len's eyes widened. "It's perfect."

"Oh good!" Gigi clapped. She pointed to Dessa's outfit. "I made yours a little more simple. You seem like you have the accessories down."

"Speaking of..." Dessa reached into her purse and pulled out two gold necklaces, each with a sparkling metal net on the end, stuffed to bursting. "Wear these whenever possible. They're spell bags. It should make it harder for the Mechoida to find you."

Gigi donned the first and handed the second to Rainey. "I doubt they're looking for us, but I guess better safe than not."

"They're pretty," Rainey said as she lowered her

head to her cup. She slurped the top of her drink a bit ungracefully until it was low enough to pick up without spilling. When she rose, her face was surprisingly serious. "I haven't heard anything," she said, breaking the focus from the outfits.

"At least it wasn't found," Harlow said quietly.

Rainey held her cup close to her. "I wish I could help more."

"You've helped plenty," Harlow said.

Len and Dessa both nodded vigorously in agreement.

Dessa's cheeks were full of muffin. From the side of her mouth, she said, "For real. Don't even worry about it. We have a plan."

"Kind of," Len added.

Gigi leaned forward. "Can we help?"

"Can you fight with starlight?" Harlow asked, half joking.

"It'd be cooler if we could," Gigi said with a laugh.

"What's the kind of plan?" Rainey asked.

"Step one, confront the Queen about missing memories," Harlow said.

Rainey and Gigi waited.

Harlow shrugged. "Step two... TBD."

Rainey hummed disapprovingly.

"It's a work in progress," Harlow said.

"How about step two is to put on your awesome new superhero clothes," Gigi said. "You can figure out step three, then, as you go."

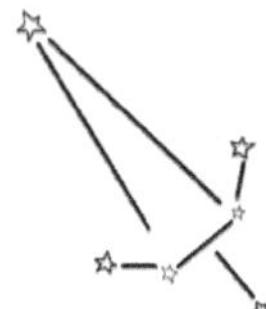

"WE REALLY DO HAVE THIS HALF-BAKED," Len said as they left the cafe.

"The plan of attack or the project in Moore's class?" Harlow asked, feigning ignorance.

"Both," Len said honestly.

"But mostly the plan for tomorrow night," Dessa said.

"Yeah. I'll figure it out." Harlow scratched the back of her neck, the feeling of cold dread creeping back up along her spine.

"You always do," Dessa said.

# THE WAY THINGS COULD HAVE BEEN

Harlow was the first to reach the roof.

The painful sound of the metal door scraping along gravel cut into the night air as she swung the door open. The crunch of the little stones beneath her feet brought her back to memories long ago, back when she was small and alone. Facing her aunt, the ruthless and legendary Queen, had never been easy. Especially on the roof. Here, overlooking the city that shined brighter than the stars above, was a dangerous place to be.

This had been the place where Harlow had spent long hours training into the night. The place she had battled dummies and summoned stars until her limbs ached. Until her knees and elbows were scraped, bloody, and bruised. This was the place her aunt took her when she had wanted to put Harlow back in her place.

But she wasn't a child anymore.

And she wasn't alone. She wasn't afraid.

Her friends at her back brought with them a renewed sense of courage. She heard their steps behind her, slow and steady. Ready for whatever might come.

Harlow pulled starlight down, weaving it into her sword.

The shimmering sound like quiet bells behind her echoed in her ears as Len crafted her shield and spear. The familiar sound of Dessa's bow drawing taunt followed.

Her aunt didn't seem to notice.

Or care.

She stood tall in the middle of the black and gray spiraling rock garden, her back to them. "My general has arrived," she said slowly. She cast a long glance over her shoulder, eyes half closed as if she couldn't be bothered to be scared. "And she brought backup."

Harlow held her sword out, pointing the glimmering tip at her aunt's back, though they all still stood several yards away. "We know what you did," she said as confidently as she could.

The Queen let out a bored huff. She turned back to overlook the city lights, ignoring the sword pointed toward her, the threat of violence from trusted allies. "I saved everyone," she said. "I brought us all here for a chance at life again."

"You killed me first," Harlow's voice quivered, though the grip on the hilt of her sword was strong.

Her aunt didn't even flinch. The cool breeze picked up, carrying her skirt around her ankles like waves in the ocean. "And how did you manage to unlock such painful memories? Memories I have worked hard to seal."

At Harlow's side, Dessa's eyes narrowed. Her gentle arm pulled the bow string closer to her body. It dragged along her cheek. "So you *have* been keeping information from us," she said through clenched teeth.

Len moved closer to Harlow, her broad shield shining in the moonlight. She was silent, but Harlow could feel her pain radiating from her. The admission that the Queen had known about their memories, that she had been responsible for their absence, had cut Len to her core.

Len was loyal. Up to the end, she was sure that Len believed this was all some kind of strange misunderstanding. As her shield drew up, Harlow knew that all goodwill was gone.

Harlow took a step toward her aunt with Len close at her side. "Moonlight," Harlow answered.

"Stolen magic *is* more powerful," her aunt said with a slight shrug. She finally turned to look them in the eyes. A small smile fell on her lips.

"We don't need it," Len said. "We can do this ourselves."

"Do what, exactly?" The Queen's eyes fixed on Len. "Now that you know what I've done... are you here to kill me?" Her focus shifted to Dessa, her gaze narrowing on the tip of the arrowhead. "Get your revenge for saving our kind?" At last, she settled on Harlow. "I did what any leader would do. I cut away the chaos before it could destroy everything."

Harlow's heart ached dully beneath her ribs. *Cut away.* As though her loss of life was a simple equation. But then, Fox was telling the truth where the Queen had lied.

She was the chaos.

She was the spark that set off the destruction of their world.

Or, she was the sword. The heavy fall of the blade before the silence.

"We're here for answers," Dessa said.

The Queen kept her sights on Harlow. Her mouth twitched into a grimace. Disgust. Anger. "You have been corrupted by the light of the moon," she said, clear and strong. "There is only one way to eradicate the disease. I must cut it out before it tears us all apart."

"The moon isn't corruptive, you are!" Harlow thrust her sword forward, arm long and strong against the cold of the night. "You've been keeping its secrets from us because you're afraid of it!"

"I am!" The Queen's voice boomed through the darkness, as though she was everywhere, and nowhere all at once. "And if you aren't, then you've learned nothing from me and nothing from your past." She lifted her hand up to the sky. "You are doomed to repeat the same mistakes. But I will not."

Starlight descended from the navy sky in glimmering rain, flooding the roof with bright, rainbow light. The Queen's hands twisted, fingers expertly shaping the light into two long swords, broad and sharp, impossibly large for her to hold without magic.

They shimmered vividly, illuminating her face from below in a sinister glow.

Harlow steeled herself. She gripped her own sword tighter. She had her starlight, too.

She could do this...

The first blow came so quick and brutal that Harlow had hardly registered that her aunt had even moved.

Instinct drew her sword up to parry the hit. The clash of the swords hitting something much heavier rang out in her ears as sparks burst around her head.

Len stood in front of Harlow, heels digging into the ground as her shield held strong and high against the Queen's blades. She turned her head over her shoulder and smiled at Harlow, though her jaw was tight with exertion. She looked back at the Queen, a cry escaping her throat as she shoved her shield as hard as she could against the swords.

The Queen stumbled.

The high-pitched whistle of Dessa's arrow shot past Harlow, her hair moving as it passed her cheek.

Blood, dark in the moonlight bloomed where it hit the Queen in the shoulder.

Dessa drew another arrow.

It launched, but the Queen blocked this one with ease.

She always was a fast learner...

*No time to waste.*

Harlow side stepped Len. She swung her sword down, hard and fast.

Burning starlight sparked around them as the swords made contact.

Harlow swung again.

Again.

Again.

The Queen blocked. Moved back. She drew her swords up to block again.

But Harlow was quick.

The relentless onslaught caused the Queen to stumble. Gravel underfoot crunched, gave way to their heavy steps.

An arrow narrowly missed both of them.

One of the Queen's swords found an opening.

Harlow tried to react, to adjust her sword up and out, but it was too late.

The shield came down between Harlow and the blade.

Then... it faded away. Stars drifted like fireflies between them, then up, and gently floating back into the sky.

Harlow's eyes widened with horror.

The shield of starlight was gone.

Len stumbled forward, her hand on her shoulder

where the wound from Harlow's sword was too deep and dark.

Len fell to her knees.

Harlow heard a scream. A furious, angry, painful cry. From her, from Dessa, from what sounded like the Earth itself.

Len's body hit the ground.

Heart pounding like a war drum in her ears drowned out the sound of Dessa's screams. Blood and adrenaline, hot and burning, flooded every muscle. "I didn't–" Her words barely broke free of her throat.

She attacked too carelessly – tried to block when she should have trusted that Len was beside her.

She was blinded. By wrath, by fear, by trying to *win*.

Dessa rushed to Len's side as the Queen's second blade spiraled, brilliant gold burning brightly as it weaved into a long spear.

Harlow's sword went up with a loud roar that broke free from her throat, though her muscles strained to lift it as a freezing encased her heart.

It was too late.

This time, she was too slow.

The head of the spear pierced through Dessa's side, cutting through the material as though it was nothing but paper. The force of it shoved her to the ground beside Len.

Dessa looked up at Harlow. Fear etched into every line in her face. She tried to stand, but the spear held her pinned. Like an animal in a trap, unable to free itself, unable to live if it did escape. She let out a shaking breath, then lifted herself to her knees. She drew her arrow. At the sudden movement, she flinched in pain and the arrow let loose into the sky.

She stumbled backwards. One step. Then another. She held her side with one hand, the other clutched the length of the spear. Her eyes were wide, disbelief taking hold of her now as she stared at the wound, her breath ragged.

Harlow collapsed to her knees beside her. She held Dessa in one arm and with the other, she forced her sword out to the Queen, a feeble attempt to keep her away as she pulled Dessa closer. "Dessa, please," she begged through a shuddering breath. The corners of her vision faded rapidly as she desperately tried to gulp in air but found her lungs were empty.

Dessa's eyes drew up to Harlow. The hand on the spear moved to Harlow's face, though she couldn't quite reach. A tear spilled down Dessa's cheek. "I'm sorry..."

"Look at what you have done." The voice was booming now, drowning out Dessa's last ragged breaths, the horrible beating of Harlow's heart. It came from all around her, surrounding her like shadows. The world was going dark, and Harlow couldn't see. "You have brought one planet to its destruction. I will never allow that to happen again."

The Queen's sword landed just as Harlow thought her own heart might break beyond repair.

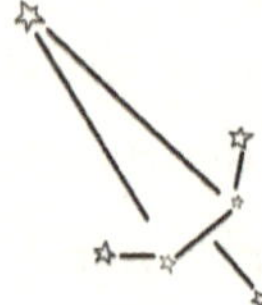

Harlow's mouth was wide. A silent scream.

The stubborn beating of her heart told her that she was still alive.

For now.

She searched the dark of her bedroom for Carina as gasping breaths finally began to clear the lingering dust of the nightmare.

The cat pressed her head into Harlow's outstretched hand. "A nightmare?" she asked quietly.

"A vision," Harlow gasped. Her fingers contracted around Carina's form, feeling the soft fur, the gentle vibration of her purrs. All reminders that she was here. Now. "I saw how tomorrow ends."

Carina's head lifted. Her large eyes scanned her face, reflecting back the streetlight from the window like two little moons. "Are you sure? You've never had a vision this strong before."

Harlow nodded. She closed her eyes and threw herself back onto the pillow, damp with sweat. "We're not strong enough," she whispered. "If we confront her, she'll discover what I've done. It ends the same way. But this time... Len. Dessa..."

"We'll find a different way." Carina curled up beside Harlow, nuzzling into her ribs.

Harlow's gaze found a point on her ceiling. A dot of pale yellow light in the darkness. She wondered, briefly, what it was on her desk that reflected the streetlight up when she remembered the locket Dessa had given her.

Len had tidied the room. She must have left it on the desk, a not-so-subtle reminder for her to wear it.

Rosemary for protection. Thyme for bravery. Fennel. For her fuckery.

"I know the way," she murmured at last.

Carina burrowed deeper. "Then I'll help you."

# CHAPTER 26

# STOLEN STARLIGHT

"For the record, I don't like this plan," Carina said quickly as Len and Dessa's mouths hung open.

The group sat in Harlow's living room, each with a mug of mediocre coffee in front of them. The morning sun cast gentle rays through the sheer curtains, obscuring the dirty sliding glass door. A galaxy of silver steam drifted up from their mugs, reaching up and out before disappearing into the cool air.

After explaining her nightmare, and the change in

plans, their coffee had all sat, untouched, growing cold slowly.

As if by lighting strike, Len jolted out of her shock, her expression resolute. "I don't either. Harlow, you can't do this."

Harlow flinched, fighting her instinctive response to argue. Instead, she took in a deep breath and waited.

Dessa looked from Len to Harlow. Her eyes narrowed slightly. "Fox gave you this idea. I knew we shouldn't have trusted him."

Harlow let her breath out. "It's not like that," she said, voice calm as she could muster. "I saw how this ends. How our plan ends. And it's... terrible."

Len shook her head. "Just be more mindful of where you're swinging your sword."

"And I'll look out for spears," Dessa added quickly.

"No," Harlow said. Her tone was suddenly stern. She had been their leader once. She could do it again. She sat up straighter, squared her shoulders. "My aunt is strong, but the moonlight is stronger. I won't risk you both when I could do this alone."

Carina jumped up beside her.

Harlow gave her a quick pat on the head. "Not completely alone."

Len's gaze shifted to Carina. "You said it yourself, you trained a lifetime to harness the power of the moon.

What's Harlow going to do with all that power and no direction for it?"

"Let's say you *do* take her on like this," Dessa cut in. "And let's say you *do* win. Best case, all goes according to plan. What then? Wait for the moonlight to eat you away like all the others?"

"Fox is fine–"

"Fox!" Dessa spat. She leaned in closer, eyes fierce. "For all we know he's been playing a long game. Trying to weaken you. Weaken *us*. We fought a whole war over this, Harlow. A war that destroyed our home."

"I know." A sour feeling rose up in Harlow's stomach. It pulsed through her, igniting her blood. Her fingers twitched. "But what if it wasn't really like that? Didn't you say that the Queen uses knowledge for her own control and power? Dessa." She reached out for her hand, but Dessa withdrew quickly. "Len." Her eyes moved to her friend. She searched her face for any clue into her thoughts but found nothing.

Len looked away.

"What if we wait?" Dessa said. "We don't have to do this right now. We can give you time to train."

"What's one month to a lifetime?" Len mumbled. Her eyes moved up slowly. "The Queen planned the assault before the next moon. If we don't take out as many as possible, you know she will."

Dessa's jaw clenched.

"You really won't reconsider?" Len prompted in one final attempt.

Harlow shook her head. "It's the only way to keep you both safe."

"So what? We sit on the sidelines and wait for you to come back to us?" Dessa's voice trembled.

The sound pierced Harlow's heart. She blinked away the sting in her eyes. "I'll use the moonlight. Just this once. With the Queen gone–"

"Gone?" Len spoke over her. "Harlow, you really don't..."

Carina stood taller, her long tail up. "With the moonlight, we might be able to steal the stars from her."

"Steal her starlight?" Len's eyes widened. "And what if that's just a hypothetical?"

Dessa let out a little puff of frustration. "Why can the guards not do this alone?" She glanced at Ara and Vela. "I mean, you have the training."

Carina's tail flicked. "First of all, she wouldn't let me even suggest it."

"That's true," Harlow said, sipping her cold coffee.

"And also," Carina went on, "the idea of stealing starlight is... theoretical. I fear that only another starlight wielder could accomplish it. First and foremost, we would need to gather it, then harness it."

"It should work," Ara said, validating Carina's theory. "I don't much care for the idea on its whole, but combining the stars and the moon ought to work."

Dessa and Len exchanged a long look.

"You really want us to wait on the sidelines while you attempt a theoretical hostile takeover? What if... what if you fail?" Dessa curled her knees to her chest.

Harlow smiled.

The sidelines should have felt natural to them at this point. Harlow had always done things alone, as much as she could. They were safer when she was alone. Safer back at home instead of picking fights in alleyways and deserted parks. Safer when they didn't need to worry about Harlow picking up her part of a group project, even.

This was no different. Just a normal weekday fighting monsters before clocking in at the observatory.

An observatory that had been blown to pieces by a war she didn't quite understand...

"I'll come back. I always do."

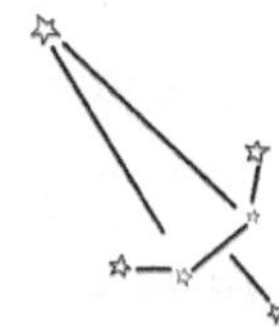

Harlow left them, their apartment, and the afternoon sunlight behind her. She hadn't told them where she was going, too worried about the fallout and too tired to deal with their scolding.

Carina had told her she would help Harlow harness the power of the moon. But she had only one chance to get this right. She had seen what happened when a minor error, a small lack of planning, cascaded into tragedy. She couldn't afford that here.

It wasn't just her life at stake.

And there was only one other like her who could show her the way.

Her stomach turned, her hands icy, every muscle screaming to run as she crested the hill along The Old Wall. Her heart slammed into her chest when she saw Fox there, waiting for her in a golden glow of the midday sun.

He smiled, eyes softening at her presence, then rolled the sleeves of his plain button-down shirt up to his elbows as if he was about to get to work. He looked back up at her and tilted his head, a gesture to call her closer.

Harlow forced her feet to move, to carry her the rest of the way until she was standing close enough to touch him. She looked out over the city, at the gleaming buildings and the small, white, puffy clouds that drifted above the rooftops. She looked everywhere but at him. As her hands gripped the top of the wall, she wasn't sure she could face him. Couldn't look into those dark eyes that seemed to truly know her. Not without bursting into tears of anger, frustration... and though she didn't want to admit it, hurt.

"I'm glad you agreed to meet me," Fox said. He leaned down beside her, exposed forearms resting on the wall beside her hands. Heat of his skin radiated out, warming her gently. "I missed you."

Harlow's eyes drifted from the landscape to his fingers, loosely interlaced, to his strong hands. She followed the trail of veins beneath his skin up to his arms... the same arms that had held her close a few nights before. The same arms that had been bloodied and beaten saving her. The same arms that transformed...

She shivered at the thought of her own body morphing, becoming something she had feared for so long. She sighed her anxiety out slowly through parted lips, trying to steady the tremble in her fingers, the swirling mess in her stomach.

Fox leaned down, his dark curls falling into his eyes as he tried to capture her gaze.

"I'm meeting the Queen tonight," Harlow said quickly, before she could second guess herself. She closed her eyes, feeling the sun on her skin, her hair tickling the back of her neck as a small breeze blew around them. She opened her eyes when he said nothing else, her gaze drawn back to the stone wall. "I'm going to confront her. And take her starlight."

The muscles in Fox's arms twitched, his fingers curled. "Is that possible?"

Harlow shook her head. "I don't know. I'm going to try."

"Then I'll help you."

Harlow pushed off the wall with both hands, she swayed a little on her feet, then turned to sit along the wall's edge, ignoring the long drop on the other side. "I'd like your help... using the moon." She watched him from the corner of her eye carefully as he turned to sit beside her.

"Then tomorrow would be better," he said. "We are strongest when the moon is full."

Harlow sighed. "She's planning an attack on the Mechoida tomorrow. If there are others..." She tried to find the right words, but they escaped her mind. She went forward anyway. "Others like you... you'll need to warn them to not engage with her. Tell them not to come for her."

Fox opened his mouth to speak, but Harlow raised a hand to quiet him.

"I don't know how she's planning it... It's some sort of trap," she said quickly. "But she's powerful. More powerful than any of us." The memory of the burning planet slipped through a crack in her thoughts. She smelled the fire, planted her feet as if the Earth was shaking from it. Harlow pushed through the memory. "And she's on to us. She knows we're not aligned with her anymore. I can feel it."

"Alright. It has to be tonight," Fox said quietly. "I trust you."

Harlow snorted. She wanted to say the same back. But while she had given him no reason to distrust her, he had provided her with plenty. "Yeah, okay," she said.

"You trust me, too." Fox cocked his head. His tone was calm, good natured despite her opposition. "Otherwise, you wouldn't be here."

Harlow glanced at him. "Well, you did save me... Twice, I guess."

Fox's smile was warm. "Well," he said, mimicking her tone, "I do love you still, I guess."

Harlow bit her lip, her hands tightening to fists at her sides. "Then you'll teach me how to access the moonlight?"

"Of course." Fox's hand covered hers. He ran his thumb along her knuckles.

A spark of fire ignited in her veins, so bright it felt

like starlight. Her breath hitched in her throat, her gaze lifting to his. She searched his expression for a long while, trying, and failing, to read his mind.

The corners of Fox's eyes creased playfully. He squeezed her hand. "Oh, do you mean now?"

A small laugh burst from her lips as her face reddened. "That might be best," Harlow managed, slipping her hand from beneath his.

He tapped his knee, as though he was unsure what to do with his hand now. "I usually prefer a more hands-on approach," he said with a surprisingly cocky half-smile. "But I suppose this can't wait for nightfall."

Harlow's ears turned red beneath the mess of hair. "You're getting bold for a math nerd," she said.

Fox rose, extending his arm to help her up. "I'm just getting back to the way we used to be."

Harlow hopped off the wall, pushing past his arm with a sway of her hip.

He laughed, his hand coming to the back of his neck. "I always tried to make your life a little easier. To no avail." He gestured for her to follow him down the path. "You know when you're Queen, you'll need to be better about bossing me around."

Harlow raised a brow, her pace hurried to catch up to him. "Oh yeah? And why's that?"

Fox put his hands in his pockets. He leaned down as

they walked so they were eye level. "I'm impossible to control otherwise," he said with a wink.

Harlow thrust her head up as he rose back to his full height. "I don't want to control anyone," she said. "And I don't want to be Queen."

"That's what makes you fit for the role, don't you think?"

"I thought you were going to teach me," Harlow said, looking around them as they continued down the stone pathway. "Not lecture me."

"Lecture?" Fox's tone was thick with feigned offense. "Harlow, I'm flirting with you."

Harlow's eyes narrowed, but a flutter raced through her. "Well..." She had no follow up. She was completely off balance, entirely unsure of what to say or how she felt or even what her next thought was.

"Maybe you'll remember when you access your truest form," he said at last. "You can tell me all about it when it's done."

*Done.*

It sounded so final.

Harlow's work would never be done, no matter how the night turned out for her. So long as she didn't die on that rooftop, she'd never know a day without struggle.

Overhead, a bird called, the leaves on the long branches hissed in the wind.

And beauty, she reminded herself. She'd never know a day without appreciation for her new home. Even with her old memories, she hoped.

Fox pointed to an empty park at the bottom of the hill, breaking her thoughts. "Look quiet enough?"

Harlow nodded. "Does it need to be quiet?"

"Hard to say. Most pick up the skill easily here since they've done it before – back home. But a little space for quiet and focus can't hurt."

They began their steady decline down the narrow path together.

"You said that I had harnessed moonlight before," Harlow said. "That bodes well, right?"

"I think you're a fast learner."

At the base of the hill, the stone walkway stopped abruptly, overtaken by thick grass and tall dandelions. The park was mostly just a large patch of grass with a few empty benches, scattered ancient trees full of long reaching branches, heavy with bright green leaves.

It was a space Harlow had never seen before and she only realized now just how silly it was that she had never followed the path of The Old Wall down to its end when she has explored every nook and cranny of the university, from the old photography building, to the hidden stairwells and hard to get to roofs of the newer buildings.

She thought she had seen it all in her years here. And no matter how silly it was, this small, hidden park shined a light on the fact that she still had much to find. There was always something new to explore. Something else to learn. Like the password for an underground bar below a bookstore, or the location of an empty field of grass and weeds. Or how to use moonlight.

Harlow followed Fox to a shadow beneath one of the tallest trees as he took her hand and guided her to sit across from him.

The grass was cool beneath her, the sunlight warm as it speckled across her shoulders.

"Ready?"

# CHAPTER 27

# THE LOVE WE LOST

Harlow was never ready. But it also never stopped her.

Though she couldn't actually transform with the sun still up, she found the process to be surprisingly simple. All she had to do was call the moon. And let its light in.

She didn't even have to see it for it to work.

Internally, she had sworn at herself for spending years perfecting the spinning of starlight when she had this at her fingertips the whole time. If only she had known just how easy it could have been.

Before she left the shadow of the tree, Fox leaned in and gently kissed the crown of her head. He breathed in deeply, a pained expression on his face when he pulled back at last, though his confident smile covered it well.

"Let me come with you," he whispered, his words echoing now in her mind. "It might still be a challenge to access the light once you're there."

"I'm up for the challenge," she told him with the same bold grin.

Though, the way he said goodbye made Harlow question if it was really much, much harder than he made it seem.

At least she'd have Carina at her side.

Harlow changed into the outfit Gigi fashioned for her. She secured her knife in her boot and stretched before the bathroom mirror, inspecting the fabric for any tears or openings. When she found it safe enough, Harlow turned her phone off and cracked open an energy drink.

Not that she needed it.

Her heart was already bursting, her body wholly alert. Her eyes snapped to any motion from her peripherals, her ears twitched at the sounds from the street below. In her hand, the tiny popping of the fizzy bubbles as they met the air sounded like an avalanche.

She downed it, trying to ignore Carina's hard stare from the threshold of the door.

"If this goes poorly," Carina said, sounding a little bored, "do you really want your last meal to be pink poison? What flavor is that anyway?"

Harlow looked the can over. She burped. "It's *pink*, Carina."

The cat tossed her head to the side, nose upturned at it.

"And we're not dying tonight," Harlow said as the can crumbled in her grip. "If I die and can't finish this month's print, Jensen will kill me."

"Not if I do first," Carina said with as much of a laugh as a cat could muster. "You can't leave me here alone with those other strays. Got it?"

Harlow smiled despite the drowning dread. "Got it."

Carina darted down the hallway on silence paws. "The moon's up," she called.

"And so are we..." Harlow cast her phone another long look. It would be easy to turn it back on and call her friends. They would come willingly. Enthusiastically, even. She could call Fox. Tell him to bring himself, his allies, all of them for backup.

But the sound of Len's shallow breath, of Dessa's screams in her dream stopped her.

It had started with the Queen and her sword. It had ended with the Queen and the moonlight. It was the two of them, dancing in a circle of fate with a trail of brutal casualties left behind in their aftermath.

At least this time, Harlow could stop the damage from spreading out to those she loved.

Harlow took a deep breath in until she couldn't anymore. For the first time in weeks, she felt...

"Ready?"

Harlow stared at her reflection, at the face so familiar, and yet, so foreign. She flashed herself a half-smile and tucked her short hair behind her ears. The same choppy style in shades of pink and blue that her aunt had always hated. In the same crappy apartment that her aunt thought was beneath them. On the counter, an open notebook lay next to toothpaste and an open jar of face cream. It was full of notes and scribbles for her latest pitch. For a graduate degree that her aunt thought was a waste of time and money...

It was in the little rebellions that Harlow had always found her power.

And now it was time for the big one.

Harlow left the bathroom wordlessly. She passed Carina, checking that the sliding door was locked.

"I'm ready," she said at last, her hand on the cold door handle. She looked around her messy apartment, the place she called home. "Hey, Carina..."

The cat looked up at her as Harlow opened the door a sliver.

"I just transform, then spin her starlight to me, right?"

"In theory." Carina's ear twitched.

"And if that doesn't work?"

The cat's eyes narrowed. "We run like the earth below us is breaking and hope we can live off the grid until we're strong enough to come back."

Harlow nodded, the door opening a little wider as she planted herself between the hallway and Carina. "Right. Tell the others if I'm not back by dawn, to do that second part, okay?"

Carina was on her feet in an instant. She sprinted for the door.

Harlow slipped through the crack and slammed the door behind her.

Carina's cries were muffled through the door. Scratching sounds clawed at the wood as she shouted for Harlow.

Harlow's heart ached at the sound, but she held it firmly closed, more resolute than ever. She locked the door tightly and threw her key in her pocket as she hurried down the hallway.

Thank the stars Gigi had the forethought to add pockets...

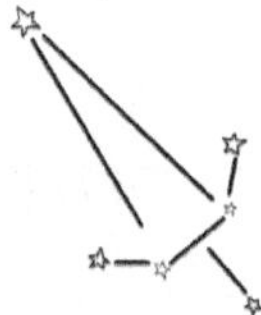

Harlow entered the highrise as deep golden twilight melted into a navy blue evening. The lobby was empty. Its usual bustle was eerily still. A shiver ran up Harlow's back as she made her way up the elevator, thoughts of her aunt calling in a bomb threat or renting the whole structure only to clear it out on this night ran through her mind.

Her thoughts were like space dust, floating freely fast but without dimension or purpose.

It didn't matter how the space was clear. Only that it meant there was less chance of someone else getting hurt. And for that, she was grateful.

But as the doors opened to an empty penthouse apartment, Harlow understood the gravity of her situation at last.

*The roof.* Her aunt would be on the rooftop rock garden, waiting for her. Perhaps, even, waiting for *them.*

With the failure of her sword to deliver the message, the Queen would have done it herself. And left far fewer survivors.

With each step up the narrow stairs, Harlow's thoughts were with the Mechoida.

She thought of the woman who she had watched turn before her eyes.

*Click.* The sound of her boot on the next step echoed in her ears, in tune with her heart. Steady. And terrified.

She thought of the one who had pinned her to the wall, taunted her as she suspended, helpless without her starlight.

*Click.*

She thought of the one who threw moonlight. Of the ones who came in pairs.

*Click.*

She thought of Fox.

Harlow's hand was on the cold lever handle. It only took one push. One push and one step forward into the moonlight. A small decision to move forward would change her world forever.

Her whole life as a speck on the earth, a speck in the galaxy, a speck in the empty universe, a speck in time itself.

There was no turning back now.

Harlow pushed the door open.

The air was cold against her skin as a calm wind lifted her hair from her neck. The crunch of rock beneath her feet, the thump of her heart, her breathing steady, it was a symphony she was familiar with. A lullaby for her weary mind.

The Queen was looking out onto the city, at the starlight and twinkling city lights. She didn't turn to face Harlow. Her hands were laced loosely behind her back, her stance tall.

Harlow approached her with long strides. She stood at her aunt's side, silent. From here, everything seemed so small. She could not make out the individual people, or the details of the buildings. The wide expanse of the city, a labyrinth of tall buildings, busy streets, and narrow alleys, all looked purposeful from here. Everything was perfectly planned.

Like an ant colony.

Her fingers itched to call her sword.

But as she found the moon overhead, covering them in a silver glow, she knew she had to wait.

Her aunt looked her up and down from the side of her eyes. She looked disgusted. "What is that ridiculous attire?"

"A friend made it," Harlow answered honestly.

The Queen scoffed. "A friend." The word was laced with venom. "You are making a lot of those these days."

Harlow's scalp tingled as her body responded to the danger beside her. "Only a few," she said.

The Queen's eyes narrowed. "You have failed in your task. But the monks got it done."

Harlow tried to stifle her surprise. She bit her lip. "Carina neglected to mention–"

"I will end this once and for all," the Queen cut her off. "With or without you."

"End it... Just like last time? Will you kill a whole planet to maintain your control?"

The Queen turned to Harlow with such swiftness, that Harlow flinched before she even understood why.

She stepped back, away from the edge of the roof as her aunt advanced on her. "Do not speak to me of things you do not know. You were not there when the world collapsed on itself. You were not there when your kind needed you." Her words hit Harlow like punches.

She took in a quick breath and dug her heel into the gravel, steeling herself to stand her ground. "I know what you did," she said as the words from her prophecy echoed in her mind, filling her heart with anger. *We know what you did*, she had said.

This time was different. This time, she was alone.

The Queen's eyes narrowed on Harlow. "Tell me, then," she said, her voice a low whisper. "What did I do?"

Harlow stepped forward. "You killed me."

The Queen cocked a single brow, her chin raising slightly. "I did."

The admission was stark. Like morning light on misty mountains, it cleared the rage in Harlow's chest until there was only a single thought. A single word.

"Why?"

The Queen faced Harlow, unafraid. "So you only have the part of the story where you are blameless. Tell me, did you use the moon to reveal this truth to you?"

Harlow's jaw clenched. "Yes," she said through gritted teeth. "I did. And I want to know *why*."

The Queen laughed, a hollow, broken sound. "I killed you because I had to."

Stinging in Harlow's fingertips raced up her arms. The light of the stars warmed her veins, the moonlight swallowed her skin in ice. "I don't understand."

"You wouldn't," the Queen said plainly. "You had been too far corrupted by then. As you grew closer to that soldier... I should have seen it coming. In a way, it was my own fault. I should have killed him as soon as I suspected him. Perhaps all of this could have been avoided."

Cold froze Harlow's heart. *Fox.* She was talking about Fox...

The Queen's eyes narrowed, a crease formed

between her brows. "I see now that your first death was not enough to teach you. You will always be seduced by lesser gods offering pretend power no matter how I raise you."

Harlow reached up, pulling starlight, grasping desperately at moonlight. *Call the moon. Call it in.* Her thoughts screamed. *Let the light in.*

"Fate is a collapsing star, reborn again, and again–" The Queen spun falling stars into blades, glimmering chains wrapped around the hilt and up her arms, fixing them to her by a strong magic.

*Let the light in!*

Moonlight flooded through Harlow's muscles and deep into her bones. She felt weightless, a moment of time stopping for her as her skin burned and froze all at once, lighting the space between them in an iridescent flash.

"And again!" The Queen's voice cracked like thunder.

Harlow collapsed onto the ground as gravity exerted its will on her once again. She felt strange as she lifted herself from the rocky ground, like she was not really in herself. Her body was light as she rose up, towering over the Queen. The night around here was tinted in a strange shade of purple. She could hear her aunt's heart beating, and couldn't feel her own.

Starlight wrapped around her, its familiar power pulsing through her. In one final pull, she crafted the sword in her hand.

In her massive, monster-like hand.

The Queen swung her double blades at Harlow. Cuts landed on Harlow's arm, spilling bright moonlight from the wound.

It hurt. But not like she expected it to. Harlow watched the wound reseal itself with ease.

Harlow smiled.

# THE SHIELD AND THE BOW

Harlow parried the next strike with ease, her sword pushing back the Queen's as sparks shimmered around them.

"So this is what you've become?" The Queen growled, dodging the next attack as she backed up quickly, smirking at Harlow's speed. "And when I'm gone, what do you plan to do then?"

Harlow's sword swung up over head. It came

crashing down on the space the Queen had just occupied, black and white rocks exploded around them.

The Queen rushed forward, one sword high as the other struck Harlow's leg. "Let the monsters roam free?"

Harlow roared. Not with pain, but with frustration. No matter how hard she sparred with her aunt, the other woman was always faster, always stronger, always one step ahead as she could predict Harlow's every move.

The Queen's blade tore around Harlow's other leg. From behind her, she heard the Queen's voice again. "And when the planet is consumed with deception and falsities, will you wish you could make the same choice as I did?"

Harlow spun on her heel, but the Queen was already too far to strike.

The breeze cast sparkling starlight between them as the damage to their swords began to repair slowly.

"I'm not trying to kill you!" Harlow bellowed, her new mouth moving strangely though her voice sounded the same to her ears. "And this knowledge is for all!"

The Queen's blades rose to her face, casting pale shadows across her brows.

Harlow's free hand reached out to her aunt. She steadied her stance, planting herself to the rooftop as best she could. The pull of the starlight in her aunt's hands was strong. It fought to stay connected, forced away from Harlow's determined influence. She grimaced, extending her hand further as traces of starlight wrapped around her fingers.

"You cannot take my starlight!" The Queen drove her body forward, the blades moving faster than Harlow could react. She sliced one leg, then an arm, the palm of her hand, a deep gash formed on her back.

Harlow stumbled, a pained scream ripped through her as she fell to her knees. Her vision narrowed, obscured by the haze of swirling purple and blue as the colors intensified.

She looked up as the Queen stepped forward, sharp swords ready to deal the final blow.

Harlow struggled to her feet, scrambling up as swiftly as she could. She called forth more moonlight as her wounds more slowly stitched themselves together.

She had to keep fighting.

And if the Queen wouldn't give up her starlight... Then Harlow would have to show her the same amount of mercy she had been given.

The Queen left her with no choice.

Harlow harnessed moonlight as she stood tall once more. She let it all in. She let it guide her body, let it consume her sword.

A high cry pierced the night air.

Carina, huge and sparkling with the light of galaxies spinning within her, landed at Harlow's side. She looked up at Harlow with barred teeth, a smirk. Then, she turned to face the Queen with a long, angry growl.

A blossom of hope filled Harlow's chest. She stood taller, pressing her shoulders back. She had just begun to think she wouldn't make it off the roof alive when her guardian arrived.

It wasn't too late...

But her peace didn't last long, replaced with a swift sense of dread that coursed through her body. With Carina here, she now had to worry about the dangerous fact that neither of them would come out of this unscathed.

The Queen turned to Carina, her own scowl forming. "You serve the starlight, monk." She raised her blades higher. "Think hard before you commit a treasonous act."

Carina bristled. "There are Mechoida swarming the building," Carina told Harlow. Her voice was low and calm, though her body was wound tight. She crouched down, ready to spring on the Queen if she needed to. "The others are trying to hold them back. I don't know how long they will last without us."

Fear rushed up Harlow's body, her limbs prickled painfully at the thought of her friends below, fighting for their lives. Her thoughts raced faster than she could track. Images of them below, their weapons drawn, breath heavy with fear, infiltrated every corner of her mind.

Why had they come?

She gripped her sword tighter.

The Queen's neck craned to look over the edge of the building. Her scowl quickly shifting to a smirk as she pointed a sword at Carina. "Have you come to atone for abandoning your Princess in the last life?"

Carina paced between her and Harlow, her head low, pupilless eyes focused steady on her target. "I won't let Harlow fight alone."

"Then you will join her in death." The Queen's blades sliced toward them, flinging from their chains on her arms, they launched like missiles in the dark.

Carina ducked low, her shoulders protruding from her back as she sank as low as she could before launching herself up into the air. She ran along the periphery, swiping at the Queen when she could.

The Queen was faster. The swords in her hands morphed into small rope darts, dangerously sharp and quick. They shot out from her arms with precision like a second set of fists.

One struck Carina in her back leg as Harlow's sword blocked the second.

The pointed arrowhead stuck to her as the Queen forcibly pulled, knocking the cat off her feet.

Carina's front claws dug into the loose rock as she desperately tried to keep her distance. "Her starlight!" Carina cried out over the sound of tumbling stones and her straining breath.

The Queen's focus was on Carina as she continued to ensnare her closer. But her other hand launched her dart, almost too swiftly to see.

This time, Harlow's sword came up vertically. The tip of the dart grazed along Harlow's forehead, slicing her massive head as the chain circled close around the blade, tangling it until it was stuck.

Harlow yanked her sword toward her, her other hand rising to pull the starlight from her aunt's hands. She envisioned it so clearly she could feel it pulse in her hand. She saw it, each pinpoint of starlight going out as it drained from the Queen. It would be dark soon, with only her sword and her moonlight to light the way... Everything would be hers. Everything.

The Queen's eyes widened, her mouth open to a scream, though no sound broke free.

Starlight flickered until, at last, the Queen's starlight extinguished.

The rooftop was dark, except for the faint glow casting off Carina and the sword in Harlow's grip. If the moon still shone above them, its light did not reach them. The scene before them was grayscale, dull, details lost in the shadows.

Carina limped away, carrying herself with slow, heavy steps back toward Harlow. She looked up at her, ears flattened against her head, moonlight dripping from her wound, then disappearing into the cold air.

Ahead, the Queen shrunk back, her shoulders collapsing in on herself as she struggled to bring down more starlight in vain. She stepped forward as Carina continued her slow march to Harlow's side. "Stay away from her!" With one hand outstretched to them, the other wrapped around herself, she looked small. Alone. Weak.

Harlow hardly heard them in the muffled quiet of her own stillness. She was far away, the empty darkness of space expanded around her, traveled through her until there was no telling where her body ended and the universe itself began. A surge of power deep within her core hurled her mind outward, pulling her skin from her muscles. She released herself to the expanse and the feeling of cold overtaking her heart and thoughts soothed all concern and care. She fell back, floated, and came together in the quiet nothingness.

It was gentle. Peaceful.

She knew what she needed to do to keep it.

To keep it all.

All of it.

*All.*

Harlow's sword, a pale light so bright it blinded her, rose up. She didn't need to see. She could hear the fear in the dark, ringing so loudly around her that its vibrations burrowed into her. She wanted to silence it.

Because she had to.

Because she could.

"Harlow, stop!" Carina's voice was muted, a scream drowned beneath vast, deep water.

A sound like crashing waves burst through the night.

Harlow's sword hung in the air mid-swing.

Len's shield held firm against the blade.

Harlow pressed her all strength into the starlight shield, but she could gain no more forward momentum. Sparks misted around her as she dragged the sword down, running the sharp length of it across the shield slowly.

Nothing was going to stop her.

Nothing.

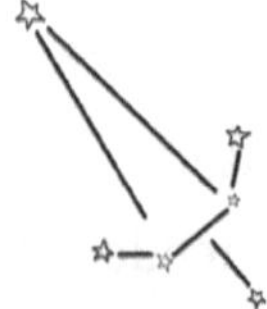

LEN'S LEGS strained to hold her ground. Deep lines in the loose rocks formed as she was slowly, painfully pushed back. She grit her teeth, her arms shook as her muscles all tensed, trying to keep the sword from breaking through her shield.

Sparks fell around her.

She was already so tired.

Her shield was failing.

Len let the weight of the sword press her down. She crouched low, watching its heavy blade through the star shield. She tried to make out Harlow's face, but it was too hard to tell what she was looking at. A monster, or her friend?

How had she gone so far so fast?

She readied herself, muscles coiling, body tight. A final burst of strength, Len launched herself up, her shield repelling the sword and causing Harlow to stumble backward.

Dessa took her place. Her bow and arrow were gone, her arms outstretched wide. Fear gripped her body. But she wasn't afraid of the monster in front of her, or those below them, climbing up the side of the building, swiping and gnawing at their guardians as they fought to push past them.

No, as she held her hands out, chest open, she felt the fear of loss. Of losing Harlow to the empty. Of losing out on all the possibilities that life on Earth had in store for them, even if it wasn't together.

Harlow was good. And fierce. And stupid. And kind. She was loyal and silly. She made terrible choices but always worked to remedy them. The world was better for their humanity. For their love and their anger. For their happiness and their tears.

Harlow wasn't what she had been before. Not a princess or a warrior. Not a god among soldiers. She wasn't... *this*.

She was human.

Pain drilled into Dessa's chest, resting there as if finally at home among the fear, the worry, the love, the hope. A magnitude of emotion swelled within her, spilling out into a small smile. She didn't know what to do with it all, with the intensity of it all. So she smiled as she stared defiantly at her friend.

Harlow was stubborn.

And so was she.

Harlow steadied herself on powerful legs. Her pupilless eyes, blank and glowing, stared back at Dessa. Her sword drew high.

Dessa's breath was shallow as her lips parted, her heartbeat pounding in rhythm with her whispering words, nearly lost in the snarling and the chaos around them. She tried, even if Harlow couldn't hear, even if it was the last thing she ever did. "Look at me, Harlow…" Tears burned her eyes as her vision clouded. "Look, Harlow. Please."

Harlow's sword was frozen, hanging in the air between them.

"We love you," Dessa whispered. "Please. Look at what we have to save here."

CHAPTER 29

# THE SPACE
# BETWEEN

Dessa didn't believe in fate. Fate was an excuse people used when they failed. It was something to blame because the pain of acknowledging that their own shortcomings or lack of preparation or misjudgment was too great to hold. Consequently, people failed to learn their hard lessons and continued to make the same tired mistakes over and over again, never improving or reflecting, never moving past their mentality that fate was against them.

Fate was what people applauded when they succeeded and didn't want to admit it was on the backs of others. It was something to point to and declare their right when the reality was, they were no more special than the next person – just able to better wield their influence and privilege.

Len disagreed.

Adamantly.

Fate was just the opportunity that presented itself, a pause in the road of life that jutted off in different directions. Fate was the forced stop. It couldn't be helped. But there were still options. It was what one did with the choices that fate provided that determined the outcome. Everyone needed a little nudging from time to time and hopefully they would take the road that was right for them.

It was that evening, as the sun began to set in the western sky, that Dessa started to think Len might be right. Maybe she would admit it if they lived long enough to talk it through.

Dessa had promised herself that she wasn't going to go to Harlow's apartment that night. She wasn't going to beg her to reconsider the plan, no matter how idiotic she found it. She was done trying to out stubborn her. It only led to heartache.

And a headache.

A massive one.

So as she walked by Harlow's door on the way to pick up her cheesecake delivery order, she put on her headphones and blasted music as loud as she could handle it. She fixed her gaze to the end of the hallway and marched past with long strides.

It took exactly one song to walk down the stairs, pick up the plastic bag of comfort cheesecake from the delivery driver, and walk back up to their hallway. The song changed just as Dessa passed Harlow's door. But when she expected the second of silence, what she heard instead, was Carina's distressed cries from the other side of the flimsy wood door.

The next song began, a series of loud drums and angry screaming filled her ears.

Dessa ripped the headphones from her ears.

The screaming continued.

Dessa's brows furrowed, the plastic bag crinkled in her grasp as she moved closer to the door. "Carina?"

The cat's cries ceased instantly, replaced by small scratching on the door. "Dessa! Harlow left! Let me out!"

"She left without you?" She cringed at her own question. That much was obvious. But she was still shocked that Harlow would do that. Why would she go alone? They had a plan...

"Yes!" Carina sounded just as annoyed as she was with herself.

"Hang on, I'll get my key!" Dessa called back from halfway down the hall, bag smacking along her thigh as the clear plastic box inside burst open. The door to their apartment smacked the wall and she flung her bag into the sink where it bounced dully in the cheap metal basin.

"Whoa." Len peeked from behind the wall, her head sidewise. "What–"

"Harlow left already," Dessa said. She was already ducking around Len as she hurried down the hall to change into her new battle outfit.

"She what?" Len ventured slowly into Dessa's bedroom as she shimmied into the bodysuit.

Dessa tucked her arms into the long sleeves, fitting her thumbs through the little holes to keep it secure. "She left without Carina. Locked her in the apartment and left." She glanced up at last at Len, her heart beating rapidly as her thoughts.

Len nodded, as if that all made sense and was across the hall to her room a moment later. "Can aliens get Darwin Awards?" she called from her room.

"Let's make sure it's just an honorable mention," Dessa said as she laced up her boots.

"Let's just get Carina out before the moon comes up

and she busts down the wall," Ara corrected, slinking into the hallway, her lean body curving up along the doorframe.

Len and Dessa entered the hallway in unison. Each looked the other up and down, admiring for a moment, their new looks.

"Hope this stuff works," Dessa said.

"It will."

"Ever the optimist."

The two women dressed in shimmering and strange outfits, with three frantic cats close behind, ran down the street just as the sky above them faded into a navy blue.

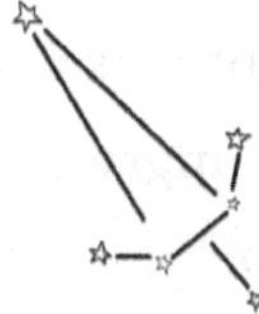

THE SKYSCRAPER LOOKED EVEN TALLER NOW that the entire block was lightless. The streetlights, the interiors of the surrounding buildings, were all dark. All empty.

Dessa and Len stood at the base of the apartment building, looking up at the desolate structure as the three giant cats, glowing pink, purple, and blue in the darkness around them, stalked the sidewalk.

Dessa reached up, pulling starlight down around

her. The stars filled her with the familiar warmth and comfort as she spun her hand and crafted the bow.

Len's shield, narrow and contained for now, rested along her arm. She held her star spear in the same hand, keeping it close to her as she pried open the large glass doors to the lobby with a small grunt and the group slipped through to find the room the same as the outside – silent, devoid of life and color.

"Where is everyone?" Len asked as they journeyed deeper into the room with light steps.

Around the cats, their faint glow illuminated the way, casting darker shadows across the floor.

Dessa's eyes scanned the space, her scalp tingled with anticipation as fear crept up her chest, polluting the space where her righteous anger had been.

It was easier to be angry at Harlow. She imagined she would storm up to the roof, swoop in as the ultimate assist, win the day and then feel extra smug as she told Harlow what was what. But this feeling of uncertainty, of everything being slightly off-putting and still...? That was harder to contend with.

She hadn't predicted that the entire block would be without power. That the building would be empty. That they'd have to climb *a lot* of stairs.

That all of this probably meant that the queen had long foreseen this outcome.

She cast a glance at Len who gave her a quick nod toward the emergency exit at the far end of the lobby.

"Ready for some cardio?" Len said, her tone surprisingly carefree.

Dessa raised a brow at her and held her bow closer. "You know my stance on running."

"Not unless there's zom–" Len started but was silenced by her guardian's quick pounce in front of them.

The cat's tail flicked, so high it nearly hit Len in the chest. "Quiet," she hissed as her body readied low to strike at something ahead in the dark.

From the shadows, a tall figure emerged with two others flanking either side. They walked closer, but stopped far enough that their faces were still hidden in the shadow.

But Dessa didn't need a face to see who was standing in the middle.

Tall, slim, and hands resting in his pockets as though he was kind of bored with their arrival. His shoulders were broad, his head tilted up to see them better past the glow of the cats. "Fox."

Len squared her shoulders as the two figures beside him advanced slowly. Their movements were purposeful, but... strange. As though they were stiff. She raised her shield, her spear in her other hand elongating. Her stare was fierce. "Please tell me you're here to help Harlow," she said as her grip on her spear tightened.

"I am," Fox said.

Carina growled, low and primal in the dark. She moved to stand at Dessa's side as Ara stalked to the outskirts.

"But not to help us?" Dessa's fingertips traced the string of her bow, checking the arrow carefully.

"That would be more accurate."

Dessa drew her bow up, her arrow ready.

The two in front of Fox began to tremble, their bodies shaking in the darkness.

Dessa aimed at the one on the left. She waited.

Moonlight filled their bodies, their limbs expanding, their snarls piercing the night.

Dessa's arrow flew as they finished their transformation, striking the first in the shoulder.

Ara leaped onto it, claws hooking in its neck as she bit down and moonlight spilled onto the floor, then disappeared. The creature dissipated before them as the second crouched down low, then on all fours, ran toward them.

From behind, glass shattered as a hoard of Mechoida stormed into the room.

Len turned, shield ready as Vela raced to the

entrance, meeting the monsters with a frenzy of claws and teeth.

An eruption of growls and gnashing and cries echoed around them.

There were too many. There was no way...

"Carina!" Dessa caught her attention just as she was about to spring into the fray. "Go help Harlow!"

Carina gave her a quick nod and jumped high into the air. She ran, feet floating just above the battle below and out the broken doors.

Dessa spun on her heel, launching another arrow at the space Fox had been.

The empty space.

Len's shield held back the second one that had been by Fox's side. Its clawed hand thrashed against her starlight, igniting sparks of fire around them. Her spear came up and she cut into the swirling skin.

Dessa's arrow hit it from the side, and just like the first, it faded away as quickly as it had arrived. She grabbed Len's shoulder. "The stairs," she said quickly. "We'll funnel them there."

Len's breath came out in small bursts as more monsters poured into the room, claws and moonlight meeting in brilliantly bright flashes. She nodded quickly and pushed Dessa ahead of her with her shoulder.

Dessa narrowed her attention to the sound of her

boots smacking against the tile, the long huff of air as she exhaled all her fear from her chest. She ran into the door, her arm smacking the large push lever as hard as she could.

It burst open and Dessa turned back as her stomach dropped.

Len inched backwards, her shield deflecting giant scratching hands as a few slipped past Ara and Vela's defensive attacks.

Dessa checked the darkened stairwell for any signs of Fox. But he was long gone. She just had to hope he would take his time getting to the roof...

She turned back, an arrow already drawn back. It whizzed past Len's shield and hit her target, drawing the Mechoida's head back in pain.

Just enough time for Len to rush to the door.

She held it open, her shield blocking the entrance and her spear atop, pointed out dangerously. Her strong voice cut through the chaos, calling their cats back to them.

Vela and Ara swept through the air, their glow brighter than any of the monsters around them. They worked together, spinning and twirling between each other and the Mechoida in a silent comradery. Each swipe of their claws hit a target. Each bite was so quick that the other was able to maneuver between to draw the attack away.

The Mechoida, on the other hand, were unruly. They drew forward, pulled back. Some attacked relentlessly, sacrificing their own safety for the offensive strike while others backed away at the first sign of Ara or Vela.

But they were many.

Dessa set loose another arrow, striking one who had managed to grab ahold of Vela's tail.

At last, the cats made their escape to the stairwell with the Mechoida sprinting toward them.

Ara pushed Len and Dessa back with her massive body, nudging them further into the narrow darkness as Vela spun around to continue her attack just the first Mechoida was close enough to strike.

She knocked its hand back with her clawed paw, backing away into the doorframe as she did.

"Go," she told Dessa, her voice calm as the violent onslaught continued ahead of them.

Ara jumped over Vela, her sleek body able to fit between her and the top of the door. She barred her teeth. "Hurry."

Len's eyes narrowed. Her spear pulled in close, she looked back to Dessa.

Dessa's heart stuck in her throat. She didn't want to leave them. But...

"Harlow. Carina. They need us," Len said, though her voice broke, her expression was stern. She nodded for the stairs. "Start climbing. I'll be here for you if any break through."

Dessa blinked away a tear. Her eyes stung.

"Stay safe." But her words were lost in the pounding sound of her feet propelling her up on every step. Her legs burned, her lungs on fire as she rushed away from the sound of battle below to the unknown above.

# CHAPTER 30

# THE CLOSEST STAR

Hatysa stared at someone she thought she knew once. Her hands were outstretched, a small smile on her lips. Through a mist of deep purple, they stood there, alone. Her vision tunneled, blackening her periphery.

No, not alone.

Another joined her side. Their hands slipped into each other's. They both looked up at her.

Fearlessly.

She looked at their hands, empty but for each other's.

Fearless, yet calm. No weapons. No anger. Nothing but an emotion she could not name. She wasn't sure she knew how.

She stepped back, and they stepped forward.

Together.

A blinding light burst between the three of them, it ignited the space in a blaze of pale white light, so bright it blinded her.

She backed away, her clawed hand up to block the rays of light.

It went out just as fast.

Between them, Fox's massive form rose up to his full height. Along his body, swirls of light drifted slowly across his skin. His head turned toward them, fox-like with a long snout and large, galaxy filled eyes locked on them. "You want to save life here?" he asked Dessa, though his mouth moved in a different time from his voice. "Your Queen keeps us from our truest potential. She keeps the light for herself. If you want to save this earth, let Hatysa end her reign once and for all."

Len pulled her shield from the sky with one smooth motion. It lit around them, casting shadows across the ground.

Carina darted close, positioning herself between the

trio and Fox. "Harlow took her starlight. She's no threat now."

Fox tilted his massive head toward the Queen.

She stood, resolute with her head held high and shoulders back. Though at her sides, her hands hung limply.

Fox chuckled. A sinister sound from his monster-like mouth. "Then we have won." A hand reached out for Hatysa's. He bowed to her. "Come with me, my Queen."

Hatysa looked down at her own hands, the sword she held there, glowing faintly in her grasp.

They had done it.

Won.

"With you at my side, we can awaken the others. Once we are all enlightened, we can finally be free," Fox said, his arm reaching closer to her as he rose, an empty smile cutting through his face slowly.

She waited, watching him with a strange detachment. He looked just as she remembered him. Confidence in his stance. Ease in his movements. Intensity of his gaze.

But his smile...

It used to be kind.

She was hit by image after flashing image. Their time together on a long destroyed planet. Their short, fated meeting here. She watched his smile through space and time, through easy afternoons and painful midnights, through all forms he took and all lifetimes together.

It didn't look like this.

It couldn't be like this.

Hatysa's sword fell. Moonlight and starlight shattered, then, slowly, flickered out.

Fox's hand recoiled, a snarl replaced his smile.

Dessa and Len rushed to her side as Harlow felt her body collapse. Her knees hit the rough rock, her body transformed back, mind still reeling with the flood of memories.

Her friends' hands slipped into Harlow's as they huddled close.

Human hands.

Weak and small.

They lifted her up onto her unsteady legs.

Resilient and hopeful.

On the horizon, the sapphire sky brightened into a pale citrine as sunlight crested the tops of the buildings.

Carina crouched low, moving between them and Fox.

Harlow looked up at the dawning, starless sky. Desperation tightened in her chest.

The moon was still bright...

"If you cannot let your humanity go," Fox's voice rumbled through Harlow as if he was speaking from within her, "I will cut it out."

The rooftop door burst open, a surge of Mechoida battled to squeeze through, their bodies contorting and writhing to break their way to them.

Harlow pushed her friends back, her arms coming up defensively, though she was not sure where to direct her movements. Her mind went blank as Fox took a step closer and growls and whispers filled the rooftop.

There was no starlight. She couldn't keep her friends safe. After all this... Every choice had led her here. To disaster.

Carina circled them, her large paws shimmering as more light shined down between her and the monsters who had surrounded them.

Harlow's eyes followed her movements. She looked into the face of each monster, all waiting as if for a command to strike. They had them pinned down, corralled in a ring with no escape.

"It's over. The stars are gone." Fox stepped closer, his monstrous form haloed by the rising sun, so bright, Harlow instinctively raised her arm up to block the light.

The sunlight.

A smirk flashed across her face as she reached past

him, and her body filled with warmth, a surge of strength, a sense of calm. She twisted her hand, pulling the sunlight toward her, and her fingers clasped around the hilt of her sword.

Fox recoiled.

Harlow held her sword out, bright as the morning dawn.

"It's only one star," a Mechoida growled from her side, their claws swiping at Carina's back.

She dodged, hissing loudly. She did not strike back, their standoff still in place as each side waited for the other to make the first contact.

"You can still come back," Fox said as he took another careful step.

Harlow frowned. A dull pain nipped at her heart as she looked up at him, silhouetted by the sun. A thousand things that could have been merged into the emptiness of their reality.

There was no more possibility between them.

Only an ending.

It was just a matter of how. And who would make the first destructive move.

"I want to go forward," Harlow whispered at last.

All around her, the Mechoida closed in, inching closer, tightening the ring around them.

Fear seeped into her as she eyed them, her sword out long, but her hands trembling.

And then, she felt a gentle hand on her shoulder.

Then another.

Harlow turned to Len on her left. The corner of her friend's lips tilted up, a calm smile despite their dire circumstances. She squeezed Harlow's shoulder and strength poured into her.

On her right, Dessa winked at her. Confidence replaced the last of her fear.

The sword. The shield. The bow.

Harlow's sword shimmered brighter, bursting in bright sunbeams as a shield surrounded them, and rays of light broke free, blinding them all in brilliant starlight.

# THE MORNING

Harlow blinked furiously into the sunlight burning over the tops of the surrounding buildings. Warmth caressed her cheeks, gentle and loving. She heard the sound of bird calls from somewhere far away.

She had expected screams. And a claw to the face. She expected to open her eyes to a demolished roof, a bunch of monsters pouncing, and her friends bloodied.

But as she looked around them, her eyes adjusting to the morning light, the rooftop looked surprisingly undisturbed, her friends were smiling at the cerulean sky, and any trace of Fox or the Mechoida, or even of their guardians in their giant forms, was gone.

Her brows furrowed at her empty hands. "Are we...? Did we...?" She did her best to speak, but the sentence wouldn't form. She had too much to ask, too much to say.

From the other side of the roof, Ara and Vela slunk through the door, their small house cat forms restored.

"Ara!"

"Vela!"

Carina raced to their sides as Vela limped along, her back leg dragging behind her, though she seemed to be smiling. "Way to hold them off," she said, half scolding, half impressed.

Vela shook her body out, her leg's unnatural angle righting itself. "Next time there's a massive swarm, you see how easy it is."

Carina nudged her head with her own as Ara rubbed her long body along them both.

Len put her hands on her hips, her smile brightening at the sight of their cats, safe and sound. She surveyed the rooftop, then sighed. "You know," she said, answering one of Harlow's unspoken questions, "I don't know where they go when they disappear like that."

Dessa's gaze narrowed. "Hey, guys..." She pointed to

the empty space where the Queen had stood. "Where'd she go?"

The three looked at the corner of the roof, each with an equally dumbfounded expression.

"What? Did she repel from the side of the building?" Harlow threw her hands up as the cats all joined them.

"Maybe she teleported?" Carina offered, casting a glance up at Harlow. "Got her starlight back and spelled her way out?"

Harlow raised a brow. "*Can* she get her starlight back? That wasn't a one-time thing?"

Carina's tail flicked. "Why're you looking at me? I'm just the idea cat. I don't know how this stuff works."

"You *literally* studied it for a lifetime," Dessa said.

Carina's jaw snapped. "Not starlight. We studied moonlight. It's completely different."

Harlow sighed. She let the sounds of their debate and teasing fade into the background. The Queen was gone. Somewhere. And so was Fox. Though, she was certain that she would only ever see one of them again.

She didn't know what happened to Mechoida when they were struck with starlight. But she had never seen the same one twice.

Deep in her chest, her heartbeat reminded her that she was still alive. And, as painful as it was, she was glad to feel it all.

Though, right now, she also felt hungry. And a little distraction probably wouldn't hurt. She was grateful for the emotions, the many truths she held tightly at once, but... she also knew that all of that would be waiting for her soon enough.

It would come in waves. All of it was going to hurt for a long time. It was just the way of things. Eventually, the hurt would turn to a dull, persistent ache. The ache would turn to tender melancholy. There would be moments of forgetting, and the savage crashing around her when she least expected it.

"What time does Go Nuts Donuts open?" Harlow asked, cutting her own thoughts short.

"4am," Dessa answered, though she had just been in the middle of her own sentence. "Why?"

Harlow shrugged. "Nothing to do now except get breakfast. Preferably the sugary kind."

Len scratched the back of her head, her smile widened. "Well, there's a lot to do, actually. But I vote we fill up first."

"Seconded," Dessa said brightly.

THE BUILDING WAS STILL empty when they walked out. Which Harlow was thankful for. Coming from the roof in strange outfits to a wrecked lobby with broken glass, hanging wiring, and gutted couches would have been, at the very least, an uncomfortable conversation.

They stepped over shards and stuffing carefully and quickly, hurrying out into the street before anyone came to check on the place.

The power appeared to still be out on the entire block, judging from the lack of light from any window, and the emptiness of the sidewalk.

How the Queen had managed it, or was able to evacuate the entire building, Harlow still couldn't be sure. She thought about how she would go about asking. If she should ever see her again, that is.

"You know, Len, if you still need a pitch, I think that the localized power outage and vandalized luxury condo building might be a good piece," Dessa said as they turned the corner, greeted by sunlight beaming between two buildings.

"Hey, I was going to write about that," Harlow feigned protest.

Len shrugged. "I actually think I'll do some interviews. Students here have some hidden talents. It'd be fun to highlight them."

"Since when do you write for fun?" Dessa teased.

Len raised her hands in surrender. "Since today."

Harlow quickened her pace ahead of them as Carina trotted along at her side.

"We'll search for the Queen, and anyone else we can find," the cat said quietly.

Harlow shook her head. "Don't. Just rest for now. You have all more than earned it."

"That's what you said last time," Carina grumbled.

"Well, I mean it. Then and now." She stuffed her hands into the pockets of her battle outfit. "Not that you even *need* to earn it. Rest is just as vital as food and water. It's just good strategy."

"Tell that to your caffeine habit."

Harlow snorted. "How about we both work on that, then?"

Carina nodded. "Donuts, then rest for the humans. Just rest for us cats." She turned quickly without a break in her pace and got the other cats' attention.

"I'll bring back some wet food," Harlow called after them as the cats hurried away. "The good stuff!"

"Don't you come home without it!" Carina's voice carried down the street, and then, they were gone.

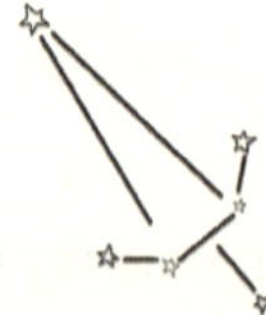

THE THREE SAT on the curb of the sidewalk outside the donut shop. The sky above was growing lighter with each bite, the cerulean fading into a pale light blue. Beyond the tops of the skyscrapers, the moon was sinking slowly on the horizon.

"I think if I had to do my life over again, I think I'd order the maple," Harlow said as she spoke from the side of her mouth, glaring at the pink sprinkle donut in her hand.

"That all?" Dessa prompted, her own mouth full.

Harlow nodded, picking off little sprinkles and tossing them into the empty street one at a time. "Yep, that's all."

Len leaned in, her silver hair spilling over one shoulder. "I would've thought it'd be to not succumb to the power of corruptive light and try to kill us all, but hey, I'm glad you're on team no regrets."

Harlow smiled as she stuffed the last of the donut down. "Should I get a tattoo to commemorate the night? 'No regerts'?"

Dessa pointed at Harlow's forearm. "Just get 'Dessa is always right' here. So you remember."

Harlow hummed playfully as she imagined it there. "I will if you pay for it. I'm still out of a job, *remember*?"

Dessa nudged her with her shoulder. "We're going to be alright, Harlow."

"Sure as the sunrise. We're going to be alright." Len's arm came up over the two of them. She pulled them in close, Dessa's cheek smooshed against Harlow's as she squeezed them tightly.

A flush blazed across her cheeks and ears as Dessa nuzzled closer into the curve of Harlow's neck. Despite all the pain, the loss, and the overwhelming exhaustion, Harlow's heart raced so loud beneath her ribs she was certain it would wake the entire block. The smell of sweat and sweet sugar and warm, rich dough surrounded them like a protective blanket.

They were going to be alright...

"I still wish I ordered maple." Harlow did her best to pout, but a big belly laugh broke out of her instead as Len shoved the two of them away cheerfully.

"Stars, you're insufferable. Just go get a maple donut," Dessa said once she was free of Len's embrace, her body working to right herself as she rebalanced on the curb.

"I can't. I'm poor," Harlow said with a mischievous grin. She thought she saw the hint of Dessa's nose turn a slight pink. Her smile grew.

"I'll spot you." Len grumbled as she rose from her spot.

Just as swiftly as it had come, Harlow's smile softened.

Len's legs seemed stiff, her movements careful. She stretched her back out before she looked down at Harlow with a serious expression. "But you do owe us both for cheesecake."

Dessa's hand flew to her forehead. "The cheesecake! Ugh, it's probably festering in the sink…"

Harlow raised a brow. "What cheesecake?"

Dessa threw her head back. Her eyes were closed tight. "I had ordered cheesecake to make ourselves feel *something* other than worry for you last night," Dessa said with an exaggerated huff. "And I had to abandon it to go save your life."

"The ultimate price," Len said solemnly with her hand over her heart.

Harlow lowered her head in shame. The gesture was playful, but the emotion was genuine. She had a feeling she'd be grappling with a lot of it soon. "I owe you cheesecake. And a donut. And my life. In that order."

"Yeah, yeah. You can keep your life for now." Len stood on her toes, a final stretch before she disappeared into the donut shop, the little bell over the door chiming as it closed behind her.

"I'll let the cheesecake slide, too," Dessa said quietly. "For a fee."

"Still don't have any money…"

Dessa caught Harlow's eyes; they burned brightly,

as if she had captured the sunlight within herself. "Just an answer to a question."

Harlow's brows furrowed.

Dessa smiled in the face of Harlow's skepticism, the corners of her eyes creasing gently. "Do you think if I kissed you now that it would ruin things?"

Harlow's stomach dropped, her lips parted as she sucked in a shallow breath. Whatever questions she had been expecting, perhaps what it felt like to harness moonlight, why she had gone off on her own, where she thought the Queen was, if she thought they'd have to keep battling at night... Nothing could have readied her for *that*.

Years ago, when Dessa had said she didn't want to ruin their friendship, Harlow had begrudgingly agreed. It made sense then, even if she hated it. She supposed it still made sense now...

Except that now, she wasn't the same as she had been back then, scared and confused in a darkened photo gallery. Now she was strong. Comfortable in her uncertainty. And her love felt bottomless, selfless. Despite her turbulent past and unknown future, she *knew* that the life she wanted to live was this one. She *knew* that she was capable of a love that would cross lifetimes.

A love that was vulnerable.

A love that asked for help.

A love that welcomed others into the tiny corners she had once been too afraid to show.

At last, Harlow shook her head. "We're older now. Wiser. Well, you not me," she choked out, unsure if she had even said any of it at all. She shifted her body to move closer, her chest wide, hands planted on the sidewalk as though she were afraid she'd float away if she let go. "You've seen me at my worst."

Dessa's eyes fell. "Same..." She drew in a long inhale, her chest rising slowly as the morning sun. "I'm not proud of how I've acted these past weeks. I've been... wrong about a lot of things." Her gaze shot up. "Don't tell Len. I'll deny it and call you a liar."

"I know you will." Harlow laughed, and Dessa's smile flickered back to life as a flush of pink blossomed in her cheeks. Harlow leaned in closer, heat expanding in her heart, radiating out to every limb. "What made you change your mind?"

"You did." Dessa met her halfway, a small gasp escaping her lips as they met Harlow's.

The bell chimed, breaking them apart.

Len stood just outside the shop with a large, rectangle box a dozen in her hand, held aloft as if she was showing them off like a trophy. She laughed, a light and airy sound. "What?" Her eyes bounced between the two, each with a guilty expression etched into their faces. "Oh, you two thought I didn't notice sophomore year?" She stepped closer, then offered her hand to help Dessa up.

Dessa took it slowly, her face burning a bright red as Len hoisted her up.

Harlow struggled to her feet; her legs felt boneless, her muscles weak. She swayed, unsteady as she finally straightened her back. She did her best not to hide her pained grimace, though a smile overtook her as she rubbed the back of her neck. "That obvious?"

Len rolled her eyes, but her smile was kind, if not a little teasing. "Painfully. I'm glad you two are finally getting over yourselves. And all it took was a world-ending catastrophe." She lowered the box to Harlow's eye level. "I got us four of each. Let's go home."

"Don't forget we have to stop at the pet store," Dessa said. Her hand slipped into Harlow's easily as they set off down the sidewalk. "You promised them the good stuff."

Harlow sighed, her shoulders deflating.

"Maybe you can pick up an application while you're there," Len suggested.

Harlow looked up at the morning sky. "I'll just rob convenience stores. It's easier." She waited, then sighed when neither of her friends spoke up. "Get it? Easier. Convenience stores."

"Ha ha," Len fake-laughed.

"One thing at a time," Dessa said. She swung Harlow's hand up playfully. "First, cat food. Second, donut feast. Third, sleep for a million years."

Harlow felt herself smile despite the nagging of her own ever-growing to-do list that began to loop annoyingly in the back of her mind. Three items sounded nice. Hers was much longer... and much more daunting.

Item one: Find a job. Preferably one that paid decently. And often.

Two: Get her articles turned in. And hopefully not have to go through rounds and rounds of revisions.

Three: Check on her friends. And probably buy more wine and flowers since that was the least she could do to repay them. Though to do that, she had to see list item number one.

Four: Search out the Queen before she could do any more damage. Though, for all she knew, it was possible she'd never see or hear of her again.

Five: Find others like them as they began to wake up.... There would be more. In her heart, she knew there would be many more.

Whatever Fox had done that night to bring so many to them, it had echoed out. She could feel the magic in the air, the ripple that would grow into a wave. If she could get to them before they turned... Well, then she might have a chance at stopping the cycle before it grew beyond her. Then, they might have a chance to save the Earth before it even knew it was in danger.

Dessa squeezed her hand. The sound of her friends' laughter flooded into her as the sun rose higher into the morning sky.

All around them, the city was starting to wake up.

Harlow sighed it all out.

*One thing at a time.*

# CHAPTER 32

# THE STUDY HARD CLUB

The tricky thing about knowledge was that it didn't always lead to understanding. Harlow had always found it strange that two people could read the same article, see the same statistics and facts, and come to completely and wildly different understandings.

Harlow, Len, and Dessa had all entered the same program, taken the same classes, and yet they all wrote for different reasons.

Len for justice.

Dessa for truth.

And if Harlow was being real with herself, she wrote for the fight of it. For the challenge of taking something that people held firm and shaking it up and laying it bare before them to really contend with it.

Of course, she found that most people dug their heels in when presented with information that contradicted their own beliefs.

And that was the strangest part to her. How knowledge could be a powerful tool against disinformation and corruption. But only so much as people were willing to understand it.

*Otherwise...*

"Knowledge is power and power reveals," Gigi said as she sat up on her knees from her position on the floor. She leaned her body over the coffee table, eyes wide with excitement as though she had just told a joke and was waiting for everyone to laugh at it. Her bandage was gone; the long wounds on her face were still red despite her bright smile. At last, she drew back onto her knees, waving her hand as though they were all too slow to keep up with her. "So," she went on, "we study hard. Learn everything we can about how the magic works and chart all the data points we can find. And hopefully, we'll reveal super cool aliens! And not the planet-ending kind. We'll call it 'The Study Hard Club'!"

From behind the high counter, Rainey pinched her brow. The steam from the large pot obscuring her more subtle annoyance. "No offense, but–"

"I love it!" Len called from the other side of the kitchen. She was busy whisking flour into a small pot of melted butter. "It's unassuming, nerdy, and just silly enough. We shouldn't be taking ourselves so seriously."

Harlow's apartment was buzzing with the happy sounds of life.

From the small kitchen, metal and ceramic meeting in quick chimes as Len and Rainey worked hard and fast on preparing food echoed into the living room.

The cats chased each other about the hallway, their nails tearing up the carpet as they propelled themselves forward in an epic play-battle.

Gigi's voice carried over it all as she threw out ideas, each wilder than the last.

The familiar scratching of Dessa's pen diligently scribbling them down in her notebook like soft white noise...

Her apartment. Alive with love and care.

*Home.*

The smell of warm butter and sweet berries boiling

in sugar and starch filled the space like a sprinkle on top of chaotic joy.

Harlow was curled up in the corner of her couch, her legs drawn up to her chest, head resting on her knees as she watched her friends with a quiet contemplation.

In the days since the full moon, Harlow had heard nothing of the Queen.

Or Fox.

She had seen no monsters roaming the streets, though she hadn't actually been looking. Still, she flinched every time her phone beeped, waited far too long to check who had tried to reach her. She hurried back to her apartment every evening before the stars came out, checking over her shoulder as she slipped into the front door of the apartment complex. She kept her lights on, her curtains shut, and even asked for a sleepover like the old days, which Dessa and Len had graciously agreed to. They arrived with new matching pajamas for the three of them, bottom-shelf wine, and deli cheese, and entirely too many pillows.

Harlow's fear frustrated her.

She couldn't help it.

But at least she had summoned the courage to ask for help. That felt like a win.

Perhaps the biggest one of all.

She was sure that there would be more nights like

these. Where she was both happy and hurting. Fulfilled and craving. Together... and a little lonely. Maybe that was just the way it was. Life was full of contradictions.

Like the battle between knowledge and power. If one corrupted the other, it was entirely up to the individual person to decide what to become, how to use their awareness. All she could do was continue to spread the right information when she had it and hope for the best.

That night, in Harlow's little apartment, they were all trying to find a way to do just that.

Forming a network for people who were waking up had been Carina's idea. There had to be a better way to operate than just allowing people to fall into danger because of misinformation or lack of understanding.

"Besides," Carina had said, "I am getting used to these nights off. It'd be nice to have more of them."

Harlow had reluctantly agreed that sitting inside and eating snacks and watching junk TV was easier on her body than spending all night fighting giants.

Using the internet, they could access people all over the world, provide support for them, teach them what they knew, and, as Len pointed out, help them feel less lonely.

Harlow pitched the idea to her friends, who all jumped in to help with its creation. Rainey had set up the technical side, Gigi the design. Len and Dessa focused on the writing, ignoring their schoolwork entirely, as they channeled their energy into anything but their articles.

Now, all the network needed was a name.

Dessa tapped her pen against the paper. "'The Study Hard Club'… I kind of like it too," she said at last.

"Do I have veto power?" Harlow asked from her corner.

Rainey pointed a wooden spoon at her over the high countertop. "Thank you! That's two votes for no."

Gigi waved her hand. "Len likes it."

"I do," she said, peeking out from the side of the kitchen, the large bowl cradled in the crook of her elbow.

"That should count as two," Gigi said.

"What? Why?" Rainey protested.

Gigi ignored her, her nose thrust up in the air defiantly. "And same for me. I get one vote for each scar."

"'The Study Hard Club'?" Rainey repeated, back to work on the steaming berries.

"Yeah, I mean, we are based out of a university."

"I fear we've been outvoted," Harlow said.

"I fear as well." Rainey stirred the berry mixture, launching another bright burst of fragrance through the room.

Dessa squeezed Gigi's shoulder gently as rose from her position on the floor beside her. She motioned to Harlow with her notebook as she approached the couch with light steps, her bangles jingling delicately on her wrist. "Scooch."

Harlow unfolded herself, making a space in the corner for Dessa.

She settled in beside Harlow, head resting comfortably on her shoulder. They stayed like that for a while, watching their friends argue about the merits of naming systems, collaborate on the shared dish, and laugh about all of it and nothing at all.

The cats pranced about the floor, checking in on each of them with silent, upturned tails and twitching noses as they sniffed at shoes and corners. They had calmed down from their previous shenanigans, though Harlow was certain it would start up again soon.

Carina talked about settling down, pretending to be a house cat most nights. But she knew, just as she felt in her own bones, that the guardians were itching to get back out into the moonlight.

Harlow softened into Dessa's closeness. There would be plenty of time for battles. Plenty of time to call down starlight and feel her sword in her hand. There were plenty of long nights ahead. For now, she put aside her urge to get up and move. For now, this moment could just be home.

On a planet she loved.

With people she loved.

"Any ideas on how to find people through the network yet?" Dessa's voice was soft beneath the bustle in the small apartment.

The tip of Harlow's nose grazed along Dessa's hair. She closed her eyes. "No idea. I'm just making this up as I go."

"That's the human way," Dessa said softly.

Harlow smiled. "Yeah, I guess so."

# EPILOGUE

Speculation as to what had happened to the half destroyed high-rise apartment building ranged from 'government conspiracy to destroy evidence of a spy headquarters' to 'major gas leak' to... most accurately, 'aliens'. But no one theory ever dominated another, except on campus where most students, and some staff, agreed that *something strange* was going on. After all, the observatory *and* the city building felt like too much of a coincidence to ignore.

The city seemed, at least publicly, more interested in

fixing it up quickly and quietly than providing any answers. There was hardly any news about either the destruction or the restoration. Seemingly as swiftly as their battle tore it apart, the repairs were completed, and people in tailored clothes carrying expensive leather bags moved back in.

On their nights out, Harlow, Len, and Dessa simply avoided that block entirely in an unspoken agreement to turn at the corner instead. They had enough to worry about without adding the stress of looking up at the penthouse to see if the lights were on.

But still...

A tangle of pain and wistfulness tugged on Harlow's chest as if a string made of memories had been hooked around her sternum, tethering her to places and feelings that she desperately wished she could destroy with the swing of her sword. The longer she fought the pull, the harder she found herself unable to avoid the places she never wanted to see again. Like being battered about in an undertow for so long, Harlow figured that it was probably best to just let go and follow the current of her curiosity.

And so, fueled by far too much pink bubble caffeine, and a sprinkle of audacity, Harlow set out alone into the glow of city lights underneath the dark new moon.

Instead of turning the corner where they usually

did, she kept walking forward. She focused her attention on the sounds of her own booted feet on the sidewalk, the murmur of people passing by, the occasional rumble of music booming from within the restaurants and bars… She latched on to anything she could to ground herself in the moment.

In the dull beat of her heart.

In the tickle of her hair along her chin as a cool breeze drifted down the street.

In the glittering reflections of neon lights along the glass windows.

She walked until she reached the other end of the street.

The same street she had traveled down so many times with clenched fists and her head held high.

Now, she looked up at the top of the building with her fingers loose, her shoulders squared. It was hard to see the all-glass walls of the penthouse from here, and despite all her growth, she still felt small standing at its base.

Harlow backed up a few steps to get a better look at the top floor.

She blinked.

And the light turned on.

# The End...

# UNTIL WE TRANSFORM AGAIN

# About the Author

Wren Jones hates writing bios.
She changes hers as often as she
changes her hair (which is quite often).
She lives in the Sonoran Desert with
her wild family and two tame cats.
She tells stories with happy endings for
mildly unhappy protagonists.

She is aggressively kind & surprisingly spiteful.

# Acknowledgements

First, I would like to thank you for reading. Especially if you are reading this part. That's some dedication! Or some epic curiosity...

Either way, it should be rewarded. Here's the gift I have for you: Today is going to be a magical day. Go look for it. If it's late at night and you stayed up all night to read this like you did when you were a kid, that's even better! Tomorrow is going to be so incredibly magical for you!

Truly, storytellers are just people talking to the void without readers like you. I'm glad you came with me on this journey. I wrote this for me, because it's more of what I'd like to see in the world. But I also wrote this for you. So you can remember that you are wonderful, that the world is worth fighting for, and that we can make great change through small acts of love and friendship.

I would like to thank all the magical girls (gender neutral) who are out there fighting injustice wherever they see it. This book is for the ones who seek out light in the darkness, the ones who keep trying when it's hard, and the ones who sometimes make their own lives difficult for the sake of their community. I hope you get back what you put out there a thousand times over.

Thank you to my husband who believes in me and reminds me of my strength and how far I've come when I am being self-defeating. Thanks for never letting me get too far down into the weeds and occasionally reminding me to sleep. Even if I'm too stubborn to listen.

Thank you to my friends. You're all crushing it out there and I'm so in awe of every single one of you. Thank you for your support throughout this (and my many other) adventures. Life is really short and often difficult, but with you guys in my corner, I feel like no matter what, it's a beautiful day because you and I are here at the same time, on this same tiny speck, just hurling through space. Together. How lucky am I to be born in a place where I had the opportunity to know you all?

To the Local Girls (who aren't so local anymore). I am thankful every single day that I happened to go to that random meet up ten years ago. You have all profoundly changed my life for the better. I don't believe in fate. But, I mean... come on.

Thank you to my nemesis. You know who you are and what you did. May our epic battle never end.

Thank you to my daughter for reminding me what's important and never failing to ask me questions until I am forced to confront the nature of the vastness of life. You make me take things slower because of how fast you move and how quickly you are growing up.

Thank you to my son for making my days full of laughter, even though I'm pretty sure at this point that you're purposefully depriving me of sleep so I'm weaker when you ask for snacks. I'm on to you.

I love you both more than all the stars in the universe.

Thank you to my family for sticking this out with me. I promise I'm trying to work hard, be honest, and help people every single day. Yes, I'm still writing.

A big thank you to Carly at Booklight Editorial for getting on a call with me to gently point out the plot holes and helping me make sense of the chaos. Editors are amazing and you guys have a hard job. I appreciate it more than you know!

Huge thanks to my sister for body doubling with me and chasing their dreams. It's because of you that when

I felt like giving up, I reminded myself that this is going to be "our year". We got this.

Thank you to the writing community, the readers I have met, and the lovely booksellers who've had my back. Thank you to the Beta readers, the ARC readers, to all the readers. We need all of us here and I'm so proud to be part of such a loving, supportive, and kind group of humans.

Thank you to coffee. When the nights are long, I know that it will be okay. Because there's coffee waiting for me in the morning. Thank you to the roasters, the farmers, the folks who transport it, the friendly faces who sell it. Without coffee, I am just a big old mess.

Shhhh. This one is a secret. Most of my students don't know I'm an author. Don't tell them. To the students who found out, thank you for keeping my secret identity safe.

Thank you to everyone who supports public education for all.

Thank you to the helpers. The fighters. The supporters. Those who practice empathy and those who stay curious.

And lastly, a big middle finger to Pokopia. You're the reason I blew past my internal deadline. It had nothing to do with my burn out, taking on too much, or other obligations (of which, I am told, are many). I blame YOU and I refuse to do any self-reflection on this matter. So much ash to clean up.

Really.

So.

Much.

Ash.